SUMMER OF '69

SUMMER OF '69

MICKEY STRUNAK

ReadersMagnet, LLC

Summer of '69.
Copyright © 2021 by Mickey Strunak.

Published in the United States of America.
ISBN Paperback: 978-1-956780-52-9
ISBN eBook: 978-1-956780-49-9

All rights reserved. No part of this publication may be reproduced, stored in a retrieval system or transmitted in any way by any means, electronic, mechanical, photocopy, recording or otherwise without the prior permission of the author except as provided by USA copyright law.

The opinions expressed by the author are not necessarily those of ReadersMagnet, LLC.

ReadersMagnet, LLC
10620 Treena Street, Suite 230 | San Diego, California, 92131 USA
1.619.354.2643 | www.readersmagnet.com

Book design copyright © 2021 by ReadersMagnet, LLC. All rights reserved.
Cover design by Kent Gabutin
Interior design by Renalie Malinao

CONTENTS

Chapter 1	"The Amazing Mets" 1
Chapter 2	Baltimore Orioles regular season 11
Chapter 3	Braves take first National League West Crown 18
Chapter 4	The 1969 World Series 24
Chapter 5	National League Championship Series 1969 43
Chapter 6	American League Championship Series 1969 53
Chapter 7	Epilogue 63
	Gil Hodges *63*
	Tommie Agee *74*
	Ken Boswell *80*
	Don Cardwell *82*
	Ed Charles *85*
	Donn Clendenon *87*
	Duffy Dyer *93*
	Jack DiLauro *96*
	Wayne Garrett *97*
	Gary Gentry *100*
	Jerry Grote *101*
	Rod Gaspar *109*
	Bud Harrelson *111*
	Cleon Jones *116*
	Cal Koonce *121*
	Jerry Koosman *122*
	Ed Kranepool *128*

	J.C. Martin 134
	Jim McAndrew 138
	Tug McGraw 139
	Amos Otis 148
	Bobby Pfeil 150
	Nolan Ryan 152
	Tom Seaver 165
	Art Shamsky 175
	Ron Swoboda 179
	Ron Taylor 183
	Al Weis 184
Chapter 8	Various Statistics and Game by Game Results 188
Chapter 9	Mets' Career Statistics 199

CHAPTER 1

"THE AMAZING METS"

The New York Mets opened and closed the 1969 season with losses, which was hardly unusual since they never won on opening day since they joined the National League, as an expansion team in 1962. Those lovable Mets in 1962 who lost 122 games with first baseman-Marv Throneberry and manager, Casey Stengel. In the seven seasons since 1962, including 1968, the Mets had 737 losses, average of over 104 losses per year. In 1969, the Mets won 100 games, perhaps the most miraculous pennant title in a major league season.

The 1914 Boston Braves came back from last place in midseason to win the National League pennant. Baseball historians will point out that the Braves had a 5th place finish the season before. The year before in 1968, the year of the pitcher, the Mets finished in 9th place in a 10 team league.

And not to mention the National League pennant winning New York Giants, the Miracle Giants, the team with Bobby Thompson's shot heard around the world. They were established with superstars - Willie Mays, Monte Irvin, Alvin Dark, Sal Maglie, Thompson, and Larry Jansen.

Who were the New York Mets of 1969? A bunch of non star players. A bunch of kids. Outside of maybe, pitchers-Tom Seaver and Jerry Koosman, plus left-fielder Cleon Jones, there wasn't a regular with on the team that other clubs wanted. The previous season with basically, the same team, the Mets finished 73-89. They hit only .228, as a team with only 81 home runs. However, yes the Mets had pitchers that everyone wanted in Koosman and Seaver with a young Nolan Ryan. They had two of the best pitchers in the league. Over the winter, General Manager - Johnny Murphy repeatedly turned down trades for those pitchers. They did not deal.

When the season started, the Mets lost to expansion team, the Montreal Expos at home in Shea. It looked like another dismal season. How could anyone forecast the miracle season that was about to unfold.

And miracle it was because the Mets won the World Series in '69 never happened before. No team had ever went from 9th place the year to before to a pennant and World Series victory the next season. The Boston Red Sox went from 9th to first for an American League pennant in 1967, but lost in the World Series in seven games to the St. Louis Cardinals.

And no team ever drank and wasted champagne, as the New York Mets, who within three weeks had three clinchings to celebrate- the NL East Division, the NL pennant, and the World Series crown.

Through it all, the calmest person was manager, Gil Hodges, who one year before prior to the day of clinching the NL East division, had suffered a heart attack in Atlanta. If Hodges' doctor had ordered him not to get excited, let it be known that Gil followed his doctor's advice to the tee.

Only twice during the Mets unbelievable season did Hodges lose his cool-once behind closed doors of the locker room and another time was in front of the Shea Stadium faithful during a game.

The first time was in mid July when he locked the clubhouse doors and read his team the riot act. A perfectionist who cannot tolerate mistakes on the field that he knows should not happen. Hodges had seen too much to remain quiet. So he sounded off and yelled, and the entire team got the message.

The second time was a double header on July 30th when the Mets suffered their most lopsided defeats. It was against Houston who had been tormenting the Mets, ever since they both came into existence in 1962. Houston won the first game, 16-3 with a record breaking pair of grand slam home runs in the 9th inning. They were in the process of winning the 2nd game, when Houston scored 10 runs in the 3rd inning. Suddenly, Gil Hodges emerged from the dugout.

At first it looked liked like a routine pitching change, but when Hodges got to the mound, he did not stop. He continued walking in slow methodical steps on to left-field, where he chatted briefly with Cleon Jones. The manager, Hodges then turned and headed back to the dugout with the contrite Jones walking with his head down about 10 steps behind Hodges.

Hodges did not feel that Jones was hustling on a hit into the left field corner. He was supposedly lifted because his leg was bothering Jones, but everyone in the park knew it was disciplinary move and Jones said that, later in the evening.

If Hodges was trying to wake the team up, it did not work. They lost 11-5, and lost again the next day, 2-0 to end July with a 55 - 44 record (.556 Pct.), but hardly one capable of winning the pennant.

MICKEY STRUNAK

If Houston gave the New York Mets fits and they did so that year by winning 10 of 12 games they played that season. Against the clubs they were supposed to beat, they were superb.

After St. Louis, the defending NL Champs, got a slow start out of the gate, it appeared that the Chicago Cubs would run a way with the NL East division. They led from opening day until September 10th, when the Mets, finally for the first time in their history, caught Chicago and moved into first place by themselves. They had beaten Chicago and continued a blistering pace (22-5) down the stretch.

The Mets first thought they had a chance to win the NL East crown was in early July. They had two series with the Cubs in Shea Stadium and Wrigley Field, with only a 3 game set with Montreal in between. The Cubs firmly entrenched in first place and were not taking the Mets seriously. Even though New York sports-writers were saying the two series were **the first crucial** series in New York Mets history.

And the Mets were hot at the time. They had just returned from a special trip in which they had won 6 of 8 from St. Louis and Pittsburgh. Also, they had a 5 game winning streak when the Cubs arrived on July 8th.

The Mets came from behind with three runs in the tenth in the opener to nip the league leaders, 4-3 with Ed Kranepool driving home the clinching run with a bloop single. Don Young's failure to catch a drive near the left-center field wall set up the winning rally and also started dissension among the Cubs. Captain, Ron Santo sounded off that the ball should have been caught in left-center field.

The next evening, 59,083 jammed the park for what was a historic night. For 8 1/3 innings, ace, Tom Seaver pitched a perfect game and also had 11 strikeouts of Cubs batters. The Met fanatics could hardly controlled, as the ninth began.

When Randy Hundley opened the ninth with a bunt and was thrown field out by Seaver, the customers were near hysterics. But then, pinch-hitter, Jimmy Qualls lined Seaver's first offering, cleanly into left center field and the spell was broken. The large crowd groaned, but then cheered as Seaver retired the next to batters and wound up wit a 4-0 victory. Again, the Mets had beaten the league leaders.

Chicago recovered to win a 6-2 victory the next day with a 5 run fifth inning in which the Mets booted the ball around. After the victory, someone asked manager, Leo Durocher, "If these were the real Cubs?" Leo could not resist the chance to take a shot at the Mets. "No," he said, "those were the real Mets."

The Mets did not forget the famous quote and a week later in Chicago after Chicago won the opening game, 1-0, the Cubs figured they had silenced the Mets. But they hadn't. All year long, Hodges had pointed out that the Mets had more resiliency than any team he had been associated with, including Brooklyn. Sure enough, they came against Chicago.

The next day, July 15th with 38,608 watching, the Mets won, 5-4, with light-hitting shortstop, Al Weiss driving in 3 runs with his first home run of the season. It was his second home run in the last 2 seasons, which was even more startling.

The Mets did it, again the next day with Weiss hitting home run number two. This was the first time since 1964 that Weiss hit two home runs in a season. Art Shamsky and Tommie Agee also hit home-runs that day and the Mets trounced the Cubs, 9-5.

The Mets were not about to lose to Chicago, again until the pennant race was over. In mid September, in what was the final showdown between the two contenders, the Mets won two games against the Cubs and completely demoralized the league leaders.

Again a light hitting infielder, beat the Cubs, 3-2 on September 8th. Tommie Agee hit a home run for 2 runs, then the Cubs tied it in the sixth. But in the last of the sixth, Agee doubled and Wayne Garrett, a rookie third baseman with a .218 batting average, singled home the winning run for Jerry Koosman.

The next night, Tom Seaver, or Tom Terrific, as called by New York writers, beat the Cubs, 7-1. The following night the Mets swept Montreal in a twi-night double header to take over first place.

If the Cubs had any doubts about the Mets being for real, they had it spelled out for them the following week, as the pennant race was settled.

In a space of one week, they won three games from Montreal, a pair of 1-0 victories in a double-header with Pittsburgh. Both runs were scored on run batted in base hits by pitchers. The Mets then won a game, 4-3 against St. Louis in which left-hander, Steve Carlton struck out 19 batters. Finally, the Mets did lose on a no-hitter by Pirates pitcher, Bob Moose. However, they did not lose ground in the pennant race.

Clearly, the Mets could not do anything wrong down the stretch in late September.

From August 13th - when they lost 3 straight in a series with Houston - until the end of the season, the Mets won 38 of 49 games. Three of the losses came in a series with Pittsburgh on September 19th and 20th. The Mets lost the first three, then came back to win the final pair on September 21st. That started them on a 9 game winning streak, including a September 24th victory over the reigning NL Champs - the St. Louis Cardinals. This clinched the National League Division Championship.

If the players went wild in the clubhouse, it was nothing like the 56,586 Shea partisans did to the ball park. They ripped up the sod and took it home as souvenirs. They stole the bases, including home plate. Seven years of expansion growing pains were over.

The team that lost 120 games in its first season in 1962 were now number one in the East Division.

Seaver, despite more than a month with a tender shoulder in which he lost 4 of his 7 games, came on strong at the end and won his last 10 starts in a row to finish with a 25-7 record. He was the Winningest pitcher in the big leagues.

Jerry Koosman, a 19 game winner in his rookie season, also was bothered by a sore shoulder. His problems began in spring training in St. Petersburg and it was not until late May that he pitched well. It started with a 15 strikeout performance in a no decision game with San Diego. From then on, the left-hander was great. He finished with a 17-9 record.

Gary Gentry was up and down his rookie year, but did finish at 13 - 12. Other starters were, former Pirate, Don Cardwell (8-10), Jim McAndrew (6-7), and occasionally, Nolan Ryan (6-3). McAndrew, who figured as a regular starter, was out half the year with a sore arm. The Mets were without problems on the mound. Still they managed to win 100 games, only the 4th team in the decade to do this. The other teams were the New York Yankees and Baltimore Orioles. The bullpen was led by left-handed, Tug McGraw. McGraw, Ron Taylor, and Calvin Koonce did most of the relief pitching. The pitching staff turned in 16 complete game shutouts and had a total of 28 for the season which was high in the major leagues.

The Mets had two .300 hitters in left-fielder, Cleon Jones (.340) and right-fielder, Art Shamsky (.300). Shamsky hit for .300 batting average platooning with World Series star, Ron Swoboda, who hit against left-handers. Art hit 14 home runs and knocked in 47 runs in 100 games. My dad told me once that Shamsky, then with Cincinnati hit 3 consecutive home runs against the Pirates at Crosley Field one Saturday night in 1966. The next day on Sunday afternoon in his first at bat, he hit another home run to make 4 consecutive home runs in four at bats. Swoboda hit nine home runs and drove in 52 runs. Cleon Jones contended for the batting title all season, but had hamstring problems and could not keep up with **Charlie Hustle,** Pete Rose, who won the batting title. Jones finished at .340, a career high.

The steadiest player was center fielder, Tommy Agee. He hit .271 and led the club with 26 home runs and 76 RBI's. His defense in center field was superb.

The only change in club personnel came on June 15th, when GM, Johnny Murphy secured a deal for first baseman, Donn Clendenon of Montreal that sent 4 minor leaguers to Montreal. Clendenon platooned with left-handed hitting, Ed Kranepool and hit 13 home runs and 37 RBI's in half a season.

The Mets magic continued with an unbelievable 3 game sweep of the Atlanta Braves in the National League Championship Series (NLCS). This was the first NLCS after both leagues split into two divisions after the 1968 season with expansion of two teams to each league.

The Mets went on to defeat the American League Champs, Baltimore in 5 games to win their first World Series. Some called it *the Impossible Dream* others called it *The Preposterous Dream.*

1969 Regular Season Batting Records New York Mets (100-62 record)

Player	G	AB	R	H	HR	RBI	BA	SB
LF Cleon Jones +	137	483	92	164	12	75	.340	16
RF Art Shamsky +	100	303	42	91	14	47	.300	1
SS Bob Heiss	4	10	1	3	0	0	.300	0
2B Ken Boswell +	102	362	48	101	3	32	.279	7
CF Tommie Agee	149	565	97	153	26	76	.271	9
C Duffy Dyer	29	74	5	19	3	12	.257	0
C Jerry Grote	113	365	38	92	6	40	.252	2
1B Don Clendenon	72	202	31	51	12	37	.252	3
SS Bud Harrelson #	123	395	42	98	0	24	.248	1
1B Ed Kranepool +	112	353	36	84	11	49	.238	3
RF Ron Swoboda	109	325	38	77	9	52	.235	1
3B Bobby Pfeil	62	211	20	49	0	10	.232	0
3B Wayne Garrett +	124	400	38	87	1	39	.218	4
MI Al Weiss #	103	247	20	53	2	23	.215	3
C J.C. Martin +	66	177	12	37	4	21	.209	0
3B Ed Charles	61	169	21	35	3	18	.207	4
OF Amos Otis	48	93	6	14	0	14	.151	1
2B Kevin Collins+	16	40	1	6	1	2	.150	0
OF Jim Gosger +	10	15	0	2	0	1	.133	0
Team Total (8)	162	5427	632	1311	109	598	.242	66
Pittsburgh (1)	162	5626	725	1557	119	651	.277	74
Cincinnati (2)	163	5634	798	1558	171	750	.277	79

Pitching Records New York Mets 1969

Pitcher	W	L	Pct.	ERA	G	IP	H	R	SO	BB
Tom Seaver	25	7	.781	2.21	36	273	202	75	208	82
Tug McGraw +	9	3	.750	2.24	42	100	89	25	92	47
Jerry Koosman +	17	9	.654	2.28	32	241	187	66	180	68
Jack Dilano	1	4	.200	2.40	23	64	50	19	21	18
Ron Taylor	9	4	.692	2.72	59	76	61	23	42	24
Don Cardwell	8	10	.444	3.07	30	152	145	63	60	47
Gary Gentry	13	12	.520	3.43	35	233	192	94	154	81
Jim McAndrew	6	7	.462	3.47	27	135	112	57	90	44
Nolan Ryan	6	3	.667	3.53	25	89	60	38	92	53
Cal Koonce	6	3	.667	4.99	40	83	85	53	48	42
Team Total	100	62	.617	2.99	162	1468	1217	541	1012	577
St. Louis	87	75	.537	2.94	162	1460	1289	540	1004	511

+ *means left-handed and* # *means switch hitter*

CHAPTER 2

BALTIMORE ORIOLES REGULAR SEASON

A strange thing happened on their way to becoming a baseball dynasty. They stumbled against the amazing New York Mets, after winning 112 out of 165 games, including the ALCS.

Until then, when the Mets polished off Baltimore in 5 games, people were comparing the 1969 Orioles to the great old Yankee teams.

A team without a weakness that was stronger than the 1966 team, which swept the Los Angeles Dodgers in 4 straight in the World Series. So strong that Merv Rettenmund, *the Sporting News Minor League Player of the Year* in 1968, could not crack the starting lineup.

The Orioles were in first place since April 16th on and they finished 19 games ahead of defending champion, Detroit in the first East race. The only team that won by more games was the 1936 New York Yankees, who won by 19 and ½ games.

Certainly that was enough to proclaim that a dynasty was in the making. But after a 3 game sweep of Minnesota in the ALCS, the Orioles were out-hit, out-pitched, and out-fielded by the Mets in the World Series.

The Orioles would go on to win the World Series against Cincinnati in 1970 and then lose to Pittsburgh in 1971. They were definitely the best baseball club from 1966 to 1971, a six year period - 2 championships and 4 American League pennants.

In 1969, it was great year for the Orioles. 4,000 fans swarmed the airport to welcome the team after the big disappointment to the Mets. Just like the Baltimore Orioles, NFL title holders in 1968 (13-1 record), who lost to the New York Jets in the 1969 Super Bowl III, 16-7. The Jets were the media darlings and 18 point underdogs in the game. They came from the 10 team AFL (American Football Conference) before the merger in 1970 of the NFL and AFL into two 13 team conferences.

Back to the airport in Baltimore, one banner read: "We're still # 1." The players, responded by sharing loyalty and appreciation and touched the fans through the fence. It was very emotional for some and brought tears to their eyes.

The city of Baltimore took its share of criticism before and during the Series over attendance. How did Baltimore support this fine team to the tune of only 1,058,168 during the season? The response was one million fans was not bad for a city and market the size of Baltimore, plus Washington was 90 miles away for the Washington Senators baseball club.

Searching for reasons, people pointed to the fact that the Orioles made shambles of the AL East race. They were on top by 6 ½ in mid June, by 14 at the All-Star break, and 15 ½ in mid August. On September 13th with 17 games left, the O's clinched the first AL East crown in history.

The pennant victory was a personal victory for manager, Earl Weaver, the youngest manager in the league at 39. Weaver was in the minors for years and was brought up to coach under Hank Bauer in 1968.

Earl never made the majors, as a player. He started his managing career, while still an infielder in the late 1956 season at Knoxville, where he inherited a last place team that finished last.

After a fourth place finish in a 6 team league the next season, Weaver managed 19 teams, including winter ball. He never finished out of the first division. All but one of his last 15 ball clubs, including the 1969 Orioles, finished first or second.

In mid-season, 1968, he replaced Bauer. Cynics said that the 1969 Orioles had so much talent anyone could manage them to a pennant. The club gave him a one year contract at $40,000 for one year.

Hoping that his string of one year contracts would be as long, as Walter Alston's in Los Angeles, Weaver bought a house in Baltimore.

There was a sign in spring training that the Orioles would win it all, but no one paid much attention to spring training. Baltimore went 19-5 in exhibition season.

The Orioles started close to that pace at the start of the season by going 16-8 and were ahead by 3 games. Opposing teams in the East awaited for a slump or injuries, but there was none of either.

Only 10 players were left from 1966 Championship team, but the key men remained. They also added Mike Cuellar in December 1968.

Cuellar came in a trade that sent outfielder, Curt Blefary to Houston. Cuellar was 31, a left-hander with a screw-ball and labored through the first half of 1968 with a sore arm. In 4 seasons with Houston, he never won more than 16 games.

"He's an artist," said Jim Russo, "the Oriole scout who mentioned, Cuellar was the greatest thing to come out of the National League since Frank Robinson. He throws all kinds of pitches and gets them over the plate."

No one placed much stalk in Russo's words until mid-season. Cuellar went on to win 13 of 15 decisions during the 2nd half. He got club records for wins (23) and innings (291). In nine complete games, he held opposing hitters to 4 hits or less.

The key man on the team, again in leadership, as well as performance was Frank Robinson. In 1967, he had a base running collision with Al Weis and as a result had vision problems through most of 1968.

In 1969, he came back, leading the club with a .308 batting average, driving in 100 runs, and hitting 32 home runs for a career total of 450, 12th on the all-time list through 1969.

Yet, Frank said he would not vote for himself, as MVP. He would vote for Boog Powell.

The 247 pound first baseman had his best season, since coming up to Baltimore in 1962. He led the team in home runs (37), RBI's (121), and was second to Frank Robinson in batting average at .304.

Powell also led in key runs produced stat. This stat is driving in runs that brought Baltimore within one run, into a tie, or put them one or two runs, ahead. He did it 70 times, 25 times in the 6th inning, or later.

Other players, also improved.

Mark Belanger, the sure handed short-stop, raised his batting average from .208 in '68 to .287. He gave batting coach, Charley Lau much of the credit.

Center fielder, Paul Blair raised his batting average from .211 to .285. Dave Johnson, second baseman, despite a bad back that plagued him, raised his average from .242 to .280 and led the Orioles in doubles.

Don Buford, who was the best leadoff hitter in Orioles history, collected 96 walks, 19 Stolen Bases, and scored 99 runs. He hit for a .291 batting average.

Jim Palmer, who did not pitch in the major leagues in 1968, registered a 16-4 record and led the AL in winning percentage (.800), despite spending 42 days on the disabled list with back problems. Four days after coming off the Disabled list, Palmer pitched the only no-hitter in the American League in '69 against Oakland.

Dave McNally, the number 2 starting pitcher behind Cuellar, did improve and was almost as good as the 1968 season (22-10). In 1969 he won 20, including 15 in a row.

He tied league records, set by Johnny Allen in 1937, for most wins at the start of the season (15) and consecutive wins (17), from September 22nd, 1968 to July 30th, 1969. The Orioles were calling him Dave McLucky.

Tom Phoebus, the number 4 starting pitcher went 14-7, but did not appear in the ALCS or World Series.

The bullpen did not have a king, but had exceptional balance. It was bullpen by committee. Ed Watt, Pete Richert, Dick Hall, Dave Leonhard, and Marcelino Lopez combined for a 29-15 record and 35 saves.

Catching, hitting wise, was the teams weakest department. Andy Etchebarren and Elrod Hendricks shared the position and drove in 64 runs. They also got 6 RBI's from Clay Dalrymple in 37 games.

The Orioles were very strong on defense. Detroit manager, Mayo Smith said, "Trying to hit the ball through the Baltimore infield was like trying to throw hamburger through a brick wall."

It was anchored, as it had been since 1959, by Brooks Robinson at third base. Brooks was great in the field, again in '69, but had an off year at the plate by hitting only .234. He did drive in 84 RBI's in the clutch, however.

Batting Records Baltimore Orioles - 1969 (109-53 record)

Player	G	AB	R	H	HR	RBI	BA	SB
UT Terry Crowley +	7	18	2	6	0	3	.333	0
RF Frank Robinson	48	539	73	140	32	100	.308	9
1B Boog Powell +	152	533	83	162	37	121	.304	1
OF Curt Morton	56	89	15	27	6	21	.303	3
IF Chico Salmon	52	91	18	27	3	12	.297	0
LF Don Buford #	144	554	99	161	11	64	.291	19
SS Mark Belanger	150	530	76	152	2	50	.287	14
CF Paul Blair	150	625	102	178	26	76	.285	20
2B Dave Johnson	142	511	52	143	7	57	.280	3
C Andy Etchebarren	73	217	29	54	3	26	.249	1
OF Merv Rettenmund	95	190	27	47	4	25	.247	6
C Elrod Hendricks	105	295	36	72	12	38	.244	0
RF Dave May +	78	120	8	29	3	10	.242	0
C Clay Dalrymple +	37	80	8	19	3	6	.238	0
3B Brooks Robinson	156	598	73	140	23	84	.234	2
IF Bobby Floyd	39	84	7	17	0	1	.202	0
Team Total(2)	162	5518	779	1465	175	722	.265	82
Minnesota(1)	162	5677	790	1520	163	733	.268	115

Pitching Records - 1969 Baltimore Orioles Records

Player	W	L	Pct.	ERA	G	IP	H	R	SO	BB
Eddie Watt	5	2	.714	1.65	56	71	49	18	46	26
Dick Hall	5	2	.714	1.92	39	66	49	14	31	9
Pete Richert+	7	4	.636	2.20	44	57	42	17	54	14
Al Sorensen	1	1	.500	2.29	12	20	14	6	13	10
Jim Palmer	16	4	.800	2.34	26	181	131	48	123	64
Mike Cuellar +	23	11	.676	2.38	39	291	213	94	182	79
Dave Leonard	7	4	.636	2.49	37	94	78	28	38	37
Dave McNally +	20	7	.741	3.22	41	269	232	103	166	84
Tom Phoebus	14	7	.667	3.52	35	202	180	89	117	87
Jim Hardin	6	7	.462	3.60	30	138	128	62	64	43
Marcelius Lopez+	5	3	.625	4.41	27	69	65	34	57	34
Team Total (1)	**109**	**53**	**.673**	**2.83**	**162**	**1474**	**1194**	**517**	**897**	**498**
New York (2)	**80**	**81**	**.497**	**3.23**	**161**	**1441**	**1258**	**587**	**801**	**522**

CHAPTER 3

BRAVES TAKE FIRST NATIONAL LEAGUE WEST CROWN

The Atlanta Braves won the first NL Wild, Wild, West in style with 93 wins. Manager, Luman Harris simply would not be denied. It was their fourth season in Atlanta, Georgia after relocating from Milwaukee in 1966 to a brand new stadium.

They won the division by winning 17 of 20 games during one stretch in September, including 10 in a row. The tenth coming on the on the next to last game of the season when they clinched the West against Cincinnati.

"Nobody lost in the West. The Braves won it …… That's all you can say, " said Red's manager, Dave Bristol.

"We played good baseball down the stretch," said Clyde King, Giants manager. "It was simply the case of the Braves not losing. They were not…. You have to hand it to them."

As hot as the Braves were to close the season, they were just the opposite when they played the Mets in the National League Championship Series (NLCS). They lost three straight. Their pitching failed them.

Despite the NLCS, the 1969 season was the Braves most successful since they relocated to Atlanta, Georgia in 1966 from Milwaukee.

It was clear to all it was a special season on opening night, when for the first time in Atlanta history the Braves won the season opener by edging the Giants, 5-4 on a RBI single by reserve, Mike Lum in the bottom of the ninth inning.

They preceded to sweep the Giants, three in a row, including one by knuckleball pitcher, Phil Niekro. Phil would go on to win 23 games, prompting Vice President, Paul Richards to say, "Niekro's knuckleball is not hittable."

The Braves knew they had a catcher who could handle Niekro's tricky knuckleball - 20 year old - Bob Didier. Hank Aaron said after the season, "Didier made Niekro a big winner. He was always a good pitcher, but he had to find someone to catch him."

The Braves came from behind and won several games to be in contention for the NL West title.

First baseman, Orlando Cepeda, was obtained in the controversial trade with St. Louis for catcher, Joe Torre on March 17th. Torre was coming off an off season for him - 10 Home Runs and just 55 RBI's in 1968. Cepeda showed the way in the early going.

"Cha-Cha" Cepeda who played on two straight pennant winners at St. Louis knocked in some big runs in the early going and had the Braves thinking World Series title. His rah-rah style of play was infectious with teammates. When opposing pitchers cooled off Cepeda, someone else started to hit. Of course, there was always Henry Aaron, Mr. Consistency, taken for granted. Aaron was usually referred to **Hammerin Hank** from Mobile, Alabama, enjoyed one of his best seasons. He hit 44 home runs, plus three more in the NLCS with New York. Aaron also had 97 runs batted in and ended up with 554 home runs through 1969 for 3rd on the all-time list.

Ron Reed, a tall-pitcher who three years ago decided to quit his NBA basketball career, won 18 games, including 9 of 11 down the stretch. Cecil Upshaw, a submarine delivery pitcher, was the bullpen ace with 27 saves. George Stone, Jim Britton, Pat Jarvis, Paul Doyle, Milt Pappas, and Claude Raymond, former Expo all contributed.

Second baseman, Felix Millan made the all-star team. He teamed with Gil Garrido to give the Braves a very steady double play combination.

Clete Boyer, third baseman was imported from the Yankees, also contributed big hits, despite going 0 for 39 in April. His fielding at third base was exceptional.

Rico Carty, left-fielder came back from missing 1968 with tuberculosis, hit .342 and pretty much carried the club in September.

Bob Tillman, a reserve catcher, hit three home runs in a game.

General Manager, Paul Richards made a key deal on June 12th, when he acquired CF-Tony Gonzalez for young catcher, Walt Hriniak and minor league players. Gonzalez was what Atlanta needed for center field.

Later in the season, Richards acquired another knuckle ball pitcher - Hoyt Wilhelm from the Angels on waivers. In September, Wilhelm recorded 4 saves and 2 victories.

On August 19th, the Cubs Ken Holtzman pitched a no-hitter against the Braves and dropped the team to fifth place - 3 games back.

But then, Atlanta got hot. After the no-hitter, they won 27 out of 37 games, similar to New York in September.

On September 30th, they clinched the west with a 3-2 victory over Cincinnati in front of 44,000 fans in Atlanta.

Aaron replied, "We are going to be a tough club for a few more years, yet."

Atlanta Braves Batting Records - 1969

Players	G	AB	R	H	HR	RBI	BA	SB
LF Rico Carty	104	304	47	104	16	58	.342	0
RF Hank Aaron	147	547	100	164	44	97	.300	9
UT Tito Francona+	51	88	5	26	2	22	.295	0
OF Tony Gonzalez+	89	320	51	94	10	50	.294	3
CF Felipe Alou	123	476	54	134	5	32	.282	4
SS Gil Garrido	82	227	18	50	0	10	.272	0
OF Mike Lum+	121	168	20	45	1	22	.268	0
2B Felix Millan	162	652	98	174	6	57	.267	14
1B Orlando Cepeda	154	573	74	147	22	88	.257	12
C Bob Didier#	114	352	30	90	0	32	.256	1
UT Bob Aspromonte	82	198	16	50	3	24	.253	0
3B Clete Boyer	132	496	57	124	14	57	.250	3
UT Tommie Aaron	49	60	13	15	1	5	.250	0
SS Sonny Jackson+	98	318	41	76	1	27	.239	12
LF Ralph Garr+	22	27	6	6	0	2	.222	0
C Bob Tillman	69	190	16	37	12	29	.195	0
Team Total	**162**	**5460**	**691**	**1411**	**141**	**640**	**.258**	**59**

Pitching Statistics - Atlanta Braves - 1969

Player	G	W	L	Pct.	ERA	IP	H	R	SO	BB
Hoyt Wilhelm	8	2	0	1.000	0.73	12	5	1	14	4
Paul Doyle+	36	2	0	1.000	2.08	39	31	9	25	16
Phil Niekro	40	23	13	.639	2.56	284	235	93	193	57
Cecil Upshaw	62	6	4	.600	2.91	105	102	36	57	29
Ron Reed	36	18	10	.643	3.47	241	225	103	160	56
Milt Pappas	26	6	10	.375	3.63	144	149	66	72	44
George Stone+	36	13	10	.565	3.65	165	166	82	102	48
Jim Britton	24	7	5	.583	3.78	88	69	38	60	49
Gary Neibauer	29	1	2	.333	3.90	57	42	28	42	31
Pat Jarvis	37	13	11	.542	4.43	217	204	113	123	73
Ken Johnson	9	0	1	.000	4.97	29	32	17	20	9
Claude Raymond	33	2	2	.500	5.25	48	56	34	15	13
Total	**162**	**93**	**69**	**.574**	**3.53**	**1445**	**1334**	**631**	**893**	**438**

Chicago Cubs - Batting Records - 1969
2nd Place in East

Player	G	AB	R	H	HR	RBI	BA	SB
2B Paul Popovich	60	154	26	48	1	14	.312	0
LF Billy Williams+	163	642	103	188	21	95	.293	3
2B Glen Beckert	131	543	69	158	1	37	.291	6
3B Ron Santo	160	575	97	166	29	123	.289	1
SS Don Kessinger #	158	664	109	181	4	53	.273	11
C Randy Hundley	151	522	67	133	18	64	.255	2
1B Ernie Banks	155	565	50	143	23	106	.253	0
CF Jimmy Qualls#	43	120	12	30	0	9	.250	2
UT Willie Smith+	103	195	21	48	9	25	.246	1
CF Don Young	101	272	36	65	6	27	.239	1
RF Jim Hickman	134	338	38	80	21	54	.237	2
CF Oscar Gamble+	24	71	6	16	1	5	.225	0
CF Adolfo Phillips	28	49	5	11	0	1	.224	1

SUMMER OF '69

C Gene Oliver	23	27	0	6	0	0	.222	0
RF Al Spangler+	82	213	23	45	4	23	.211	0
UT Ken Rudolph	27	34	7	7	1	6	.206	0
2B Nate Oliver	44	44	15	7	1	4	.159	0
C Bill Health+	27	32	1	5	0	1	.156	0
Total	**163**	**5530**	**720**	**1400**	**142**	**671**	**.253**	**30**

Pitching Records - 1969 Chicago Cubs

Chicago pitcher	G	W	L	Pct.	ERA	IP	H	R	SO	BB
Bill Hands	41	20	14	.588	2.49	300	268	102	181	73
Hank Aguirre+	41	1	0	1.000	2.60	45	45	13	19	12
Ken Johnson	9	1	2	.333	2.84	19	17	8	18	7
Ted Abernathy	56	4	3	.511	3.16	85	75	38	55	42
Ferguson Jenkins	43	21	15	.583	3.21	311	284	122	273	71
Ken Holtzman+	39	17	13	.567	3.58	261	248	117	176	93
Dick Selma	36	10	8	.556	3.63	169	137	74	161	72
Phil Regan	71	12	6	.667	3.70	112	120	49	56	35
Rich Nye+	34	3	5	.375	5.11	69	72	43	39	21
Total	**162**	**92**	**70**	**.568**	**3.34**	**1454**	**1366**	**611**	**1017**	**475**

New York Mets 1969 Records Against National League Teams

East Division	W	L	Pct.	West Division	W	L	Pct.
Chicago	10	8	.556	Houston	2	10	.167
St. Louis	12	6	.667	San Francisco	8	4	.667
Pittsburgh	11	7	.611	Atlanta	8	4	.667
Philadelphia	12	6	.667	Cincinnati	6	6	.500
Montreal	13	5	.722	Los Angeles	8	4	.667
East Division	**58**	**32**	**.644**	San Diego	11	1	.917
				West Division	**43**	**29**	**.597**

It should be noted that New York was 0-6 in the Astrodome in Houston, Texas.

CHAPTER 4

THE 1969 WORLD SERIES

In contrast to the previous season, when the World Series opponents were determined by mid September - Detroit in the American League and St. Louis in the National League. The matchup for the 66th Fall Classic was not finalized until October 6th.

The Major League adoption of divisional play and playoff games - league championship series, moved the World Series back by better than a week. Both league championship games were decided in three straight games. New York sweeping the Atlanta Braves and Baltimore sweeping Minnesota.

The Orioles were the winningest team in 1969 with 109 regular season wins, the most since Cleveland won 111 games in 1954. The Orioles were installed as heavy betting favores and were 5/9 favorites in Las Vegas.

The Mets advanced to the World Series on strong arms of a fine pitching staff. They sent 25 game winner, Tom Seaver to the mound for the first game in Baltimore's Memorial Stadium.

Mike Cuellar, leading the Baltimore staff with 23 games won, was the Oriole starter. The left-handed Cuban screw - ball pitcher was better than Seaver and ended his 11 game winning streak.

Baltimore left-fielder, Don Buford, making his initial appearance in the World Series sent a drive over the bullpen gate in right field, just out of the reach of Ron Swoboda who leaped at the gate for a home run. Boog Powell then got a harmless single later in the inning. Then Seaver, recovering his excellent control, did not allow another hit until two were out in the top of the fourth.

Catcher, Ellrod Hendricks singled then Seaver walked Dave Johnson. His only issued base on balls. The walk was costly, as Mark Belanger singled to right to plate Hendricks with the second run. Swoboda's throw was off target to home plate. This was the winning run. Johnson ran to third base on the play. Then Cuellar helped himself with a bloop single to center that scored Johnson, making it 3-0, Baltimore.

That brought up Don Buford, again and he delivered Baltimore's last run with a double to right.

Cuellar, meanwhile fed New York, a steady diet of screwballs. They did not do anything until the last of the seventh, down 4-0. First baseman, Don Clendenon opened the frame with a single, then Swoboda walked. Catcher, Jerry Grote then hit a one out single past Belanger at shortstop to load the bases. Mets' shortstop, Al Weiss then hit a sacrifice fly to left that ruined the shutout by Cuellar.

The Mets would not score again, helped by third baseman, Brooks Robinson great play on pinch-hitter, Rod Gasper's dribbler down the third base line.

Robinson hustled in, barehanded the ball, and threw to first base, beating Gasper by ½ step. The Mets had a minor flurry in the ninth, when Swoboda singled, then with two out Weiss walked. Cuellar then got pinch-hitter, Art Shamsky on a ground out to second base to end the game, 4-1 Baltimore. Cuellar was only the second Cuban to win a World Series game. The other was Adolfo Lugue of the New York Giants who defeated the Washington Senators in 1933.

While Baltimore fans applauded Cuellars - 6 hit pitching game, which was led by Buford's hitting and Brook Robinson's fielding. However, the big three - Frank and Brook Robinson, plus Boog Powell only got a single in 12 at-bats. It was an ominous sign for Baltimore of the future.

Box Score Game 1 in Baltimore
October 11th, 1969
Attendance: 50,429

	1	2	3	4	5	6	7	8	9	R
New York	0	0	0	0	0	0	1	0	0	1
Baltimore	1	0	0	3	0	0	0	0	X	4

New York	AB	R	H	RBI	Baltimore	AB	R	H	RBI
Agee, cf	4	0	0	0	Buford, lf	4	1	2	2
Harrelson, ss	3	0	1	0	Blair, cf	3	0	0	0
Jones, lf	4	0	1	0	F. Robby, rf	4	0	0	0
Clendenon, 1b	4	1	2	0	Powell, 1b	4	0	1	0
Swoboda, rf	3	0	1	0	B. Robby, 3b	4	0	0	0
Charles, 3b	4	0	0	0	Hendricks, c	3	1	1	0
Grote, c	4	0	1	0	Johnson, 2b	2	1	0	0
Weiss, 2b	1	0	0	0	Belanger, ss	3	1	1	1
Seaver, p	1	0	0	0	Cuellar, p	3	0	1	1
Dwyer, ph	1	0	0	0	Total	30	4	6	4
Cardwell, p	0	0	0	0					
Gasper, ph	1	0	0	0					
Taylor, p	0	0	0	0					
Shamsky, ph	1	0	0	0					
Total	31	1	6	1					

2B: Clendenon and Buford.   HR: Buford.   SF: Weiss.
DP: Baltimore.   LOB: New York (8), Baltimore (4).
Att: 50, 429.   Time: 2:11.

New York Pitching	IP	R	H	SO	BB
Seaver (Loser)	5	4	6	3	1
Cardwell	1	0	0	0	0
Taylor	2	0	0	3	1
Total	8	4	6	6	2

Baltimore Pitching	IP	R	H	SO	BB
Cuellar(Winner)	9	1	6	8	1

The hitting concern for the Orioles grew in game two, when Brooks and Frank Robinson, and Boog Powell (the Orioles big three) went a collective 1 for 10 against the 26 year old left-hander, Jerry Koosman, who flirted with Series immortality by holding the Orioles hitless for 6 innings.

Baltimore center fielder, Paul Blair ruined the no-hitter in the seventh inning with a single. Koosman retired the next two batters, but Blair engineered a dairing steal of second base and Brooks Robinson hit a ground ball single into center to plate the Orioles only run. This was the only other hit of the game.

That tied the score at 1-1. The Mets only run came in the fourth on former Pirate and Expos, Don Clendenon's home run to right field off Dave McNally in the fourth.

Going into the top of the ninth, McNally, a 20 game winner, retired the first two Met batters, easily. But, third baseman, Ed Charles gave New York a life with a single to left. Grote also, singled bringing up the light hitting, Weis (.215 batting average). Oriole manager, Earl Weaver, who ordered Weis walked, earlier to get to Koosman, elected to have McNally pitch to Weis this time.

McNally's first pitch was a high slider that Weis ripped into left-field to score Charles to give New York a 2-1 lead.

As the ninth unfolded, Koosman needed help from Ron Taylor who pitched two innings of relief in the first game, before Jerry would get the 2-1 victory.

Koosman retired the first two Orioles in the ninth, then walked Frank Robinson and Boog Powell, both on 3-2 counts. Taylor came on to pitch and after running the count to 3-1 on Brooks Robinson, retired him on a ground ball to Charles at third base.

The victory was a squeaker, but New York took it, tying the series at

1-1, with the series shifting to New York.

October 12th, 1969
Baltimore's Memorial Stadium

	1	2	3	4	5	6	7	8	9	R
New York	0	0	0	1	0	0	0	0	1	2
Baltimore	0	0	0	0	0	0	1	0	X	1

New York	AB	R	H	RBI	Baltimore	AB	R	H	RBI
Agee, cf	4	0	0	0	Buford, lf	4	0	0	0
Harrelson, ss	3	0	0	0	Blair, cf	4	1	1	0
Jones, lf	4	0	0	0	F. Robinson, rf	3	0	0	0
Clendenon, 1b	3	1	1	1	Rettenmund, pr	0	0	0	0
Swoboda, rf	4	0	0	0	Powell, 1b	3	0	0	0
Charles, 3b	4	1	2	0	B. Robinson, 3b	4	0	1	1
Grote, c	4	0	1	0	Johnson, 2b	2	0	0	0

New York	AB	R	H	RBI	Baltimore	AB	R	H	RBI
Koosman, p	4	0	0	0	Belanger, ss	3	0	0	0
Taylor, p	0	0	0	0	McNally, p	3	0	0	0
Total	33	2	6	2	Total	29	1	2	1

2B-Charles, HR: Clendonon. **SB: Blair.** **WP: McNally.**
LOB: New York 7, Baltimore 4. **Time: 2:20.** **Attendance: 50,850**

New York	IP	R	H	SO	BB
Koosman (W)	8 2/3	1	2	4	3
Taylor	1/3	0	0	0	0
Total	9	1	2	4	3

Baltimore	IP	R	H	SO	BB
McNally (L)	9	2	6	7	3
Total	9	2	6	7	3

The threat of rain hung over Shea Stadium prior to the third game, on October 14th, contrasting the excellent weather conditions they had in Baltimore.

Mets fans, despite the rain, packed Shea Stadium, something which could not be said of Oriole fans who did not sell out the first two games. The Oriole fans winning had become routine, I guess with titles in 1966 and 1970, the year after. Also, the Mets were determined as not much of a threat to the title, again for Baltimore. The Mets fans were treated to best defensive play by a center fielder in World Series history. Tommy Agee, the center fielder who played briefly, with Cleveland and the Chicago White Sox made two great catches to prevent Baltimore from scoring five runs.

Agee brought Met backers to their feet early in the first inning with a home run off Baltimore starter Jim Palmer in the first. Palmer had a stellar record, going 16-4 in regular season.

That home run was all Met starter, Gary Gentry needed, who was a rookie. Tom Agee also made key defensive plays twice bailing Gentry out of serious jams.

The Mets upped their lead to 3-0 when Gentry doubled to right center plating two runs in the second inning.

Baltimore looked like it would score in the fourth. Frank Robinson and Powell reached first and third with singles. After Brooks Robinson struck out, Hendricks lashed a line drive that appeared to be trouble into left-center. Agee was playing in right center because he was a left-handed batter. He raced more than 30 yards in the opposite direction and caught the ball back-handed in the webbing of his glove.

It was a great play for the final out of the fourth inning. With the Mets leading 4-0 in the seventh inning, Gentry was beginning to tire with fatigue and lost his control. He walked three straight batters - Belanger, pinch-hitter- Dave May, and Don Buford loaded the bases after two were out. Then Gil Hodges went to the bullpen and brought in 22 year old, Nolan Ryan.

The fire-balling right-hander got two quick strikes on Blair, but his third pitch was hit hard on a line to right-center. Again, the ball looked like a sure double. Agee dashed over and made a sliding catch on his knees, just above the grass.

Agee who played spectacular defense had taken 5 runs off the board with his key catches.

The Mets upped had upped the lead to 4-0 in the sixth on Ken Boswell's infield single, a ground out, and Jerry Grote's double.

Ed Kranepool's solo home run against Dennis Leonard completed the scoring in the 8th.

The Orioles threatened in the ninth against Ryan by loading the bases on two walks and Clay Dalrymple's infield hit after two were out. But Ryan recovered to strike out Paul Blair by throwing two fast balls past him then a curve ball to get him looking on strike 3. The Mets won 5-0 and led the World Series 2 games to one game.

October 14th, 1969
New York - Shea Stadium

	1	2	3	4	5	6	7	8	9	R
Baltimore	0	0	0	0	0	0	0	0	0	0
New York	1	2	0	0	0	1	0	1	X	5

Baltimore	AB	R	H	RBI	New York	AB	R	H	RBI
Buford, lf	5	0	0	0	Agee, cf	3	1	1	1
Blair, cf	5	0	0	0	Garrett, 3b	1	0	0	0
F. Robinson, rf	2	0	1	0	Jones, lf	4	0	0	0
Powell, 1b	4	0	2	0	Shamsky, rf	4	0	0	0
B. Robinson, 3b	4	0	0	0	Weis, ss	0	0	0	0
Hendricks, c	4	0	0	0	Boswell, 2b	3	1	1	0

Belanger, ss	2	0	0	0	Kranepool, 1b	4	1	1	1
Palmer, p	2	0	0	0	Grote, c	3	1	1	1
May, ph	0	0	0	0	Harrelson, ss	3	1	1	0
Leonard, p	0	0	0	0	Gentry, p	3	0	1	0
Dalrymple, ph	1	0	1	0	Ryan, p	0	0	0	0
Salmon ph	0	0	0	0	Total	29	5	6	5
Total	31	0	4	0					

2B- Gentry, Grote.　　HR: Kranepool (1),　　SH: Garrett,
LOB: Baltimore 11, New York 6.　　Attendance: 56,335.
Time: 2:23.

Baltimore Pitching	IP	H	R	SO	BB
Palmer (L)	6	5	4	5	1
Leonhard	2	1	1	1	1
Total	8	6	5	6	2

New York Pitching	IP	H	R	SO	BB
Gentry (W)	5 2/3	3	0	4	5
Ryan (Save)	2 1/3	1	0	3	2
Total	9	4	0	7	7

First game pitching opponents Cuellar and Seaver were matched again in the fourth contest, and both pitched good enough to win in an extra inning game that went 10 innings. The game ended in a controversial call on a bunt that gave the Mets a 2-1 decision and a commanding 3-1 lead in games.

The controversial play came with the score 1-1 with runners at first and second and nobody out in the bottom of the tenth.

The stage was set when leadoff hitter Grote's pop fly to short left field in front of Buford, who lost th ball in the background of the sky and got a late start or jump on the ball that fell for a double. Baltimore intentionally walked Weis to set up a possible double play grounder, but Gil Hodges countered by pinch-hitting, catcher J.C. Martin, a left-handed batter. The Orioles then brought in left-handed pitcher, Pete Richert.

Hodges had Martin bunt, and he did so beautifully. Richert and Hendricks converged on the ball, but Hendricks throw to first base hit Martin on the left wrist. Then the ball caromed toward second base and Gasper, pinch-running for Grote scored from second base to win the game, 2-1. Earl Weaver was not in the dugout to protest the play because he was ejected in the third inning for arguing balls and strikes by Shag Crawford.

Newpapers photographs published the following day showed that Martin was apparently running on the fair side of first base line close to the line of the grass, not the dirt before he was struck by Richert's throw. Cries of runner interference surfaced by the Baltimore team.

The Mets had gotten the scoring jump early in the game on a home run by first baseman, Don Clendenon leading off the second against Mike Cuellar. This was the first extra inning affair in the World Series since 1964 when Yankee's, Mickey Mantle ended a game, 2-1 against St. Louis Cardinal's knuckballer, Barney Shultz on a home run in Yankee Stadium.

Mike Cuellar left the game for a pinch-hitter in the eighth inning, but Seaver ended up going 10 innings and a complete game for New York. Baltimore tied in the top of the ninth on singles by Frank Robinson and Boog Powell. Then, Brooks Robinson hit a line drive slicer into right center field that Ron Swoboda made a tremendous diving catch to keep the score tied at 1-1. This set up the J.C. Martin bunt in the tenth frame that won the game for New York.

MICKEY STRUNAK

October 15th, New York, Shea Stadium
Attendance: 57,367

Baltimore	AB	R	H	RBI	New York	AB	R	H	RBI
Buford, lf	5	0	0	0	Agee, cf	4	0	1	0
Blair, cf	4	0	1	0	Harrelson, ss	4	0	1	0
F. Robinson, rf	4	1	1	0	Jones, lf	4	0	1	0
Powell, 1b	4	0	1	0	Clendenon, 1b	4	1	1	1
B. Robinson, 3b	3	0	0	1	Swoboda, rf	4	0	2	0
Hendricks, c	3	0	0	0	Charles, 3b	3	0	0	0
Johnson, 2b	4	0	0	0	Shamsky, ph	1	0	0	0
Cuellar, p	2	0	1	0	Grote, c	4	0	1	0
May, ph	1	0	0	0	Gasper, pr	0	1	0	0
Watt, p	0	0	0	0	Weis, 2b	3	0	2	1
Dalrymple, ph	1	0	1	0	Seaver, p	3	0	0	0
Hall, p	0	0	0	0	Martin, ph	0	0	0	0
Richert, p	0	0	0	0	Total	34	2	10	2
Total	35	1	6	1					

2B: Grote, HR: Clendenon (2), SH: Martin, SF: B. Robinson.
DP: Baltimore 3. LOB: Baltimore 7, New York 7. Time: 2:33

Baltimore	IP	H	R	SO	BB
Cuellar	7	7	1	5	0
Watt	2	2	0	2	0
Hall (L)	0*	1	1	0	1
Richert	0+	0	0	0	0
Total	9	10	2	7	1

*   Pitched to 2 batters in the 10th.
\+   Pitched to 1 batter in the 10th.

New York	IP	H	R	SO	BB
Seaver (W)	10	6	1	6	2

With their backs against the wall in the fifth game, the O's broke out of their hitting slump by taking the early lead against New York.

Baltimore back to being a power hitting club, scored three runs in the third inning against the Jerry Koosman. The long ball accounted for all three runs. Orioles pitcher, Dave McNally drove a Koosman pitch over the fence after a single by Mark Belanger. Then Frank Robinson hit a solo home run to make the score 3-0, Baltimore.

That was the only offense for Baltimore this afternoon, as Koosman regained his composure and control by limiting the Orioles just one hit over the final 6 innings.

McNally who scattered three hits held New York scoreless until the 6th.

Cleon Jones skipped out of the way of low inside fastball. When the ball was retieved it had smudges of shoe polish. Jones was awarded first base after umpire, Lou DiMuro, who originally called the pitch a ball. This brought Don Clendenon to the plate. Clendenon homered, his third of the Series to bring the Mets back into the game. The home run hit off the auxiliary scoreboard in left field.

McNally left for a pinch hitter after Weis hit his home run to tie the score, 3-3 in the seventh.

Koosman continued to put zeros up on the scoreboard. However, the Oriole relief pitching failed, again. Eddie Watt was now pitching for Baltimore and started the eighth by giving up a double to Cleon Jones, off the wall in left-center. After an out, Ron Swoboda hit a line drive to left that Buford trapped against the grass. Cleon Jones ran home with go-ahead run to make it, 4-3.

The fifth run was tainted for the Mets when Boog Powell misplayed Grote's smash grounder for a error, then Watt dropped

Powell's throw to the bag . While the Orioles were trying to find the ball, Swoboda scored all the way second base for a 5-3 margin.

With a 2 run cushion, Koosman walked lead-off hitter, Frank Robinson in the ninth. Powell then was safe at first after a fielder's choice ground out. Then Brooks Robinson and Dave Johnson hit routine fly outs, the last in left field to Cleon Jones.

The Mets had accomplished a baseball miracle with the 5-3 victory. They finished in ninth place the year before and were a 30-1 longshot in Las Vegas to win the World Series.

Only a quick dash by the players from the field saved them from an affectionate mauling from the frenzied New York fans running out on the field. The fans ripped up the grass sod and took it as souveners.

On the statistical sheet, the final numbers showed that the surprising Mets had outmuscled the Orioles who were number 2 in batting average in the American League. Weis, who hit .215 in the season, hit .455 for the Mets with 5 hits in 11 at bats. Swoboda hit .400 and Clendenon hit for a .357 batting average with 3 home runs and 4 RBI's. The Mets hit .220 for the 5 game series.

The Orioles only hit .146, with not one regular over .200, except Boog Powell who hit .263.

Brooks Robinson hit only .053 by going 1 for 19 and failed to produce in the clutch. He was stopped once in the turning play of the series by center fielder, Tommy Agee great play.

The Mets pitchers compiled a glistening 1.80 ERA in 5 games and Koosman won 2 games for New York. Baltimore 's ERA was a competent 2.72. However, the Mets hit 6 home runs in the series. Baltimore hit 8 doubles with the lone home run by Frank Robinson in the last game.

Even though the World Series only lasted 5 games, it was a financial success and set a record for revenue due to new league championship series round. The Mets players got $18,338 per player and Baltimore $14,904.

October 16th, 1969
At New York's Shea Stadium
Attendance: 57,397

Baltimore	AB	R	H	RBI	New York	AB	R	H	RBI
Buford, lf	4	0	0	0	Agee, rf	3	0	1	0
Blair, cf	4	0	0	0	Harrelson, ss	4	0	0	0
F. Robinson, rf	3	1	1	1	Jones, lf	3	2	1	0
Powell, 1b	4	0	1	0	Clendenon, 1b	3	1	1	2
Salmon, pr	0	0	0	0	Swoboda, rf	4	1	2	1
Johnson, 2b	4	0	1	0	Charles, 3b	4	1	2	0
Echebarren, c	3	0	0	0	Grote c	4	0	0	0
Belanger, ss	3	1	1	0	Weis, 2b	4	1	1	1
McNally, p	2	1	1	2	Koosman, p	3	0	1	0
Total	32	3	5	3	Total	32	5	7	4

2B: Koosman, Jones, Swoboda. HR's: McNally, F. Robinson, Clendenin (3), and Weis. SB: Agee. HBP: Jones (McNally). LOB: Baltimore 3, New York 6. Att: 57,397 Time: 2:14.

Baltimore	IP	H	R	SO	BB
McNally	7	5	3	6	2
Watt (L)	1	2	2	1	0
Total	8	7	5	7	2

New York	IP	H	R	SO	BB
Koosman (W)	9	5	3	6	1

Composite World Series Batting Averages for the 1969 New York Mets

Player	G	AB	R	H	HR	RBI	BA	SB
Al Weis, 2b	5	11	1	5	1	3	.455	0
Ron Swoboda, rf	4	15	1	6	0	1	.400	0
Don Clendenon, 1b	4	14	4	5	3	4	.357	0
Dave Boswell, 2b	1	3	1	1	0	0	.333	0
Gary Gentry, p	1	3	0	1	0	0	.333	0
Ed Kranepool, 1b	1	4	1	1	1	1	.250	0
Jerry Grote, c	5	19	1	4	0	1	.211	0
Don Harrelson, ss	5	17	1	3	0	0	.176	0
Tommie Agee, cf	5	18	1	3	1	1	.167	1
Cleon Jones, lf	5	19	2	3	0	0	.158	0
Jerry Koosman, p	2	7	0	1	0	0	.143	0
Ed Charles, 3b	4	15	1	2	0	0	.143	0
Art Shamsky, rf-ph	3	6	0	0	0	0	.000	0
Tom Seaver, p	2	4	0	0	0	0	.000	0
Gasper, ph,rf,pr	3	2	1	0	0	0	.000	0
Duffy Dyer, ph	1	0	0	0	0	0	.000	0
Ron Taylor, p	2	0	0	0	0	0	.000	0
Don Cardwell, p	1	0	0	0	0	0	.000	0
J.C. Martin, ph	1	0	0	0	0	0	.000	0
Nolan Ryan, p	1	0	0	0	0	0	.000	0
Total	5	139	15	35	6	13	**.220**	0

Composite World Series Batting Averages for the 1969 Baltimore Orioles

Player	G	AB	R	H	HR	RBI	BA	SB
Clay Dalrymple, c	2	2	0	2	0	0	1.000	0
Mike Cuellar, p	2	5	0	2	0	1	.400	0
Boog Powell, 1b	5	19	0	5	0	0	.263	0
Mark Belanger, ss	5	15	2	3	0	1	.200	0
Dave McNally, p	2	5	1	1	1	2	.200	0
Frank Robinson, rf	5	16	2	3	1	1	.188	0
Paul Blair, cf	5	20	1	2	1	2	.100	1
Don Buford, lf	5	20	1	2	0	0	.100	0
Elrod Hendricks, c	5	20	1	2	1	2	.100	0
Dave Johnson, 2b	5	18	1	1	0	1	.063	0
Brooks Robinson, 3b	5	19	0	1	0	2	.053	0
Andy Echebarren, c	2	6	0	0	0	0	.000	0
Jim Palmer, p	1	2	0	0	0	0	.000	0
May, ph	1	2	0	0	0	0	.000	0
Mitton, ph	1	1	0	0	0	0	.000	0
Chico Salmon, pr	2	0	0	0	0	0	.000	0
Eddie Watt, p	2	0	0	0	0	0	.000	0
Dick Hall, p	1	0	0	0	0	0	.000	0
Leonhard, p	1	0	0	0	0	0	.000	0
Merv Rettenmund, pr	1	0	0	0	0	0	.000	0
Richert, p	1	0	0	0	0	0	.000	0
Total	**5**	**157**	**9**	**23**	**3**	**9**	**.146**	**1**

Pitching Records - 1969 New York Mets

New York	G	W	L	IP	H	R	SO	BB	ERA
Gary Gentry	2	1	0	7	3	0	4	5	0.00
Ron Taylor	2	0	0	2	0	0	3	1	0.00
Nolan Ryan	1	0	0	2	1	0	3	2	0.00
Don Cardwell	1	0	0	1	0	0	0	0	0.00
Jerry Koosman	2	2	0	18	7	4	9	4	2.04
Tom Seaver	2	1	1	15	12	5	9	3	3.00
Total	5	4	1	45	23	9	28	15	1.80

Pitching Records - 1969 Baltimore Orioles

Baltimore	G	W	L	IP	H	R	SO	BB	ERA
Mike Cuellar	2	1	0	16	13	2	13	4	1.13
Dave McNally	2	0	1	16	11	5	13	5	2.81
Eddie Watt	2	0	1	3	4	2	3	0	3.00
Leonhard	1	0	0	2	1	1	0	0	4.50
Jim Palmer	1	0	1	6	5	4	5	4	6.00
Dick Hall	1	0	1	1	1	1	0	1	0.00
Dick Richert	1	0	0	0	0	0	0	0	0.00
Total	5	1	4	43	33	13	35	15	2.72

New York Mets Records by Month - 1969

Month	W	L	Pct.
April	9	11	.450
May	12	12	.500
June	19	9	.679
July	15	12	.556
August	21	10	.677
September	23	7	.767
October	1	1	.500
Total	100	62	617

Final Records of Major League Teams in 1969
National League

Eastern Division	W	L	Pct.	GB
New York	100	62	.617	___
Chicago	92	70	.568	8
Pittsburgh	88	74	.543	12
St. Louis	87	75	.537	13
Philadelphia	63	99	.389	37
Montreal	52	110	.321	48

West Division	W	L	Pct.	GB
Atlanta	93	69	.574	___
San Francisco	90	72	.556	3
Cincinnati	89	73	.549	4
Los Angeles	85	77	.525	8
Houston	81	81	.500	12
San Diego	52	110	.321	41

American League

Eastern Division	W	L	Pct.	GB
Baltimore	109	53	.699	___
Detroit	90	72	.556	19
Boston	87	75	.537	22
Washington	86	76	.531	23
New York	80	81	.497	28 ½
Cleveland	62	99	.385	46 ½

Western	W	L	Pct.	GB
Minnesota	97	65	.599	---
Oakland	88	74	.543	9
California	71	91	.436	26
Kansas City	69	93	.426	28
Chicago	68	94	.420	29
Seattle	64	98	.395	33

CHAPTER 5

NATIONAL LEAGUE CHAMPIONSHIP SERIES 1969

The National League's first experience with the two division playoff system provided one of those rare instances of an underdog winning.

The New York Mers were definitely the underdog of all of baseball. They were the darlings of Manhatten. The Yankees had their die hard fans in the Bronx. The Mets fans were the old Brooklyn Dodgers fans whose team relocated to Los Angeles in 1958 along with the New York Giants.

The Mets swept the Atlanta Braves in 5 straight games to win their first NL Pennant. The Mets had five tenth place (last place) finishes and two ninth place finishes.

In 8 of 12 regular season contests the Mets won against Atlanta. Their pitching was especially superior in complete games (51-38), hits given up (1,217 - 1,334), runs (541-631), strikeouts(1,012-893), shutouts (28-7), and ERA (2.99 to 3.53 for Atlanta).

The Braves held the edge in offense: hits (1,411-1,311), runs (691-632), Doubles (195-184), Home Runs (141-109), and batting average (.258 to .242).

In the final analysis, pitching often considered 90% of the game, predicted the outcome.

In the first game, played in front of 50,122 in Atlanta's Fulton County Stadium, October 4th, Mets' ace, Tom Seaver faced Phil Niekro, knuckleball, who won 23 games with Atlanta. The Braves were making their first post-season appearance since relocating from Milwaukee to Atlanta in 1966. The Braves last appeared in World Series in 1958 with the Yankees. Only Hank Aaron was left from that team in 1958 which lost to New York in seven games.

Neither starting pitcher finished, Niekro lasted 8 innings, giving up 5 runs in the eighth that cemented the win for the Mets. Tom Seaver departed for a pinch-hitter in the 8th.

Wayne Garrett opened the tell-tale frame with a double and tied the score, 5-5 when Cleon Jones singled. Art Shamsky's third hit sent Jones to second base. When Ken Boswell missed an attempted sacrifice, Jones was trapped off second base. Atlanta catcher, Bob Didier made the mistake of throwing behind the runner, then Jones beat the relay to third base.

When Ken Boswell grounded to the mound, the Braves could only get one runner Al Weis, who ran for Shamsky at second base. On Ed Kranepool's grounder to first base, Orlando "Cha Cha" Cepeda fired to home plate high with Jones scoring the go ahead run, 6-5.

After Jerry Grote was retired, manager Luman Harris ordered Bud Harrelson walked intentionally loading the bases for Tom Seaver. Hodges then went to his bench for pinch-hitter, J.C. Martin. Martin singled to center and when Gonzalez misplayed the ball, three runs came home making it, 9-5.

SUMMER OF '69

Game 1, Saturday October 4th at Atlanta
Attendance : 50,122

	1	2	3	4	5	6	7	8	9	R
New York	0	2	0	2	0	0	0	5	0	9
Atlanta	0	1	2	0	1	0	1	0	0	5

New York	AB	R	H	RBI	Atlanta	AB	R	H	RBI
Agee, cf	5	0	0	0	Millan, 2b	5	1	2	0
Garrett, 3b	4	1	2	0	Gonzalez, cf	5	2	2	2
Jones, lf	5	1	1	1	H. Aaron, rf	5	1	2	2
Shamsky, rf	4	1	3	0	Carty, lf	3	1	1	0
Weis, pr-2b	0	0	0	0	Lum, lf	1	0	1	0
Boswell, 2b	3	2	0	0	Cepeda, 1b	4	0	1	0
Gasper, rf	0	0	0	0	Boyer, 3b	1	0	0	1
Kranepool, 1b	4	2	1	0	Didier, c	4	0	0	0
Grote, c	3	1	1	0	Garrido, ss	4	0	1	0
Harrelson, ss	3	1	1	3	Niekro, p	3	0	0	0
Seaver, p	3	0	0	0	Aspromonte ph	1	0	0	0
Martin, ph	1	0	1	2	Upshaw, p	0	0	0	0
Taylor, p	0	0	0	0	Total	36	5	10	5
Total	35	9	10	6					

Errors: Boswell, Cepeda, Gonzalez. DP: Atlanta - 2. LOB: New York 3, Atlanta 9. 2B: Carter, Millan, Gonzalez, H. Aaron, Garrett, Lum. 3B: Harrelson. HR: Gonzalez, H. Aaron. SB: Cepeda, Jones. SF: Boyer. HBP: Cepeda (Seaver).

New York	IP	H	R	SO	BB
Seaver (W)	7	9	5	2	3
Taylor (S)	2	2	0	2	0
Total	9	11	5	4	3

Atlanta	IP	H	R	SO	BB
Niekro (L)	8	9	5	2	3
Upshaw	1	1	0	1	0
Total	9	10	5	3	3

In the second game before another sell-out crowd in Atlanta - 50,270 - October 5th, Jerry Koosman, the Mets' 17 game winner was staked to leads of 8-0 and 9-1, yet failed to survive the fifth inning.

The Mets tagged Ron Reed for 4 runs in one and 2/3 innings, added two more off Paul Doyle and then three more before the Braves offense went to work.

A home run by Hank Aaron, who homered in each of the three games, provided three runs. A single by Felix Millan, double by Cepeda and then a single by Clete Boyer accounted for two more runs. Then, Koosman departed for the showers with the score, 9-6 New York.

Ron Taylor and Tug McGraw shut out the Braves on two hit's the rest of the game. The Mets scored two more after Cleon Jones hit a home run with Tom Agee on third base. This accounted for the final margin of 11-6.

Game of Sunday - October 5th at Atlanta
Attendance: 50,270

	1	2	3	4	5	6	7	8	9	R
New York	1	3	2	2	1	0	2	0	0	11
Atlanta	0	0	0	1	5	0	0	0	0	6

New York	AB	R	H	RBI	Atlanta	AB	R	H	RBI
Agee, cf	4	3	2	2	Millan, 2b	2	1	2	0
Garrett, 3b	5	1	2	1	Gonzalez, cf	4	1	1	0
Jones, lf	5	2	3	3	H. Aaron, rf	5	1	3	2
Gasper, pr-rf	0	0	0	0	Carty, lf	4	2	1	0
Boswell, 2b	5	1	1	2	Cepeda, 1b	4	1	2	1
McGraw, p	0	0	0	0	Boyer, 3b	4	0	1	2
Kranepool, 1b	4	0	1	1	Garrido, ss	4	0	1	0
Grote, c	5	1	0	0	Reed, p	0	0	0	0
Harrelson, ss	5	1	1	1	Doyle, p	0	0	0	0
Koosman, p	2	1	0	0	Pappus, p	1	0	0	0
Taylor, p	0	0	0	0	T. Aaron, ph	1	0	0	0
Martin ph	1	0	0	0	Briton, p	0	0	0	0
Weis, 2b	1	0	0	0	Upshaw, p	1	0	0	0
Total	42	11	13	11	Aspromonte, Ph	1	0	0	0
					Neibauer, p	0	0	0	0
					Total	35	6	9	6

Errors: H Aaron, Cepeda, Harrelson, Boyer. DP: Atlanta 1, New York 2. LOB: New York 10, Atlanta 7. 2B: Jones, Harrelson, Carty, Garrett, Cepeda. HR: Agee, Boswell, H. Aaron, Jones. SB: Agee 2, Garrett, Jones. Time: 3:10. Attendance: 50,276

When the NLCS switched to New York, the Mets provided the clincher in front of 53,195 delirious Met fanatics on October 6th.

This game belonged to Nolan Ryan who replaced starter, Gary Gentry with runners on second and third with Atlanta leading 2-0.

Ryan fanned Rico Carty, as a starter, walked Cepeda intentionally, whiffed Clete Boyer and retired Bob Didier ona flyout to left field to escape damage.

The hard - throwing only mistake was in the fifth when Orlando Cepeda hit a two run home run that made it, 4-3 Atlanta.

Ryan quickly made amends for that home run, by getting a single to start the sixth inning. After Agee made an out, Wayne Garrett, whose last home run was on May 6th, exactly 5 months earlier, crushed Pat Jarvis first pitch into the upper deck in right field. That put the Mets ahead to stay.

Nolan Ryan who pitched only 89 innings in regular season, allowed just three hits in 7 innings. He also had another single in the 7-4 victory.

It was the typical Met win, timely and dramatic. Nolan Ryan went on to a very storied career - over 300 wins and seven no-hitters. Also, he got a spot in Cooperstown's Baseball Hall of Fame. Most of his success came with the California Angels and the Houston Astros.

SUMMER OF '69

Tuesday, October 7th, 1969
Shea Stadium - New York
Attendance: 53,195

	1	2	3	4	5	6	7	8	9	R
Atlanta	2	0	0	0	2	0	0	0	0	4
New York	0	0	1	2	3	1	0	0	X	7

Atlanta	AB	R	H	RBI	New York	AB	R	H	RBI
Millan, 2b	5	0	0	0	Agee, cf	5	1	3	2
Gonzalez, cf	5	1	2	0	Garrett, 3b	4	1	2	2
H. Aaron, rf	4	1	2	2	Jones, lf	4	1	2	0
Carty, lf	3	1	1	0	Shamsky, rf	4	1	1	0
Cepeda, 1b	2	1	2	2	Gasper, pr-rf	0	0	0	0
Boyer, 3b	4	0	0	0	Boswell, 2b	4	1	3	3
Didier, c	3	0	0	0	Weis, 2b	0	0	0	0
Lum, ph	1	0	1	0	Kranepool, 1b	4	0	1	0
Jackson, ss	0	0	0	0	Grote, c	4	1	1	0
Alou, ph	1	0	0	0	Harrelson, ss	3	0	0	0
Tillman, c	0	0	0	0	Gentry p	0	0	0	0
Aspromonte, ph	1	0	0	0	Ryan p	4	1	20	
Total	35	4	8	4	Total	36	7	14	7

Errors: Millan. DP: Atlanta 1. LOB: Atlanta 7, New York 6.
2B: Cepeda, Agee, H. Aaron, Kranepool, Jones, Grote.
HR: H. Aaron, Agee, Boswell, Cepeda, Garrett. SH: Harrelson. Att: 53,195.
Time: 2:24.

Atlanta	IP	H	R	SO	BB
Jarvis (L)	4 2/3	10	6	6	0
Stone	1	2	1	0	0
Upshaw	2 2/3	2	0	3	0
Total	8	14	7	9	0

New York	IP	H	R	SO	BB
Gentry	2	5	2	1	1
Ryan (W)	7	3	2	7	2
Total	9	8	4	8	3

Composite Batting Records - NLCS
1969 New York Mets

Player	G	AB	R	H	HR	RBI	BA	SB
Art Shamsky, rf	3	13	3	7	0	1	.528	0
Nolan Ryan, p	1	4	1	2	0	0	.500	0
J.C. Martin, ph	2	2	0	1	0	2	.500	0
Cleon Jones	3	14	4	6	1	4	.429	1
Garrett, 3b	3	13	3	5	1	3	.385	1
Agee, cf	3	14	4	5	2	4	.357	2
Ken Boswell, 2b	3	12	4	4	2	5	.333	0
Ed Kranepool, 1b	3	12	2	3	0	1	.256	0
Bud Harrelson, ss	3	11	2	2	0	3	.182	0
Jerry Grote, c	3	12	3	2	0	1	.167	0
Gasper, rf-pr	3	0	0	0	0	0	.000	0
Tug McGraw, p	1	0	0	0	0	0	.000	0
Gary Gentry, p	1	0	0	0	0	0	.000	0
Ron Taylor, p	2	0	0	0	0	0	.000	0
Al Weis, 2b	3	1	0	0	0	0	.000	0
Jerry Koosman, p	1	2	1	0	0	0	.000	0
Tom Seaver, p	1	3	0	0	0	0	.000	0
Total	3	113	27	37	6	24	.327	0

Composite Batting Records - NLCS
1969 Atlanta Braves

Player	G	AB	R	H	HR	RBI	BA	SB
Mike Lum, lf-ph	2	2	0	2	0	0	1.000	0
Cepeda, 1b	3	11	2	5	1	3	.455	0
H. Aaron, rf	3	14	3	5	3	7	.357	0
Gonzalez, cf	3	14	4	5	1	2	.357	0
Millan, 2b	3	12	2	4	0	0	.333	0
Carty, lf	3	10	4	3	0	0	.300	0
Garrido, ss	3	10	0	2	0	0	.200	0
Boyer, 3b	3	9	0	1	0	3	.111	0
Tillman, c	1	0	0	0	0	0	.000	0
Reed, p	1	0	0	0	0	0	.000	0
Jackson, ss	1	0	0	0	0	0	.000	0
Doyle, p	1	0	0	0	0	0	.000	0
Britton, p	1	0	0	0	0	0	.000	0
Neihomer, p	1	0	0	0	0	0	.000	0
Stone, p	1	1	0	0	0	0	.000	0
Upshaw, p	1	1	0	0	0	0	.000	0
T Aaron, ph	1	1	0	0	0	0	.000	0
Alou, ph	1	1	0	0	0	0	.000	0
Pappas, p	1	2	0	0	0	0	.000	0
Jarvis, p	1	1	0	0	0	0	.000	0
Aspromonte, ph	3	3	0	0	0	0	.000	0
Niekro, p	1	3	0	0	0	0	.000	0
Didier, c	3	11	0	0	0	0	.000	0
Total	3	106	15	27	5	15	.255	0

New York Mets Pitching Records - 1969
NLCS

Pitcher	G	IP	H	R	SO	BB	W	L	Pct.	ERA
Taylor	2	3 1/3	3	0	4	0	1	0	1.000	0.00
McGraw	1	3	1	0	1	0	0	0	.000	0.00
Seaver	1	7	8	5	8	2	1	0	1.000	6.43
Ryan	1	7	3	2	7	2	1	0	1.000	2.57
Gentry	1	2	5	2	1	1	0	0	.000	9.00
Koosman	1	4 2/3	7	6	5	4	0	0	.000	11.57
Total	3	27	27	15	26	11	3	0	1.000	5.00

Atlanta Braves - 1969 - NLCS
Pitching Records

Pitcher	G	IP	H	R	SO	BB	W	L	Pct.	ERA
Neilmauer	1	1	0	0	1	0	0	0	.000	0.00
Doyle	1	1	2	2	2	1	0	0	.000	0.00
Britton	1	2/3	0	0	0	1	0	0	.000	0.00
Upshaw	2	6 1/3	0	2	4	0	0	0	.000	2.84
Niekro	1	8	9	9	4	4	0	1	.000	4.50
Stone	1	1	2	1	0	0	0	0	.000	9.00
Pappas	1	2 1/3	4	3	4	0	0	0	.000	11.57
Jarvis	1	4 1/3	10	6	6	0	0	1	.000	12.46
Reed	1	1 2/3	5	4	3	3	0	1	.000	21.00
Total	3	26	37	27	25	15	0	3	.000	6.92

CHAPTER 6

AMERICAN LEAGUE CHAMPIONSHIP SERIES 1969

Baltimore was the best team in the American League by far. They overwhelmed the opposition in winning the East Division title by a 19 game margin over Detroit. They were equally devastating in their treatment of West Division champion, the Minnesota Twins, the first ALCS in American League history.

The Orioles disposed of the Twins in three straight games, vindicating some sports writers that said Baltimore was the best team to represent the American League since the New York Yankees halcyon days. The New York Mets had other ideas, but that was another story.

In eliminating the Twins, the Orioles proved their arsenal contained all the conventional weapons, plus a surprise or two. Baltimore's pitching was uniformly superior, its' defense the best, and they were a home run hitting ball club that won 109 games in the regular season.

The Twins were stubborn foes in the first two matches, that were played in Baltimore. The Orioles had to go 12 innings in taking the opener, 4-3 on October 4th. The next day, Baltimore won in 11 innings, 1-0. The Twins were demolished after the game and when game three moved to the twin cities, October 6th, the Orioles crushed Minnesota by an 11-0 score.

Mike Cuellar and Dave McNally were Baltimore's 20 game winners. Cuellar pitched 8 shutout innings, but did not get credit for the victory. McNally pitched brilliantly in the second game. Jim Palmer, who threw a no-hitter against Oakland during the regular season, coasted to a victory behind an 18 hit attack by their lineup.

Oriole batters were impressive, also. Frank Robinson, Mark Belanger, and Boog Powell rapped home-runs in the opener. The winning hit was perfectly executed bunt by Paul Blair, who squeezed Belanger home from third base in the 12th inning.

Blair, the swift center fielder, had 5 hits and drove in 5 runs in the 3 game rout . Left fielder, Don Buford contributed 4 hits after going 0-9 in the first two games. Oriole manager, Earl Weaver, employed a simple strategy to deal with Minnesota's, Home run and RBI-champ, which was walk him in any run scoring situation. **Killer,** his nickname, got nothing to swing at until the third game was on ice. Baltimore pitching walked Killebrew 5 times in a row in the first two games. They only pitched to him when he could not hurt them with one swing.

Rod Carew and Tony Oliva were the Twins other top hitters during the season. Carew, the AL batting champ, was unproductive, as a hitter in the playoffs, going just 1 for 14.

In the opener, Twins 20 game winner, Jim Perry held a 3-2 lead over the Orioles, entering the ninth inning. Boog Powell tied the score with a home run blast over the right field wall. Ron

Perranoski, former Dodger came in and shut down the Orioles until the 12th.

Then with 2 out and Belanger on third base in the 12th, Blair stepped to the plate. Acting on his own, he bunted toward third. Killebrew, the third baseman or catcher, John Roseboro could make the play, as Belanger raced home with the winning run. Dick Hall was the winner, who pitched 2 - thirds of an inning. Perranoski, who did have a ball leave the infield in the 12th was the losing pitcher.

Winner of 15 games in a row during the season, McNally was tagged with the *lucky* tag because Baltimore seemed to put up a lot of runs when McNally pitched, especially in games.

He pitched 11 shutout innings in game 2 and won the game when pinch-hitter, Curt Motten singled to win the game for Baltimore, 1-0. The losing pitcher was Dave Boswell, who matched McNally through 10 inning, but left in the 11th for Perranoski. Perranoski gave up the single to Motten.

For game three, Twins manager, Billy Martin, short on available pitchers, started journeyman, Bob Miller to pitch game three. Miller lasted less than three innings, and his successor faired no better. Every Oriole, except Jim Palmer hit safely in the assault which eliminated Minnesota and sent Baltimore to the World Series.

Baltimore's triumph was a strong team performance all the way. Brooks Robinson got 4 hits in the first game and played stellar defense at third base. For the Twins, catcher, George Mitterwald, a rookie, did exceptionally well by cutting down 4 Baltimore base runners attempting to steal.

Game of Saturday, October 4th, 1969
Baltimore
Attendance: 39,324

	1	2	3	4	5	6	7	8	9	R
Minnesota	0	0	0	0	1	0	2	0	0	3
Baltimore	0	0	0	1	1	0	0	0	1	4

Minnesota	AB	R	H	RBI	Baltimore	AB	R	H	RBI
Tovar, cf	4	0	0	0	Buford, lf	6	0	0	0
Carew, 2b	5	0	1	0	Blair, cf	5	0	1	1
Killebrew, 3b	2	0	1	0	F. Robby, rf	3	1	1	1
Oliva, rf	5	2	2	2	Powell, 1b	5	1	2	1
Allison, lf	3	0	0	0	B. Robby, 3b	5	0	0	0
Uhlander, lf	1	0	1	0	Hendricks, c	3	0	0	0
Reese, 1b	4	0	0	0	Motten, ph	1	0	0	0
Cardenas, ss	5	0	0	0	Watt, p	1	0	0	0
Mitterwald, c	4	0	0	0	Salmon, ph	1	0	0	0
Roseboro, c	1	0	0	0	Lopez, p	0	0	0	0
Perry, p	2	0	0	0	Hall, p	0	0	0	0
Perranoski, p	1	0	0	0	Johnson, 2b	5	0	0	0
Total	28	3	4	3	Belanger, ss	5	2	2	1
					Cuellar, p	2	0	0	0
					May, ph	1	0	0	0
					Richert, p	0	0	0	0
					Rettenmund, ph	0	0	0	0
					Echebarren, C	1	0	0	0
					Total	43	4	10	4

Errors: F. Robinson, Uhlander, Carew. DP: Baltimore 1
LOB: Minnesota 5, Baltimore 8.   2B: Oliva. HR: F.
Robinson, Belanger, Oliva, Powell.   SB: Tovar. S H :
Echebarren.   SF: Allison.
WP: Lopez. Att: 39,324. Time: 3:20.

Minnesota pitching	IP	H	R	SO	BB
Perry	8	6	3	3	3
Perranoski	3 2/3	4	1	1	0
Total (L)	11 2/3	10	4	4	3

Baltimore pitching	IP	H	R	SO	BB
Cuellar	8	3	3	7	1
Richert	1	0	0	2	2
Watt	2	0	0	0	0
Lopez	1/3	1	0	0	0
Hall (W)	2/3	0	0	0	0
Total	12	4	3	9	3

Game Sunday, October 5th, 1969
At Baltimore
Att: 41,704

	1	2	3	4	5	6	7	8	9	10	12	R
Minnesota	0	0	0	0	0	0	0	0	0	0	0	0
Baltimore	0	0	0	0	0	0	0	0	0	0	1	1

Minnesota	AB	R	H	RBI	Baltimore	AB	R	H	RBI
Tovar, cf	5	0	1	0	Buford, lf	3	0	0	0
Carew, 2b	4	0	0	0	Blair, cf	4	0	0	0
Killebrew, 3b	3	0	0	0	F. Robinson, rf	5	0	2	0
Oliva, rf	4	0	1	0	Powell, 1b	3	1	1	0
Allison, lf	5	0	0	0	B. Robinson, 3b	4	0	2	0
Reese, 1b	4	0	0	0	Johnson, 2b	4	0	2	0
Mitterwald, c	3	0	1	0	Belanger, ss	5	0	0	0

Cardenas, ss	4	0	0	0	Etchebarren, c	3	0	0	0
Boswell, p	4	0	0	0	Hendricks, ph/c	0	0	0	0
Perranoski	0	0	0	0	Motten, ph	1	0	1	0
Total	36	0	3	0	McNally, p	4	0	0	0
					Total	36	1	8	1

Errors: Cardenas. DP: Minnesota 2. LOB: Minnesota 8, Baltimore 11. 2B: F. Robinson 2. SB: Oliva. SH: B. Robinson.
WP: Boswell. Time: 3:17. Att: 41,704

Minnesota pitchers	IP	H	R	SO	BB
Boswell (L)	10 2/3	7	1	4	7
Perranoski	0*	1	0	0	0
Total	10 2/3	8	1	4	7

Baltimore pitching	IP	H	R	SO	BB
McNally (W)	11	3	0	11	5

Game - Tuesday, October 6th, 1969
At Minnesota
Attendance: 33,735

	1	2	3	4	5	6	7	8	9	R
Baltimore	0	3	0	2	0	1	0	2	3	11
Minnesota	1	0	0	0	1	0	0	0	0	2

Baltimore	AB	R	H	RBI	Minnesota	AB	R	H	RBI
Buford, lf	5	3	4	1	Uhlander, lf	5	0	0	0
Blair, cf	6	1	5	5	Carew, 2b	5	0	0	0
F. Robinson, rf	4	0	1	1	Oliva, rf	4	1	2	0
Powell, 1b	5	0	2	0	Killebrew, 3b	3	1	1	0
B. Robinson, 3b	5	1	1	0	Reese, 1b	4	0	2	2
Johnson, 2b	4	2	1	0	Tovar, cf	4	0	0	0
Hendricks, c	5	2	2	3	Roseboro, c	4	0	1	0

SUMMER OF '69

Belanger, ss	5	2	2	0	Cardenas, ss	4	0	2	0
Palmer, p	5	0	0	0	Miller, p	0	0	0	0
Total	**44**	**11**	**18**	**10**	Woodson, p	1	0	1	0
					Hall, p	0	0	0	0
					Manuael, ph	0	0	0	0
					Worthington, P	0	0	0	0
					Orzendo, p	0	0	0	0
					Renick, ph	1	0	0	0
					Chance, p	0	0	0	0
					Perranoski, p	0	0	0	0
					Nettles, ph	1	0	1	0
					Total	**36**	**2**	**10**	**2**

Baltimore pitchers	IP	H	R	SO	BB
Palmer (W)	9	10	2	4	2

Minnesota pitchers	**IP**	**H**	**R**	**SO**	**BB**
Miller (L)	1 2/3	5	3	0	0
Woodson	1 2/3	3	2	2	0
Hall	2/3	0	0	0	0
Worthington	1 1/3	3	1	1	0
Gzenda	2*	4	3	2	0
Total	**9**	**15**	**9**	**5**	**0**

Minnesota pitchers	**IP**	**H**	**R**	**SO**	**BB**
Perranoski	1	3	0	1	0
Total	**9**	**18**	**11**	**10**	**0**

Composite ALCS Batting Records
1969 Baltimore Orioles

Player	G	AB	R	H	HR	RBI	BA	SB
Brooks Robinson, 3b	3	14	1	7	0	0	.500	0
Motten, ph	2	2	0	1	0	1	.500	0
Paul Blair, cf	3	15	1	6	1	6	.400	0
Boog Powell, 1b	3	13	2	5	1	1	.385	0
Frank Robinson, rf	3	12	1	4	0	1	.333	0
Don Buford, lf	3	14	3	4	0	1	.286	0
Mark Belanger, ss	2	15	4	4	1	1	.267	0
Elrod Hendricks, c	3	8	2	2	0	3	.250	0
Dave Johnson, 2b	3	13	2	3	0	0	.231	0
Eddie Watt, p	1	0	0	0	0	0	.000	0
Lopez, p	1	0	0	0	0	0	.000	0
Rich Hall, p	1	0	0	0	0	0	.000	0
Richert, p	1	0	0	0	0	0	.000	0
Merv Rettenmund, ph	1	0	0	0	0	0	.000	0
Chico Salmon, ph	1	1	0	0	0	0	.000	0
Lee May, ph	1	1	0	0	0	0	.000	0
Mike Cuellar, p	1	2	0	0	0	0	.000	0
Andy Echebarren, c	2	4	0	0	0	0	.000	0
Dave McNally, p	1	4	0	0	0	0	.000	0
Jim Palmer, p	1	5	0	0	0	0	.000	0
Total	3	123	16	36	4	15	.293	0

Composite NLCS ALCS Records
1969 Minnesota Twins

Player	G	AB	R	H	HR	RBI	BA	SB
Jim Nettles, ph	1	1	0	1	0	0	1.000	0
Woodson, p	1	1	0	1	0	0	1.000	0
Tony Oliva, rf	3	13	3	5	1	2	.385	1
John Roseboro, c	2	5	0	1	0	0	.260	0
Reese, 1b	3	12	0	2	0	2	.167	0
Uhlander, lf	2	6	0	1	0	0	.167	0
Leo Cardenas, ss	3	13	0	2	0	0	.154	0
George Mitterwald, c	2	7	0	1	0	0	.143	0
Harmon Killebrew, 3b	3	8	2	1	0	0	.125	0
Cesar Tovar, cf	3	13	0	1	0	0	.077	1
Rod Carew, 2b	3	14	0	1	0	0	.071	0
Dean Chance, p	1	0	0	0	0	0	.000	0
Bob Miller, p	1	0	0	0	0	0	.000	0
Tom Hall, p	1	0	0	0	0	0	.000	0
Charlie Manuel, ph	1	0	0	0	0	0	.000	0
Worthington, p	1	0	0	0	0	0	.000	0
Grzenda, p	1	0	0	0	0	0	.000	0
Renick, p	1	1	0	0	0	0	.000	0
Peranoski, p	3	1	0	0	0	0	.000	0
Perry, p	1	3	0	0	0	0	.000	0
Boswell, p	1	4	0	0	0	0	.000	0
Allison, rf	2	8	0	0	0	1	.000	0
Total	3	110	5	17	1	5	.155	0

Pitching Records ALCS - 1969
Baltimore Orioles

Baltimore pitching	G	IP	H	R	SO	BB	W	L	Pct.	ERA
Dave McNally	1	11	3	0	11	5	1	0	1.000	0.00
Eddie Watt	1	2	0	0	2	0	0	0	.000	0.00
Richert	1	1	0	0	2	2	0	0	.000	0.00
R. Hall	1	2/3	0	0	1	0	1	0	1.000	0.00
Lopez	1	1/3	1	0	0	2	0	0	.000	0.00
Palmer	1	9	10	2	4	2	1	0	1.000	2.00
Cuellar	1	8	3	3	7	1	0	0	.000	1.13
Total	3	33	17	5	27	13	3	0	1.000	2.13

Pitching Records ALCS - 1969
Minnesota Twins

Minnesota	G	IP	H	R	SO	BB	W	L	Pct.	ERA
Grzenda	1	2/3	0	0	0	0	0	0	.000	0.00
T. Hall	1	2/3	0	0	0	0	0	0	.000	0.00
Boswell	1	10 2/3	7	1	4	7	0	1	.000	0.84
Perry	1	8	6	3	3	3	0	0	.000	3.38
Miller	1	1 2/3	5	3	0	0	0	1	.000	5.46
Perranoski	3	4 2/3	8	3	3	0	0	1	.000	5.74
Worthington	1	1 1/3	3	1	1	0	0	0	.000	6.75
Woodson	1	1 2/3	3	3	2	2	0	0	.000	10.86
Chance	1	2	4	3	3	2	0	0	.000	13.50
Total	3	31 1/3	26	16	14	13	0	3	.000	4.02

CHAPTER 7

EPILOGUE

Gil Hodges

Gilbert Ray Hodges was an American big league baseball first baseman and manager. During an 18 year playing career, he played from 1943, 1947 to 1963. He played for the following teams:

Brooklyn Dodgers	**1943, 1947-1957**
Los Angeles Dodgers	**1958-1961**
New York Mets	**1962-1963**

He was the major leagues' outstanding first baseman in the 1950's. Only teammate, Duke Snyder had more home runs and runs batted in during the decade. For a time, his 370 home runs were a National League record for right handed batters. He held the NL record for grand slams from 1957-1974. He anchored the Dodgers' infield on 6 pennant winners and one World Series title in 1955. He won 3 Gold Gloves at first base and led the National League in double plays at first - 4 times. He led fielding percentage at first base - 3 times, also. He managed the New York Mets to the 1969 World Series title, one of the greatest in Series history. He died in 1972 of a heart attack at 48 years old.

Hodges was born in Princeton, Indiana, the son of a coal miner, Charlie and his wife Irene. The family moved to nearby Petersburg when Gil was seven. Hodges was a 4 sport athlete at Petersburg High School, earning seven varsity letters. They were in football, baseball, basketball, and track. He did not accept a contract from the Detroit Tigers in 1941. He chose instead to attend St. Joseph's college on a scholarship. He hoped to be a college coach, someday.

He signed with the Brooklyn Dodgers in 1943 and played one game at third base that year. He went into the Marine Corps during World War II after having participated in its ROTC program at St. Joseph's. He served as an anti-aircraft gunner in battles of Tinian and Okinawa and received a Bronze Star and commendation for courage under fire for his actions.

After his military discharge, he returned to Brooklyn and played catcher for a few games in 1947. He joined an already solid team of Jackie Robinson, Pee Wee Reese, Carl Furillo, and Roy Campenella, the team's catcher. Campenella's play at the catcher position made it evident he had little future behind home plate, so manager, Leo Durocher moved Gil to first base. His only appearance in the 1947 World Series was as a pinch-hitter against the New York Yankees for pitcher Rex Barney in game 7. He struck out.

As a rookie in 1948, he hit for a .249 batting average with 11 home runs and 70 RBI's. In 1948, the Boston Braves won the NL pennant, then lost to the Cleveland Indians in the World Series in 6 games. That was the last World Series title for Cleveland to date.

On June 25th, he hit for the cycle - single, double, home run, and triple. He tied the right-handed home run record for Brooklyn with 23 home runs. His 115 RBI's were 4th in the National League. He also led all first baseman with a .995 fielding percentage. Again, in the 1949 World Series with the Yankees, he batted .235, but did drive the home the only run in a 1-0 victory for Brooklyn in game 2. In game 5, he hit a 3 run home run with two out in the seventh to pull the Dodgers within 10-6 of New York, but the struck out to end the Series, 4 games to one game, Yankees.

On August 31st, 1950, against the Boston Braves, Hodges hit 4 home runs in a game, joining Lou Gehrig, as the second player since 1900 to hit 4 home runs in a game. He hit them against four pitchers, the first being Braves, southpaw, Warren Spahn. He also, had 17 total bases, including a single in 5 at bats. That year, Gil again led the NL in fielding with a .994 fielding average. He also broke the record for double plays in the National League with 159, breaking Cincinnati's, Frank McCormick (153) set in 1939. He then broke his own mark with 171 in 1951. That record stood until Pirates' first baseman, Donn Clendenon had 182 for the 1966 Pittsburgh team that featured Mazeroski and Gene Alley, as middle infielders. Hodges finished third in home runs and RBI's in 1950 with 32 home runs and 113 RBI's.

In 1951, Gil became the first Dodger to hit 40 home runs, breaking Babe Herman's club mark of 35 hit in 1930. Gil's last home run came on October 2nd in a 10-0 win that evened a three game playoff Series at 1-1. New York won the pennant the next day on Bobby Thompson's game ending home run, called "The Shot Heard around the World." His 1951 numbers were 40 home runs, 103 RBI's, 118 runs, and 307 total bases.

Hodges was an 8 time All-Star, from 1949-1955 and in 1957. With his last home run of 1952, he tied Dolph Camilli's Dodger career record of 139, and he passed him in 1953.

Snider would move ahead of him in 1956. He was 3rd in the league in home runs (32) and 4th in RBI's (102) and slugging (.500). He was a great fan favorite for the Brooklyn faithful. He was the only Dodger regular not booed at Ebbets Field. Fans were very supportive of a long slump Hodges had at the end of 1952 season and World Series. He went the last nine games hitless and ended the World Series on a 0 for 21 slide. The Yankees beat Brooklynn that year 4 games to three games. This was one of the most famous slumps in baseball history that continued into the spring of 1953. Finally, Hodges started to hit again in May, 1953 and rarely struggled in the World Series after that. Brooklyn was always in the mix in the National League pennant contenders, but they had trouble with the Yankees in the World Series.

Hodges was involved with a blown call of an umpire in the fifth game of the 1952 World Series. Johnny Sain, batting for the Yankees in the tenth inning grounded out according to first base umpire, Art Passarella. The photograph of the play, however, shows Sain touching first base before the throw to Hodges arrived in his glove. Still, Passarella called Sain out.

He ended 1953 with a .302 batting average, he had 122 RBI's, and was sixth in home runs (31). Against the Yankees in the '53 Series he got three hits in a game 1 loss, 9-5 that included a home run. He hit an impressive .364 for the Series, but Brooklyn lost to New York in 6 games. Yankees manager, Casey Stengel always enjoyed beating Brooklyn because he played outfield for the Dodgers, as a player.

Under new manager, Walter Alston, Hodges enjoyed his finest season in 1954. He set a team Home Run record (42), hit a career high .304 and had 130 RBI's. His RBI and Home Run total were second to Ted Kluzewski, first baseman at Cincinnati.

The following are records of the Dodger teams since Hodges got there. They did not win a World Series to that point:

Year	Won	Lost	Pct.	GB.	Place
1947	94	60	.610	___	1st
1948	84	70	.545	3rd	
1949	97	57	.630	1st	
1950	89	65	.578	2nd	
1951	97	60	.618	2nd	
1952	96	57	.627	1st	
1953	105	49	.682	1st	
1954	92	62	.597	2nd	

The 1955 Brooklyn Dodger team will forever be known as the ***Boys of Summer***. Hodges production dropped to a .289 batting average, 27 home runs, and 102 runs batted in, but the season ended in a most satisfying manner for the Brooklyn fans. Facing the New York Yankees for the fifth time in the World Series, Hodges started 1 for 12 in the first three games before coming around. In game 4, he hit a 2 run home run in the fourth to put the Dodgers up 4-3. Then he hit a RBI single to lead the Dodgers in a 8-5 win. He scored the first run in a 5-3 win game 5. In game 7, he had both RBI's on a single and a Sacrifice Fly in the 2-0 victory that gave the Lords of Flatbush their first World Series title, ever. Left hander, Johnny Podres pitched the shutout and scattered 8 New York hits.

In 1956, Hodges had 32 home runs and 87 RBI's, as Brooklyn won the National League pennant, again. Once again, the World Series opponent was the Yankees. In the first game, Hodges hit a three run home run to put the Dodgers up 5-2. They went on to win 6-3. In the second game, a 13-8 slugfest win, Hodges scored the run that put Brookyn ahead, 7-6 in the third inning. He then doubled twice, each time plating 2 runs in the fourth and fifth innings for an 11-7 lead. The Dodgers led in games, 2-0. In game 5, the famous perfect game by Yankees, Don Larsen, Hodges struck out, flied out to center field, and then line out to third baseman, Gil McDougald. The Yankees won the game, 2-0 when pinch-hitter, Mitchell was called out on strikes in the ninth. The Yankees reclaimed the World Series title in seven games.

In 1957, Gil Hodges set the National League record for grand slams by a National League player (14), breaking the mark by Rogers Hornsby and Ralph Kiner. In 1972, the grand slam record was tied by Braves, Hank Aaron and Giants, Willie McCovey. In 1957, the Dodgers last season in Ebbets Field in Brooklyn before they moved to Los Angeles to play in the Coliseum, Hodges hit for .299 batting average and finished with 98 RBI's and 27 Home Runs. Hodges also drove in the last run in Ebbets Field in late September when they closed Ebbets Field. The Dodgers finished in third place, 84-70 (.545 Pct.) behind Milwaukee.

In 1958, Dodger's owner decided to move the club to Los Angeles, California. The New York Giants relocated with them to San Francisco, CA.

In Los Angeles, Hodges became the seventh player to reach the 300 home run plateau in the National League. He connected off Dick Drott of the Chicago Cubs. Hodges' production fell off in '58, 22 home runs and 64 RBI's. The Dodgers finished in seventh place, 71-83 ('461 Pct.) behind Milwaukee, again. Also, Gil Hodges broke the NL record for strikeouts with 923, held by Lou Camilli.

Things turned around in 1959. The Dodgers drew record crowds at the Coliseum, as the Dodgers captured the National League pennant. Hodges hit for .276 batting average with 25 home runs and 80 RBI's. The Dodgers had to beat the Milwaukee Braves in a 3 game playoff to get to the World Series with the Chicago White Sox. Hodges solo home run in the eighth inning of game 4 gave the LA Dodgers a big win, 5-4. They won the Series in 6 games, 4 games to 2 games.

In 1960, Gil broke Ralph Kiner's National League home run record for right handed batters of 351 home runs. He also appeared on a a made for TV show, **Home Run Derby.** In his last season in Los Angeles, he became the team's career RBI leader with 1,254, passing Zach Wheat. Duke Snider moved ahead Hodges in 1961. Also, that year, Hodges received the first of three Gold Gloves ever presented from 1951 to 1959. His career fielding percentage was .992 which is outstanding .

After being chosen in the expansion draft by the New York Mets, he thought about retiring due to his known knee problems. He was persuaded to continue his playing career in New York at the Polo Grounds. He hit the first home run in New York Met history. By the end of the year, he only played in 54 games, hitting 9 home runs, 17 RBI's in 127 at bats. The Mets went 40 - 120 in their first season.

After 11 games in the 1963 season, Gil was traded to the Washington Senators for outfielder, Jimmy Piersall in late May, for the intention of replacing Eddie Yost, as Washington manager. Hodges retired, as a player so he could concentrate on being a manager. Hodges last game, as a player came on May 5th at the Polo Grounds in a double header with the San Francisco Giants. Hodges took over the Senators after they finished 14-27 under Yost in 1963. There was a slight improvement in the Senators that season and every season in Washington through 1967, as evidenced by the following records:

Year	W.	L.	Pct.	Place
1963	56	106	.346	10th
1964	62	100	.383	9th
1965	70	92	.432	8th
1966	71	88	.447	8th
1967	76	85	.472	6th

It should be noted that Washington franchise was an expansion team in 1960. The original Senator franchise relocated to Minnesota in 1961 to become the Minnesota Twins. Then the Washington Senators relocated to Texas, or Arlington, Texas in 1972 to become the Texas Rangers.

In 1968, Gil Hodges was signed to manage the perennially bad, New York Mets. They posted their best record since coming into the National League in 1962 with a 73-89. In 1969, he led the ***Miracle Mets*** to their first World Series Championship in defeating the heavily favored, Baltimore Orioles in 5 games. After losing the first game, the Mets won 4 straight, including two games by 2-1 scores. The Mets record in their miracle season was 100-62.

After identical 83-79 seasons in 1970 and 1971, when the Mets finished in third place in the NL East, Gil Hodges died suddenly of a heart attack in West Palm Beach, Florida, after playing golf with other members of his coaching staff on April 2nd, 1972, two days before his 48th birthday. He had suffered a previous heart attach during a September 1968 game, managing the Mets. He was survived by his wife, the former, Joan Lombardi, who he married on December 26th, 1948. Together they raised a son and three daughters. Yogi Berra, who managed the New York Yankees in 1964 to an Amerian League pennant, was named as Mets manager to succeed Hodges. The Mets went to the World Series in 1973 against Oakland. However, they lost in seven games. They went 82-79 to win the NL East over St. Louis by 1 ½ games.

His funeral was mass was home parish of Our Lady of Holy Christians in the Midwood section of Brooklyn. The Mets retired his his #14 uniform and wore black on the left sleeve of their uniforms during the '73 season in honor of Hodges.

Hodges batted .273 in his career with a .487 slugging percentage, 1921 hits, 1274 runs batted in, 1105 runs, 295 doubles, and 361 home runs in 2021 games. His 361 home runs were second in Dodger history behind outfielder, Duke Snider's (389). Snyder broke his National League record of 1137 career strikeouts in 1964. Snyder finished his career in 1964 at San Francisco, as a pinch- hitter. His 1,000 RBI's in the 1950's led all NL hitters, some accomplishment with Stan Musial at St. Louis. Hodges was inducted into the New York Mets Hall of Fame in 1982.

He received New York City's highest civilian honor, the Bronze Medallion in 1969. In 1978, the Marine Parkway Bridge, connecting the Marine Park area of Brooklyn with the Rockaways in Queens, was renamed the Marine Parkway - Gil Hodges Bridge in his memory.

There has been controversy over the fact that Gil Hodges has not been elected to membership in the baseball Hal of Fame. He was considered one of the best players in the 1950's. He led the National League players with 1,000 RBI's in that decade. Critics point out that Gil never lead the NL in any offensive category - home runs, RBI's, batting average, or never won a MVP award. Some of Hodges best seasons came when Brooklyn did not win the pennant. Also, his .273 batting average is frowned on by voters.

Hodge's has been regularly considered for selection by the Hall of Fames, Veteran's Committee since 1987. He just missed getting into the Hall of Fame by one vote in 1993, when no candidates were selected.

Hodges will eventually, get in in my opinion. Just this month, November 2011, Hodges was placed onto a Golden Era Veterans' Committee for consideration into the Hall of Fame. The voting will take place by a 16 member committee on December 4th and 5th in Dallas, Texas.

Bill Mazeroski, Pirates second baseman, who retired in 1972 was inducted into Hall of Fame on his defensive skills. He had about a .260 batting average and hit the famous walk off home run against the Yankees to beat them in the 1960 Series. Hodges also, had exceptional defensive skills at first base, similar to Mazeroski. He deserves to be in the Hall of Fame.

Gilbert Raymond Hodges
Position: 1st Base & Outfielder
Bats: Right, Throws: Right
Height: 6'1", Weight: 200 pounds
Born: April 4th, 1924 in Princeton, Indiana
High School: Petersburg (Petersburg, Indiana)
School: Saint Joseph's College
Signed: Brooklyn Dodgers as an amateur free agent in 1943
Debut: October 3rd, 1943
Teams: Dodgers / New York Mets 1943 - 1963
Final Game: May 5th, 1963
Died: April 2nd, 1972 in West Palm Beech, Florida
(47 years old)

Year	Team	G	AB	R	H	HR	RBI	BA	SB
1943	Brooklyn	1	2	0	0	0	0	.000	1
1947	Brooklyn	28	77	9	12	1	7	.156	0
1948	Brooklyn	134	481	48	120	11	70	.249	7
1949	Brooklyn	156	596	94	170	23	115	.285	10
1950	Brooklyn	153	561	98	159	32	113	.283	6
1951	Brooklyn	141	582	118	156	40	103	.268	9
1952	Brooklyn	153	508	87	129	32	102	.254	2
1953	Brooklyn	141	520	101	157	31	122	.302	1
1954	Brooklyn	154	579	106	176	42	130	.304	1
1955	Brooklyn	150	546	75	158	27	102	.289	2
1956	Brooklyn	153	550	86	146	32	87	.265	3
1957	Brooklyn	150	579	94	173	27	98	.299	5
1958	Los Angeles	141	475	68	123	22	64	.259	8

1959	Los Angeles	124	413	57	114	25	80	.276	3
1960	Los Angeles	101	197	22	39	8	30	.198	0
1961	Los Angeles	109	245	25	52	8	31	.242	3
1962	New York Mets	54	127	15	32	9	17	.252	0
1963	New York Mets	11	22	2	5	0	3	.227	0
18 Seasons		2071	7030	1105	1921	370	1274	.273	63

Post-Season

Year	Team	Lg	G	AB	R	H	HR	RBI	BA	SB
1947	Brooklyn	NYY	1	1	0	0	0	0	.000	0
1949	Brooklyn	NYY	5	17	2	4	1	4	.235	0
1952	Brooklyn	NYY	7	21	1	0	0	1	.000	0
1953	Brooklyn	NYY	6	22	3	8	1	1	.364	1
1955	Brooklyn	NYY	7	24	2	7	1	5	.292	0
1956	Brooklyn	NYY	7	23	5	7	1	8	.304	0
1959	Los Angeles	CWS	6	23	2	9	1	2	.391	0
7 Seasons			39	131	15	35	5	21	.267	1

Accomplishments in Gi Hodges Career

> 8 time All-Star - first base - 1949, '50, '51, '52, '53, '54, '55, and 1957.
> Three World Series Championships - 2 as a payer - 1955 and 1959, as a Dodger. One as a manager - 1969 - New York Mets.
> 1959 Lou Gehrig Award.
> Hit 4 home runs in a game on August 31st, 1950.
> Number 14 retired by New York Mets in 1973.

Tommie Agee

Tommie Lee Agee was a big league, center fielder famous for making the two greatest catches in World Series history, both of which occurred in game three of the 1969 World Series. Tommie played center field, most of his career for the following major league careers:

Cleveland Indians	1962-1964
Chicago White Sox	1965-1967
New York Mets	1968-1972
Houston Astros	1973
St. Louis Cardinals	1973

Agee was born in Magnolia, Alabama and played baseball and football at Mobile County Training School with future New York Mets teammate, Cleon Jones. After one season at Grambling State University, college baseball (1961), Agee signed with the Cleveland Indians for $60,000.

After two seasons in the Indians' farm system, Agee received a September call up to Cleveland in 1962. His first game was as a pinch hitter came September 14th at Metropolitan Stadium in an 11-0 loss to the Twins. He also played in September in 1963 and 1964 with Cleveland, playing a total of 31 games, batting .170 with one home run and 5 RBI's. Following the 1964 season, Cleveland GM - Gabe Paul sent Tommie Agee to the White Sox with Tommie John, as part of a blockbuster trade with three teams involving Cleveland, Chicago White Sox, and the Kansas City Royals that brought All-Star, Rocky Colavito back to Cleveland.

Agee batted just .226 with the Pacific Coast League's, Indianapolis Indians and then hit .158 in 10 games with the White Sox in 1965. After earning the starting center fielder job in spring training, 1966, he hit a two run home run in the season opener. He was hitting .264 with 9 home runs and 38 RBI's in mid July and was named the White Sox representaive for the All-Star game. He ended the season with a .273 batting average, 22 home runs, and 86 RBI's to earn the American League Rookie of the Year honors. He played Center Field very well and earned a Gold Glove for defense. Although he played in small parts of 4 seasons before 1966, Agee received the ***American League Rookie of the Year Award.***

At the All-Star Break in 1966, Agee was batting .247 with 10 home runs and 35 RBI's to earn his second consecutive All-Star selection in 1967. His second half numbers fell-off (just 4 home runs after the All-Star break). He finished with 14 home runs, 52 RBI's, and batted .234. The White Sox finished with in fourth place, just three games back of first place, Boston. Minnesota and Detroit were also in the race until the final day on Sunday. On a team loaded with great pitching, the White Sox lacked offensive production. No starting regular in the lineup hit over .241, possibly costing Chicago an American League pennant in 1967.

To fix the offense, the White Sox imported perenninal .300 hitter, Tommy Davis, along with pitcher, Jack Fisher and two minor leaguers from the New York Mets for Agee and infielder, Al Weis.

In 1968, Tommie Agee was beaned by flame thrower, Bob Gibson of St. Louis on the very first pitch to a Mets batter in spring training. At the start of the season, he went 0 for 10 in a 24 inning game with Houston that made his batting average drop from .313 to .192. It led to a 0 for 34 slump that brought his batting average down to .102. For the season, he batted .217 with 5 home runs and 17 RBI's.

Agee got off to a hot streak in 1969. He had his first multi home run game in the third game of the season against the

Montreal Expos. The home run went half way up section 48 of the left field upper deck at Shea Stadium, a feat that was never duplicated. Expos left fielder, Mack Jones said, "The ball was still going up when it hit the stands." To commemorate the home run, there was a printed sign in that section of the stadium with Agee's name, uniform number, and the date. He also had his first four hit game on May second (4 for 4 with a walk and a home run).

By May 21st, Agee was batting over .300 and the Mets won their third consecutive game for a .500 record after 36 games. This was the Mets first .500 record at that point in the season. They then lost 5 straight games to fall into fourth place in NL East.

The Mets went on a 11 game winning streak that included a two home run, four hit performance by Agee against the San Francisco Giants in the final game of the streak. By this point the Mets were in second place, seven games behind Chicago.

The Mets were 7 ½ games back on September 8th when the Cubs came to Shea for a crucial 2 game series with New York. Cubs starting pitcher knocked Agee down with an inside pitch in the bottom of the first. Then Jerry Koosman to start the second, hit the first Cubs batter he faced who was Ron Santo, on the hand, breaking it. Agee retaliated by hitting a 2 run home run in the third, and then scored the winning run of the game on Wayne Garrett's single in the sixth inning. The Mets swept the Expos in a double header on September 10th. Coupled with a loss by Chicago, the Mets moved into first place for the first time in their history in September 1969. The Mets finished strong and did not fall out of first place. On September 24th, the New York Mets clinched the NL East title, as Don Clendenon hit two home runs in a 6-0 victory over Steve Carlton of St. Louis. Nine days earlier, Carlton struck out 19 Mets in a 4-3 loss to New York. For the season, Agee hit .271, while leading the team with 26 home runs, 97 runs scored, and 76 RBI's. Along with Cy Young

Award winner, Tom Seaver and left fielder, Cleon Jones, he was one of three Mets to finish in the top 10 in National League MVP balloting. He was also, named *the Sporting News' National League Comeback Player of the Year.*

Agee batted .357 with 2 home runs and 4 RBI's in the Mets' three game sweep of the Atlanta Braves in the 1969 NLCS. In Game 3, with the Series tied 1-1, Agee had what *Sports Illustrated* called the greatest single performance by a center fielder in World Series history. In the first inning, Agee hit a lead off home run off Jim Palmer for what eventually was the game winning hit and RBI, as the Mets shut out the Orioles, 5-0. Interesting enough, two other Mets would also hit Game 3 lead off home runs in subsequent World Series, Wayne Garrett in the 1973 Series and Lenny Dykstra in the 1986 Series. Agee also, made 2 incredible catches that probably saved 5 runs. The first one was a two out line drive to left center field by Elrod Hendricks with two runners on base. Agee sprinted across the outfield and caught the ball in the webbing of his glove before running into the wall. The second catch was on a fly ball hit by Paul Blair with the bases loaded in the seventh inning off Nolan Ryan. This was the only World Series appearance by Ryan in his storied 27 year career. Agee sprinted towards right center field warning track. When the wind blew the ball down and away from him, he lunged a headfirst dive for the catch. He rolled on the warning track, but held onto the ball. With Blair rounding second base moments after the catch, Agee may have saved an inside-the-park, grand slam home run.

Agee began the 1970 season by going on a 20 game hitting streak from April 16th to May 9th. He enjoyed one of his finest games of his career on June 12th, when he went 4 for 5 with two home runs and four runs scored. He then hit for the cycle on July 6th. Agee displayed his daring base running in the 10th inning of a Mets, 2-1 victory over the Los Angeles Dodgers, when he stole second, took third on a wild pitch. He then surprised everyone, when he stole home for the victory. For the season, Agee batted .286 and established a Mets season record for hits with 182, runs with 107, and stolen bases with 31. He also won his second Gold Glove Award, making his first African-American to win a Gold Glove in both leagues.

Chronic knee injuries hampered Agee in 1971 and 1972, though he still batted .285 and tied the Mets lead with 14 home runs in 1971. In 1972, he finished second on the Mets with 47 RBI's, even though he hit only .227. In 1970 and 1971, the Mets finished 83-79.

Folowing the 1972 season, Agee was traded to the Houston Astros for Rich Chiles and Buddy Harris. He faced the Mets for the first time on April 24th and went 2 for 3 with a walk, a run scored in a 4-2 Astros win. He was batting .235 with 8 home runs and 15 RBI's, when Houston dealt him to the St. Louis Cardinals on August 18th. The Cardinals were in a pennant race with the Mets and Pittsburgh. The Mets would win the NL pennant in 1973. Following the 1973 season, he was traded to the Los Angeles Dodgers, but was released in spring training. Tommy Agee then retired from baseball.

After retirement, he operated the Outfielder's Lounge near Shea Stadium . Agee was also known as the most active Met in charitable events and baseball clinics. He appeared as himself in a 1999 episode of **Everybody Loves Raymond** with some other teammates from the 1969 Mets.

Agee had a heart attack while leaving a Midtown Manhattan office building in the late morning on June 22nd, 2001 and died at Bellevue Hospital Center in Manhattan, New York at age 58. He is survived by his wife, Maxine, and daughter, Janelle. He was inducted into New York Mets Hall of Fame in 2002.

Tommie Agee
Position: Center Fielder
Bats: Right, Throws: Right
Height: 5'11", Weight: 195
Born: August 9th, 1942 in Magnolia, Alabama
High School: Mobile County (Grand Boy, AL)
School: Grambling State University
Signed by Cleveland Indians as an amateur free agent in 1961
Debut: September 14, 1962
Teams: Mets, White Sox, Astros, Indians, Cardinals - 1962-1973
Final Game: September 30th, 1973
Died: January 22, 2001 New York, New York (Age 58)

Year	Team	Lg	G	AB	R	H	HR	RBI	BA	SB
1962	Cleveland	AL	5	14	0	0	0	2	.214	0
1963	Cleveland	AL	13	27	3	4	1	3	.148	0
1964	Cleveland	AL	13	12	0	2	0	0	.167	0
1965	Chicago	AL	10	19	2	3	0	3	.158	0
1966	Chicago	AL	160	629	98	172	22	86	.273	44
1967	Chicago	AL	158	529	73	124	14	52	.234	28
1968	New York	NL	132	368	30	80	5	17	.217	13
1969	New York	NL	149	565	97	153	26	76	.271	12
1970	New York	NL	153	636	107	182	24	75	.286	31
1971	New York	NL	113	425	58	121	14	50	.285	28
1972	New York	NL	114	422	52	96	13	47	.227	8
1973	Hous./St.L.	NL	109	266	38	59	11	22	.222	3
12 Seasons			1129	3912	558	999	130	433	.255	81

Post Season

Year	Team	Lg	G	AB	R	H	HR	RBI	BA	SB
1969	New York	NLCS	3	14	4	5	2	4	.357	2
1969	New York	WS	5	18	1	3	1	1	.167	1
2 Post-Seasons			8	32	5	8	3	5	.250	3

Accomplishments for Tommie Agee

Two time All-Star (1966 and 1967) - Chicago White Sox.
World Series Champion (1969)
Two time Gold Glove award winner (1966 White Sox and 1970 Mets)
1966 American League Rookie of the Year.
1969 National League Comeback Player of the Year.

Ken Boswell

Ken Boswell was born February 23rd, 1946 in Austin, Texas and was a former big league - second baseman who played with the following teams:

New York Mets 1967-1974
Houston Astros 1975-1977

Ken was a member of the Sam Houston State University. During his big league career (11 years), he hit for a .244 batting average and 31 home runs with 244 RBI's in 930 games. He was the second baseman on he '69 Championship team and '73 National League pennant New York Mets teams.

Ken Boswell
Kenneth George Boswell
Positions: 2nd baseman, pinch hitter, and 3rd baseman
Bats: Left, Throws: Right
Height: 6'0", Weight: 170 pounds
Born: February 23rd, 1946 in Austin, Texas (Age 65)
School: Sam Houston State University

Drafted by New York Mets in the 4th round of the 1965 amateur draft
Debut: September 18th, 1967
Teams: Mets / Astros - 1967-1977
Final Game: October 1st, 1977

Year	Team	Lg	G	AB	R	H	HR	RBI	BA	SB
1967	New York	NL	11	40	2	9	1	4	.225	0
1968	New York	NL	75	284	37	74	4	11	.261	7
1969	New York	NL	102	362	48	101	3	32	.279	7
1970	New York	NL	105	351	42	89	5	44	.254	5
1971	New York	NL	116	392	46	107	5	40	.273	5
1972	New York	NL	100	355	35	75	9	33	.211	2
1973	New York	NL	76	110	12	25	2	14	.227	0
1974	New York	NL	96	222	19	48	2	15	.216	0
1975	Houston	NL	86	178	16	43	0	21	.242	0
1976	Houston	NL	91	126	12	33	0	18	.262	1
1977	Houston	NL	72	97	7	21	0	12	.216	0
11 Seasons			930	2517	266	625	31	244	.248	27

Post-Season

Year	Team	Lg	G	AB	R	H	HR	RBI	BA	SB
1969	New York	NLCS	3	12	3	4	2	5	.333	0
1969	New York	WS	1	3	1	1	0	0	.000	0
1973	New York	NLCS	1	1	0	0	0	0	.000	0
1973	New York	WS	3	3	1	3	0	0	1.000	0
2 Seasons			8	19	5	8	2	5	**.421**	0

Don Cardwell

Donald Eugene Cardwell was born December 7th, 1935. He was an an American right handed major league pitcher who played for the following teams in baseball:

> Philadelphia Phillies   1957-1960
> Chicago Cubs   1960-1962
> Pittsburgh Pirates   1963-1966
> New York Mets 1967-1970
> Atlanta Braves 1970

He died on January 14th, 2008 at 72 years old. He was the first pitcher in big league history to pich no-hitter in his first game after being traded. He pitched a 4-0, shutout on May 15th, 1960, two days after being traded from Philadelphia to the Chicago Cubs. After winning 15 games for Chicago in 1961, he also won 13 games for Pittsburgh in the mid '60's before helping the New York Mets win a World Series title in 1969.

Born in Winston-Salem, North Carolina, Cardwell signed with the Philadelphia Phillies, as an amateur free agent in 1954.

He debuted in 1957 and struggled in three seasons with the Phillies, winning 16 games while losing 24, as a spot starter.

On May 13th, 1960, Cardwell was traded to the Chicago Cubs for second baseman, Tony Taylor, two days later, he no-hit the St. Louis Cardinals in the second game of a double header at Wrigley Field. This was the first no-hitter thrown by a pitcher in his first start on a new team after a trade. The lone base runner was after a walk to Alex Grammas with one out in the first . Don proceeded to retire 26 straight batters. Two great fielding plays in ninth preserved the no-hitter-one by right-fielder, George Altman on a line drive Carl Sawatski for out number 1, and another by left-fielder Walt "Moose" Moryn on Joe Cunningham's sinking line drive to end the game. Moryn's catch was a sliding catch just 2 inches off the ground. Despite the no-hitter, Cardwell finished 9-16 in 1960's, although the Cubs were only 60-94, as a team. He did show power at the plate with 16 hits, as a hitter with 5 home runs in 77 at-bats for a .208 batting average.

Cardwell's best season was 1961, when he won 15 games and posted a career best 156 strikeouts. After slumping to 7-16 in 1962, Cardwell was traded on October 17th, along with George Altman. However, his stay in St. Louis never resulted in any games pitched for them. He was traded in November to Pittsburgh for short stop, Dick Groat.

Cardwell won 13 games for Pittsburgh in 1963, while posting a career best 3.07 ERA. He suffered severe arm trouble in 1964. He rebounded to win 13 games, again in 1965 before being traded to the Mets in December 1966 along with outfielder, Don Bosch for pitcher, Dennis Ribant, and utility man, Gary Kolb.

Pitching, as mostly a spot starter, Cardwell went 12-22 in his first two seasons, as a Met. In 1969, he went 8-10 in a rotation of Seaver, Koosman, Nolan Ryan, and Gary Gentry, helping them win a World Series title. In late July of that season, he had a 3-9 record, then won 5 straight, including a 1-0 victory in a second game of a doubleheader with Pittsburgh. Koosman also, won 1-0 in the first game. An oddity was both pichers in the games drove in their only runs in the game, respectively. This victory, the ninth of a 10 game winning streak for New York, came two days after the Mets took over first from Chicago.

Cardwell was sold to Atlanta in midseason 1970, then retired after the season.

In 14 seasons, Cardwell finished 102-138 with 1211 strikeouts in 2122 2/3 innings pitched.

Cardwell died on January 14, 2008 in Winston - Salem, NC. He was living in Clemmons at the time of the death.

Don Cardwell
Donald Eugene Cardwell
Position: Pitcher
Bats: Right, Throws: Right
Height: 6'4", Weight: 210 lbs.
Born: December 7th, 1935 in Winston-Salem, NC
School: Appalachian State University
Signed: Philadelphia Phillies as free agent Amateur - 1954
Debut: April 21st, 1957
Final Game: September 27th, 1970
Died: January 14th, 2008 in Winston-Salem, NC

Year	Team	Lg	W	L	Pct.	ERA	G	IP	H	R	BB	SO
1957	Philadelphia	NL	4	8	.333	4.91	30	128	122	71	42	92
1958	Philadelphia	NL	3	6	.250	4.51	16	108	99	55	37	77
1959	Philadelphia	NL	9	10	.474	4.06	25	153	135	77	65	106
1960	Philadelphia	NL	9	16	.360	4.38	36	205	194	115	79	150
1961	Chicago	NL	15	14	.517	3.82	39	259	243	121	88	156
1962	Chicago	NL	7	16	.304	4.92	41	196	203	116	60	104
1963	Pittsburgh	NL	13	15	.464	3.07	33	213	195	92	52	112
1964	Pittsburgh	NL	1	2	.333	2.79	4	19	15	9	7	10
1965	Pittsburgh	NL	13	10	.565	3.18	37	240	214	101	59	107
1966	Pittsburgh	NL	6	6	.500	4.60	32	101	112	58	27	60
1967	Pittsburgh	NL	5	9	.357	3.57	26	118	112	57	39	71
1968	New York	NL	7	13	.350	2.95	29	180	156	69	50	82
1969	New York	NL	8	10	.444	3.01	30	152	145	63	47	60
1970	Atlanta	NL	2	3	.400	7.69	32	48	62	42	19	24
14 Seasons			102	138	.425	3.92	410	2127	1044	671	1211	2009

Post-Season

Year	Team	Lg	W	L	Pct.	ERA	G	IP	H	R	BB	SO
1969	New York	WS	0	0	.000	0.00	1	1	0	0	0	0

Ed Charles

Edwin Douglass Charles was born on April 29th, 1935 in Dayton Beach, FL. He is former third baseman in major league baseball. He was a right handed hitter who played with the Kansas City Athletics (1962 - 1967) and New York Mets (1967-1069).

Charles was originally drafted by the Boston Braves in 1952. He spent 8 seasons in the Braves farm system in the still segregated deep south. He wrote poetry then about baseball and racism. Due to the long time career of All-Star, Eddie Mathews at third base, Charles was traded by the Braves to the Kansas City Athletics before the 1962 season.

In his rookie season of 1962, Charles hit for a .288 batting average, 17 home runs, 74 RBI's, and 20 Stolen Bases. All those were career highs for Charles. He was named to the *Topps All Rookie Team*. Charles would continue his steady play for the Athletics over the next four seasons. In 1963, he batted .267 with 15 home runs and a career high 79 RBI's. In 1964, he hit .241, with 16 home runs and 63 RBI's. Prior to the 1965 season, the Athletics owner, Charlie Finley moved the fences back to help his pitchers at Municipal Stadium. His power number's dropped to 17 total home runs in both seasons. He hit .269 and .286 in those seasons.

The Kansas City Athletics records were, as follows in Charles' stay there in Kansas City:

1962	**72-90**
1963	**73-89**
1964	**57-105**
1965	**59-103**
1966	**74-86**
1967	**62-99**

On May 10th, 1967, the Athletics traded Charles to the New York Mets. He was the oldest regular on his new team. In 1968, he led the Mets in home runs with 15. In 1969, he shared 3rd base with Wayne Garrett, as a member of the *Miracle Mets* team that won the World Series. That year the Mets were 10 games behind Chicago on August 13th. On September 24th, they clinched the NL East crown with a 6-0 win over St. Louis, with Charles hitting a home run off of Steve Carlton. This was Charles last home run in his career.

Charles played in 4 of 5 games in the World Series, in which the Mets defeated the heavily favored Baltimore Orioles. After losing the first game, the Mets won the next four. Charles scored the winning run in game 2 on Al Weis single in the ninth. He was the oldest player on the '69 Mets at 36. Ed Charles was in the famous photograph of the Mets' World Series celebration, as winning pitcher, Jerry Koosman leaped into the arms of catcher, Jerry Grote.

After the Series, Charles, whose nickname was "Glider" that came from his graceful base running and 3rd base play, announced he would retire. In his career, he batted .263 wity 86 home runs and 421 RBI's in 1005 games played.

Ed Charles
Edwin Douglas Charles (Ez or the Poet)
Position: 3rd Base
Bats: Right, Throws: Right
Height: 5'10", Weight: 170 lbs.
Born: April 29th, 1953 on Daytona, Florida (78)
High School: Gibbs (St. Petersburg, Florida)
Signed by the Boston Braves as an amateur free agent in 1952
Debut: April 11th, 1962
Teams: Athletics, New York Mets - 1962-1969
Final Game : October 1st, 1969

Year	Team	Lg	G	AB	R	H	HR	RBI	BA	SB
1962	KC	AL	147	535	81	154	17	74	.288	20
1963	KC	AL	158	603	82	161	15	79	.267	15
1964	KC	AL	150	557	69	134	16	63	.241	12
1965	KC	AL	134	480	55	129	8	56	.269	13
1966	KC	AL	118	385	52	110	9	42	.286	12
1967	KC/NYM	AL/NL	120	439	37	92	3	36	.240	5
1968	New York	NL	117	409	41	102	15	53	.276	5
1969	New York	NL	61	189	21	35	3	18	.207	4
8 Seasons			1005	3909	438	917	86	421	.263	86

Post-Season

Year	Team	Lg	G	AB	R	H	HR	RBI	BA	SB
1969	New York	NLCS	4	15	1	2	0	0	.133	0

Donn Clendenon

Donn Alvin Clendenon was born on July 15th, 1935 and died on September 17th, 2005. He was a major league baseball first baseman who played for the following teams:

Pittsburgh Pirates 1961-1968
Montreal Expos 1969
New York Mets 1969-1971
St. Louis Cardinals 1972

He is best remembered as being the World Series MVP of the 1969 New York Mets.

Six months after Clendenon was born in Neosho, Missouri, his father, Claude died from leukemia. Claude Clendenon was a mathematics and psychology professor at Langston University. He was also the chairman of the mathematics department at Langston, an African American University in Langston, Oklahoma. Clendenon's mother, Helen demanded high academic achievement from her son in deference to his father's accomplishments.

When he was only 6 years old, his mother, Helen married former Negro League's, baseball star - Nish Williams. In addition, to accademic excellence, Clendenon's new step father decided he was going to make his stepson into a baseball player. Williams served as coach on virtually every team young Donn played on, including the college team at Moorehouse College in Atlanta, Georgia. He also helped with his semi pro career with the Atlanta Black Crackers, along with Jackie Robinson, Satchel Paige, Roy Campanella, and Don Newcombe from the Negro Leagues.

Clendenon graduated as a letterman in nine sports at Booker T. Washington High School in Atlanta and received a host of scholarship offers. He was prepared to attend UCLA on a scholarship until some coaches from Morehouse College in Atlanta visited his mother and convinced her to attend school closer to home.

Moorhouse College was the premiere academic institution for young African - American men. Just before Clendenon arrived in 1952, the freshman class were assigned big brothers to help students acclimate themselves to Moorehouse and college life.

Although the policy had ended when enrolled, a Morehouse graduate volunteered to be Clendenon's big brother. His name was Martin Luther King, Jr.

Clendenon became a 12 sport letterman in football, basketball, and baseball at Morehouse. He received free agent contract offers from both the Cleveland Browns and the Harlem Globe Trotters. Clendenon decided he wanted to become a grade school teacher and taught fourth grade after graduation. Williams convinced

Clendenon to attend a Pittsburgh Pirates tryout camp in 1957, and then signed with the club.

After 5 years in the minor leagues, Clendenon was promoted to the Pirates on September 1st when rosters expanded. He made his big league debut that month. In 1962, Clendedon hit for a 302 batting average with 7 home runs and 28 RBI's in 80 games. He finished second in NL Rookie of the Year voting to Chicago Cubs, second baseman, Kenny Hubbs.

Following the 1962 season, the Pirates traded Dick Stuart, **Dr. Strange Glove,** first baseman to the Boston Rd Sox to open a position for Clendenon. Donn responded with a .275 batting average, 15 home runs, and 57 RBI's. Clendenon had big RBI years in 1965 and 1966, driving in 96 and 98 runs in those seasons. He became a big part of the Pirates offense with Roberto Clemente and Willie Stargell.

He earned the reputation as a *free swinger,* as he led the National League in strikeouts in 1963 and 1968. He finished second in 1966 and third in 1965. The Pirates record during Clendenon's stay with Pittsburgh are as follows:

Year	W.	L.	Pct.	Place
1962	93-68		.578	4th
1963	74-88		.457	8th
1964	80-82		.494	6th
1965	90-72		.556	3rd
1966	92-70		.568	3rd
1967	81-81		.500	6th
1968	80-82		.494	6th

With first prospect, Al Oliver ready to play, the Pirates left Clendenon unprotected for the 1968 expansion draft. He was then selected by the Montreal Expos on January 22nd, 1969. Then, the Expos traded Clendenon and Jesus Alou to the Houston Astros for Rusty Staub. The Astros had just hired Clendenon's former manager at Pittsburgh, Harry "The Hat" Walker with whom Clendenon had a personality issue. Clendenon refused to report to Houston.

He was traded back to Montreal and joined them on April 19th, 1969. He was batting .240 with 4 home runs and 14 RBI's when he was traded to the New York Mets on June 15th, 1969, in exchange for pitcher, Steve Renko, infielder, Kevin Collins, and two minor leaguers.

The Mets were in second place, nine games behind Leo Durocher's, Cubs in the NL East Division, when they acquired Clendenon. Splitting time wih left-handed hitting, Ed Kranepool at first base, Clendenon's batting average began to rise. On August 30th, Clendenon hit a 10 inning home run against the San Francisco Giants to give the Mets a 3-2 victory.

The Mets were 2 ½ games behind Chicago, when the Cubs came to Shea Stadium for a two game set on September 8th. The Mets swept the set to move within ½ game of first place with Clendenon hitting a two run home run in the Mets' 7-1 victory in the 9th.

The Mets won their next six in a row (ten total) to move 3 ½ games over the Cubs. On September 24th, a Clendenon single handedly beat the St. Louis Cardinals with a 3 run home run and a solo home run to clinch the National League East. Overall, the Mets won 39 out of the last 50 games to finish 100-62, 8 games in front of Chicago.

Clendenon did not appear in the Mets' 1969 NLCS three game sweep of Atlanta to reach the World Series. In the World Series with Baltimore, Clendenon played in 4 of the 5 games. He went 2-4 in game 1, scoring the Mets only run in a 4-1 loss to the Orioles. He hit a fourth inning home run in game 2 and a second inning home run in game 4 to give New York, 1-0 leads in both games.

The Orioles were ahead 3-0 in game 5, when Cleon Jones got hit on the foot with a Dave McNally pitch, however home plate umpire, Lou DiMuro ruled the ball missed Jones. Manager Gil Hodges came out of the Mets' dugout and showed shoe polish smudge on the ball. DiMuro reversed his decision, then awarded first base to Jones. Donn was the next batter and hit a two run home run to pull New York within one run. The Mets eventually, won the game, 5-3, to complete their miracle World Series championship over the heavily favored Orioles.

For the Series, Clendenon batted .357 with 3 home runs and 4 RBI's. He was chosen Series MVP by the writers. His 3 home runs in 5 games is a record, only tied by Ryan Howard of Philadelphia in the 2008 World Series.

On July 28, 1970, Donn set a Mets record by driving in seven runs with a pair of 3 run home runs and a sacrifice fly. The Mets were in second place, one game behind Pittsburgh after the game. However, they stumbled from there, ending the season in 3rd place, 6 games behind the division winning Pirates. Clendenon batted .288 with 22 home runs and 97 RBI's. The RBI mark of 97 set a New York Mets' club record.

After being demoted in 1971 to the Tidewater Tides, Ed Kranepool enjoyed a career year. With first base talent, Mike Jorgensen and John Milner coming up from the minors, Clendenon became expendable. He was released at the end of the 1971 season.

Clendenon signed with the St. Louis Cardinals in 1972, but saw very limited playing time behind Matty Alou. He was released on August 2nd with a .191 batting average, 4 home runs, and 9 RBI's. On August 23rd, the Cardinals traded Alou to Oakland, and spent the rest of the season sharing first base.

After retiring, Clendenon earned a Juris Doctorate Degree from Duquesne University in 1978, then practiced in Dayton, Ohio. He recounted the 1969 season in his book, "Miracle in New York", in which he talked about growing up in Atlanta, earning his degree, and battling drug addition, as he turned 50 years old.

He then entered a drug rehabilitation program in Ogden, Utah, and after a physical exam in connection with his treatment, learned he had leukemia. That promted a move Sioux Falls, South Dakota, in 1987, where he was a general counsel to the Interstate Audit Corporation and a drug rehabilitation councelor. Clendenon died in Sioux Falls, South Dakota at 70 after a long bout with leukemia.

He is survived by his wife, Anne, his sons - Don, Jr. and Val, his daughter - Donna Clendenon, and 6 grandsons. Shortly before his death, he was inducted into the Georgia Hall of Fame.

Donn Clendenon
Donn Alvin Clendenon
Position: first base
Bats: Right, Throws: Right
Height: 6'4", Weight: 209 lbs.
Born: July 15th, 1935 in Meosho, Missouri
High School: Booker T. Washington (Atlanta, GA)
School: Morehouse College
Signed by Pittsburgh Pirates as an amateur free gent in 1957
Debut: September 22nd, 1961
Teams: Pirates, Expos, Mets, Cardinals - 1961-1972
Died: September 17th, 2005 in Sioux Falls, SD (70)

Year	Team	Lg	G	AB	R	H	HR	RBI	BA	SB
1961	Pittsburgh	NL	9	35	7	11	0	2	.314	0
1962	Pittsburgh	NL	80	222	39	67	7	28	.302	16
1963	Pittsburgh	NL	154	563	65	155	15	57	.275	22
1964	Pittsburgh	NL	133	457	53	129	12	64	.282	12

Year	Team	Lg	G	AB	R	H	HR	RBI	BA	SB
1965	Pittsburgh	NL	162	612	89	184	14	96	.301	9
1966	Pittsburgh	NL	155	571	80	171	28	98	.299	7
1967	Pittsburgh	NL	131	478	63	119	13	56	.249	4
1968	Pittsburgh	NL	158	584	63	150	17	87	.257	10
1969	Mont/Ho/NY	NL	110	331	45	82	16	51	.248	3
1970	New York	NL	121	396	65	114	22	97	.288	4
1971	New York	NL	88	263	29	65	11	57	.247	1
1972	St. Louis	NL	61	136	13	26	4	9	.191	1
12 Seasons				1362	4648	594	1273	159	682	.274	90

Post - Season

Year	Team	Lg	G	AB	R	H	HR	RBI	BA	SB
1969	New York	WS	4	14	4	5	3	4	.357	0

Duffy Dyer

Duffy Dyer was born on August 15th, 1945 in Dayton, Ohio. He is the former major league player and coach. He played in major league baseball, as a catcher for the following teams:

New York Mets 1968-1974
Pittsburgh Pirates 1975-1978
Montreal Expos 1979
Detroit Tigers 1980-1981

Dyer played alongside Sal Bando and Rick Monday on the Arizona State Sun Devils baseball team that won the 1965 College World Series. He was drafted by the New York Mets in the 1966 major league draft and backed up Jerry Grote, as a member of the 1969 Miracle Mets that won the World Series. Duffy caught most of the games in 1972, as Grote battled injuries. In 94 games, he hit 8 home runs and had 36 RBI's. He also led

NL catchers in double plays and base runner caught stealing. He was second in assists. In 1973, he helped the Mets win the NL East Division and National League pennant. The Mets were in last place on August 30th, but rallied to overtake St. Louis with a record of 82-79.

In October 1974, Dyer was traded to Pittsburgh for outfielder, Gene Clines. He backed up catcher, Manny Sanguillen on a team that wo the NL East title. Dyer was the catcher on August 9th, 1976, when John Candelaria pitched a no-hitter against the Los Angeles Dodgers at Three Rivers Stadium. In 1977 when Manny Sanguillen was traded to Oakland, Dyer shared the catching duties with left-handed hitting, Ed Ott in a platoon system. Dyer led NL catchers in 1977 with a .993 fielding percentage, only having 3 errors in 93 games.

In 14 seasons, Dyer played in 722 games, had 443 base hits in 1993 at bats for a career .221 batting average. He hit 30 home runs and had 173 RBI's.

In 1986, Dyer was inducted into the Arizona Sports Hall of Fame.

After his playing career, Duffy was a coach for the Chicago Cubs, Milwaukee Brewers, and Oakland A's. As a minor league manager, he led the Class A - Kerosha Twins to a Midwest League Championship in 1985. In 1986, he managed El Paso Diablos to first place finish in first place in the Texas League. Dyer was hired to be a catching coordinator in 2007.

Duffy Dyer

Dan Robert Dyer
Position: Catcher
Bats: Right, Throws: Right
Height: 6'0", Weight: 187 lbs.
Born August 15th, 1945 in Dayton, Ohio (Age 66)
School: Arizona State University
Drafted by New York Mets in 1st round 9th pick of the 1966 amateur draft
Debut: September 21st, 1968 with the Mets
Teams: Mets, Pirates, Tigers, and Expos - 1968-1981
Final Game: April 15th, 1981

Year	Team	Lg	G	AB	R	H	HR	RBI	BA	SB
1968	New York	NL	1	3	0	1	0	0	.333	0
1969	New York	NL	29	74	5	19	3	12	.257	0
1970	New York	NL	59	148	8	31	2	12	.209	1
1971	New York	NL	59	169	13	39	2	18	.231	1
1972	New York	NL	94	325	33	75	8	36	.231	0
1973	New York	NL	70	189	9	35	1	9	.185	0
1974	New York	NL	63	142	14	30	0	10	.211	0
1975	Pittsburgh	NL	48	132	8	30	3	16	.227	0
1976	Pittsburgh	NL	69	184	12	41	3	9	.223	0
1977	Pittsburgh	NL	94	270	27	65	3	19	.241	6
1978	Pittsburgh	NL	58	175	7	37	0	13	.211	2
1979	Montreal	NL	28	74	4	18	1	8	.243	0
1980	Detroit	AL	48	108	11	20	4	11	.185	0
1981	Detroit	AL	2	0	0	0	0	0	.000	0
14 seasons			722	1993	151	441	30	173	.221	10

Post-Season

Year	Team	Lg	G	AB	R	H	HR	RBI	BA	SB
1969	New York	NL	1	1	0	0	0	0	.000	0
1975	Pittsburgh	NL	1	0	0	0	0	0	.000	0
2 Seasons			2	1	0	0	0	0	.000	0

Jack DiLauro

Jack Edward DiLauro was born on May 3rd, 1943 in Akron, Ohio. He is a former big league pitcher who played on the 1969 World Series Champion Mets. He also, played with the Houston Astros in 1970.

DiLauro started his professional career by signing with the Detroit Tigers, as an amateur free agent on January 1st, 1963. He never pitched in the big leagues with the Tigers. On December 4th, 1968, he was traded to the Mets for Hector Valle.

In 1969, DiLauro pitched 4 games for the Mets - AAA affiliate, the Tidewater Tides. He then came up to the Mets and made his major league debut on May 15th, 1969 against Atlanta. In 1969, he pitched in 23 games, most of them relief, and 63 innings for New York. He won 1 game and lost 4 with one save. The win, his first occurred on July 20th against the Montreal Expos . His ERA in 1969 was 2.40, better than the league average. The Mets won the World Series in 1969, but Bill did not pitch in the post-season.

After the season, DiLauro was drafted from the Mets by Houston in the rule 5 draft. In 1970, DiLauro pitched 42 games for the Astros, all in relief, pitching 34 innings. He was 1-3 with 3 saves. He was sold by Houston to San Diego's - AAA team in the Pacific Coast League, the Hawaii Islanders. In July, he was traded with Hank McGraw, brother of Tug, to Atlanta for Marv Staehle. But, he never pitched in the big leagues, again.

Jack DiLauro
Position: Pitcher
Bats: Both, Throws: Left
Ht: 6'2", Wt: 185 lbs.
Born: March 3rd, 1943 in Akron, Ohio (Age 68)
High School: North Akron (Akron, Ohio)
School : University of Akron
Signed by the Detroit Tigers, as an free agent in 1963
Debut: May 15th, 1969
Teams: Astros, Mets 1969-1970
Final Game: September 25th, 1970

Year	Team	Lg	W	L	Pct.	ERA	G	IP	H	R	BB	SO
1969	New York	NL	1	4	.200	2.40	23	64	50	19	18	27
1970	Houston	NL	1	3	.250	4.28	42	34	34	23	17	23
2 Seasons			2	7	.222	3.05	65	98	84	42	35	50

DiLauro did not pitch for the Mets in the post-season in 1969.

Wayne Garrett

Ronald Wayne Garrett was born on December 3rd, 1947 in Brookville, Florida. He was the New York Mets starting third baseman from 1972 through 1975. Garrett also, saw spot duty, as a second baseman and shortstop. He played for the following big league teams and pro team in Japan:

New York Mets 1969-1976
Montreal Expos 1976-1978
St. Louis Cardinals 1978
Chunichi Dragons 1979-1980

Garrett was on the 1969 New York Mets team that upset Baltimore in the World Series. He also started at third base on the NL pennant winning New York Mets in 1973 that lost to Oakland in the Series. In 1973, Wayne hit 6 home runs in September and then two more in the World Series. He also, tied Eddie Mathews record of striking out 11 times in the 1958 World Series. He made the final out of the Series in game 7 by popping out to short stop, Bert Campaneris.

Garrett's major league career spanned from 1969-1978. He spent half of the 1971 season on military duty. He also played for the Montreal Expos and the St. Louis Cardinals. He was traded by the New York Mets to the Expos along with Del Unser in July 1976 for Pepe Manual and Jim Dwyer. After his major league career, Garrett played two seasons for the Chunichi Dragons in Japan.

Baseball ran in the Garrett family. Wayne's brother, Adrian, played for the Chicago Cubs, the Oakland A's, California Angels, and the Atlanta Braves, mostly as a catcher, first baseman, and outfielder. Wayne's other brother, Charlie played in Atlanta's farm system. Wayne's nephew Jason, Adrian's son, played four years in the Florida Marlins' organization, AAA league in the minor leagues.

Wayne Garrett

Ronald Wayne Garrett
Bats: Left, Throws: Right
Ht: 5'11", Wt.: 175 lbs.
Born: December 3rd, 1947 in Brookville, FL (Age 63)
High School: Sarasota (Sarasota, FL)
Drafted by the Milwaukee Braves in the 6th round
of the 1965 draft
Debut: April 12th, 1969
Teams: Mets, Expos, and Cardinals - 1969-1978
Relative: Brother of Adrian Garrett

Year	Team	Lg	G	AB	R	H	HR	RBI	BA	SB
1969	New York	NL	124	400	38	87	1	39	.218	4
1970	New York	NL	114	366	74	93	12	45	.254	5
1971	New York	NL	56	202	20	43	1	11	.213	1
1972	New York	NL	111	298	41	69	2	29	.232	3
1973	New York	NL	140	504	76	129	16	58	.256	6
1974	New York	NL	151	522	55	117	13	53	.224	4
1975	New York	NL	107	274	49	73	6	34	.266	3
1976	NY/Mont.	NL	139	428	51	99	4	37	.231	9
1977	Montreal	NL	68	159	33	43	2	22	.270	2
1978	Mont./St.L.	NL	87	137	17	33	2	12	.250	1
10 Seasons			1092	3285	438	786	61	340	.233	38

Post-Seasons

Year	Team	Lg	G	AB	R	H	HR	RBI	BA	SB
1969	New York	NLCS	3	13	3	5	1	3	.385	1
1969	New York	WS	2	1	0	0	0	0	.000	0
1973	New York	NLCS	5	23	1	2	0	1	.087	0
1973	New York	WS	7	30	4	5	2	2	.167	0
2 Post-Seasons			17	67	8	12	3	6	.177	1

Gary Gentry

Gary Gentry was born October 6th, 1946 in Phoenix, Arizona. He is a famous right-handed pitcher in major league baseball, who played seven seasons for the New York Mets (1969-1972) and Atlanta Braves (1973-1975).

Gary Gentry went to Arizona State University and began his professional career at age 22 in 1969. As a rookie, he won 13 games, pitching in a starting rotation with Tom Seaver and Jerry Koosman for the Mets team that beat Baltimore, 4 games to one. On September 24th, Gentry pitched a four hit, 6-0 shutout against the St. Louis Cardinals to clinch the division title. The Mets trailed Chicago by 9 ½ games on August 13th.

Gentry was the starting pitcher for the Mets in game 3 of NLCS against Atlanta on October 6th, his birthday. Gentry struggled, but won, 7-4 to advance the Mets into the World Series.

On October 14th, Gentry was the winning pitcher in game 3 of the World Series. Gentry had a double to score 2 runs in the game, highlighted by Tommie Agee's two circus catches.

Gentry continued to pitch for New York the next three seasons. He won 28 games from 1970-1972, as the New York Mets finished in third place, each season. In 1970, they finished 6 games behind Pittsburgh.

Gentry was traded on November 1972 to Atlanta and suffered a career ending elbow injury. He pitched his last game for the Braves on May 6th, 1975 and was resigned by the Mets, but was released on July 19th. During his 7 year career, his record was 46 wins and 49 losses with an ERA of 3.56.

Gary Gentry
Gary Edward Gentry
Position: Pitcher
Bats: Right, Throws: Right

Ht: 6'0", Wt: 170 pounds
Born: Oct. 6th, 1946 in Phoenix, AZ (age 65)
School: Arizona State University
Drafted by Mets: April 10th, 1969
Terms: Mets / Braves
Final Game: May 6th, 1975

Year	Team	Lg	W	L	Pct.	ERA	G	IP	H	R	BB	SO
1969	New York	NL	13	12	.520	3.43	35	234	192	94	81	154
1970	New York	NL	9	9	.500	3.68	32	188	155	88	86	134
1971	New York	NL	12	11	.522	3.23	32	203	167	84	82	155
1972	New York	NL	7	10	.412	4.01	32	164	153	82	75	120
1973	Atlanta	NL	4	6	.500	3.43	16	86	74	37	35	42
1974	Atlanta	NL	0	0	.000	1.35	3	7	4	1	2	0
1975	Atlanta	NL	1	1	.500	4.95	7	20	25	14	8	10
7 Seasons			46	49	.484	3.56	157	903	770	400	367	615

Post-Season

Year	Team	Lg	W	L	Pct.	ERA	G	IP	H	R	BB	SO
1969	New York	NLCS	0	0	.000	9.00	1	2	5	2	1	1
1969	New York	WS	1	0	1.000	0.00	1	7	3	0	5	4
1 Season			1	0	1.000	2.08	2	9	8	2	6	5

Jerry Grote

Gerald Wayne Grote was born on October 16th, 1942. He is a former major league baseball player. He played for the following big league teams in his career:

Houston Colts 1963-1964
New York Mets 1966-1967
Los Angeles Dodgers 1977-1978, 1981
KC Royals 1981

Grote was raised in San Antonio, Texas. When he was just 10 years old, he and his family were caught in a F-4 tornado. His mother, father, and 2 sisters made it to safety. However, he lost his grandmother in the storm.

Grote attended Douglas MacArthur High School, where he played on the baseball team, as a pitcher, catcher, and third baseman. As a high school pitcher, he threw a no-hitter and an one-hitter. Grote played for Trinity University in 1962, and led the Tigers in batting average (.413), home runs (5), RBI's (19), and hits (31).

After one season at Trinity University, Grote was signed, as an amateur free agent by the Houston Colt 45's in 1962, and was assigned to play for the minor league affiliate, San Antonio Bullets. At the age of 20, he made his major league debut with the Colt 45's on September 21st, 1963, as a late inning defensive replacement for John Bateman, and hit a sacrifice fly to score Bob Aspromonte in his only at-bat. For the season, he appeared in three games, including September 27th, when every starter in the Colts line-up was a rookie.

In 1964, Grote platooned with Bateman behind the plate. The Colt 45's also, experimented with young catchers, Dave Adlesh and John Hoffman, as well because of Grote and Bateman had low batting averages (.181 and .190). Grote was the Colts catcher on April 23rd, when Ken Johnson became the first pitcher in major league history to lose a complete game, no-hitter in 9 innings, 1-0.

In 1965, the newly renamed Houston Astros that moved into the indoor astro-turf field - Astrodome started former, All-Star-Gus Triandos and prospect, Ron Brand being added to the mix.

Jerry spent his entire 1965 season with - AAA, Pacific Coast League affiliate-Oklahoma City 89ers, where he batted .265 with 11 home runs. After the season, he was traded to the New York Mets for pitcher, Tom Parsons.

The Houston franchise had the following records when Grote was there:

Year	Team	W L	Pct.	GB
1963	Houston Colt 45's	66-96	.407	33
1964	Houston Colt 45's	66-96	.407	27
1965	Houston Astros	65-97	.401	32

Houston's attendance increased to 2,151,470 in the Astrodome in 1965. They drew 725,773 in Colt Field the year before.

Jerry Grote became the starting catcher for the Mets immediately upon his arrival to New York. Though he batted only .237 with three home runs in 1966, his handling of the young Met pitching staff and his solid defensive skills were instrumental in helping the Mets avoid 100 losses and last place for the first time in their history.

In 1968, Grote was hitting over .300 at mid-season and was recognized, as one of the top catchers in the National League when he was selected to be starting catcher in the All-Star Game over Atlanta's, Joe Torre. He was only the second Met to be named starter after second baseman, Ron Hunt in 1967. Grote was held hitless in two at bats during the game. He ended 1968 with 3 home runs, 31 RBI's, and a batting average of .282.

The 1969 season was a memorable one for the New York Mets . The Chicago Cubs went a woeful, 9-17 in their last 26 games. The Cubs were hurt by a broken hand suffered by third baseman, Ron Santo, suffered during a Mets series in September. The Mets also, were very hot winning 39 of their last 50 games to overtake the Cubs by 8 games.

In 1969, Grote hit for a .252 batting average and produced career highs - home runs (6) and RBI's (40). But he was off the charts on his defense - .991 fielding percentage and a 56.3 caught stealing percentage, second in NL catchers. He was also, given credit for guiding the Mets' pitching staff, which led the team in victories, shutouts, and finished second in team ERA.

In Game 4 of the 1969 Series with the score tied, Grote doubled to start the tenth inning, then pinch runner, Rod Gasper scored the winning run an errant throw hit JC Martin on the wrist on a sacrifice bunt. With Grote calling pitches the Mets' hurlers held Baltimore to a .146 batting average during the series.

In game 4 of the 1969 Series with the score tied, 1-1, Grote doubled to start the tenth inning, then pich runner, Rod Gasper scored the winning run when an errant throw hit J. C. Martin on the wrist on a sacrifice bunt to provide the margin of victory. With Grote calling the pitches, the Mets' hurlers held Baltimore to a .146 batting average during the 5 game Series.

Grote continued to provide the Mets with good defense, leading NL catchers in 1970-1971 in putouts. In 1972, Grote played in only 64 games due to injuries. In late September, he had surgery to remove bone chips.

In May 1973, Grote broke a bone in his right arm when he was hit by a pitch and went on the disabled list for 2 months. When he returned in mid - July, the Mets began climbing winning, climbing from last place on August 30th to win the NL East pennant. One thing about the NL East race in 1973 was only 7 games separated the top team St. Louis to 6th team or bottom team in the division - New York on August 30th. What a division race it was. The Mets then defeated the heavily favored Cincinnati Reds in the NLCS. In the World Series, the Oakland A's won in 7 games.

As he had in 1969, Grote caught every inning of every post-season game for the Mets in 1973. Looking back on his two pennant winning seasons with the Mets, Grote said, "It was no miracle on the 1969 Mets. Now, '73 was a miracle."

In 1974, Grote was batting .287 with 4 home runs and 27 RBI's to earn his second All-Star selection after catcher, Johnny Bench of Cincinnati. However, injuries were starting to take their toll, so he started to share the catching position with Duffy Dyer.

Grote rebounded in 1975, posting a career - high .295 batting average in 119 games and led all catchers with a .995 fielding percentage. At Veterans Stadium on July 4th, 1975, Grote stepped in, as a pinch-hitter against former Met closer, Tug McGraw, who had been traded to Philadelphia during the off-season. With the Mets down, 3-2, Grote connected for a two run home run for the win. Tug McGraw was the Met who coined the phrase **You Gotta Believe** in the 1973 pennant season in September.

By 1977, John Stearns had taken over, as the Mets' starting catcher, as back injuries continued to mount and plague Grote. In August after 12 years with the Mets, he was traded to the Los Angeles Dodgers for two players to be named, later. Neither of these players reached the big leagues.

From 1966 - 1977 the Mets had the following records with Grote behind the plate:

Year	Won-Lost	Pct.	GB	Place	
1966	66-95	.410	28 ½	9th	
1967	61-101	.377	40 ½	10th	
1968	73-89	.451	24	9th	
1969	100-62	.617	___	1st	
1970	83-79	.512	6	3rd	
1971	83-79	.512	12	3rd	
1972	83-73	.532	13 ½	3rd	Players Strike
1973	82-79	.509	___	1st	
1974	71-91	.438	17	5th	
1975	82-80	.506	10 ½	3rd	
1976	86-76	.531	15	3rd	
1977	64-98	.395	37	6th	

Shortly, after joining the Los Angeles Dodgers, Grote struck out in his only at-bat against former teammate, Tom Seaver, who was with Cincinnati.

During his two seasons in LA, he was mostly a back-up catcher to Steve Yeager and appeared in two World Series against the New York Yankees, both losing appearances. He retired after the 1978 season, only to be lured out of retirement in 1981 by the Kansas City Royals, who was experiencing a shortage of catchers. On July 3rd, 1981, at the age of 38, Grote went 3 for 4 with a grand slam home run, a double, a stolen base, and drove home a team record seven runs. After another short stint with the Dodgers, he retired for good after 1981.

In his 16 year career, Grote played in 1,421 games, accumulating 1,092 hits, a .252 batting average along with 39 home runs and 404 RBI's. He finished his career with a .991 fielding percentage, eighth highest among catchers, lifetime. On April 22nd, 1970, Grote established a major league record for putouts in a game, when Tom Seaver struck out 19 batters against San Diego. He is the all-time leader in games at the catcher position (1,176) for the Mets. Grote caught 116 shutouts in his career.

Grote called the pitches for some of the most outstanding pitchers of his era, including Tom Seaver, Jerry Koosman, Tug McGraw, Nolan Ryan, Tommy John, Don Sutton, and Dan Quissenberry. He possessed a strong and accurate throwing arm against opposing base runners. Hall of Famer, Lou Brock, second all-time in stolen bases, found Grote to be one of the most difficult catchers on which to attemp a stolen base. Also, hall of famer, Johnny Bench, a perennial Gold Glove winner during their years in the National League together, once said of Grote, "If Grote and I were in the same team, I would be playing third base."

After retirement, Grote spent the 1985, as a manager of the Lakeland Tigers and Birmingham Barons. In 1989, he played for the St. Louis Legends in the Senior Professional Baseball Association. He was inducted into the Texas Baseball Hall of Fame in 1992.

In 1998, he was inducted into the San Antonio Sports Hall of Fame. On October 8th, 2011, Grote was inducted into the Trinity University Athletic Hall of Fame. After retirement, Grote continued to raise prize Texas Longhorns on his ranch, near Austin, Texas. He appeared as a mystery guest on the television game show - *What's my Line?*

Grote can be heard, as a color commentator with Mike Capps on Round Rock Express - PCL (Pacific Coast League) radio broadcasts (2010) on MILB.com.

Jerry Grote

Gerald Wayne Grote
Position: Catcher
Bats: Right, Throws: Right
Ht: 5'10", Wt: 185 lbs.
Born: October 6th, 1942 in San Antonio, Texas (Age 69)
High School: McArthur (San Antonio, TX)
School: Trinity University
Signed: by Houston Colt .45's as an amateur free agent in 1962
Debut: September 21st, 1963
Teams: Mets, Colt .45's, Astros, Dodgers, Royals
- 1963-1981
Final Game: October 3rd, 1981

Year	Team	Lg	G	AB	R	H	HR	RBI	BA	SB
1963	Houston	NL	3	5	0	1	0	1	.200	0
1964	Houston	NL	100	298	26	54	3	24	.181	0
1966	New York	NL	120	317	26	75	3	31	.237	4
1967	New York	NL	120	344	25	67	4	23	.195	2
1968	New York	NL	124	404	29	114	3	31	.282	1
1969	New York	NL	113	365	38	92	6	40	.252	2
1970	New York	NL	126	415	38	106	2	34	.255	2
1971	New York	NL	125	403	35	109	2	35	.270	1
1972	New York	NL	64	205	15	43	3	21	.210	1
1973	New York	NL	84	285	17	73	1	32	.256	0
1974	New York	NL	97	319	25	82	5	36	.257	0
1975	New York	NL	119	386	28	114	2	39	.295	0
1976	New York	NL	101	323	30	88	4	28	.272	1
1977	NY/LA	NL	60	142	11	38	0	11	.268	0
1978	LA	NL	41	70	5	19	0	9	.271	0
1981	KC/LA	AL/NL	24	68	4	17	1	9	.293	1
16 Seasons			1421	4339	352	1092	39	404	.252	15

Post-Season - Jerry Grote

Year	Team	Lg	G	AB	R	H	HR	RBI	BA	SB
1969	New York	NLCS	3	12	3	2	0	1	.167	0
1969	New York	WS	5	19	1	4	0	1	.211	0
1973	New York	NLCS	5	19	2	4	0	2	.211	0
1973	New York	WS	7	30	2	8	0	0	.267	0
1977	LA	NLCS	2	1	0	0	0	0	.000	0
1977	LA	WS	1	1	1	0	0	0	.000	0
1978	LA	NLCS	1	0	0	0	0	0	.000	0
1978	LA	WS	2	0	0	0	0	0	.000	0
4 Post-Seasons			26	81	8	18	0	4	.222	0

Rod Gaspar

Rodney Earl Gaspar was born on April 3rd, 1945 in Long Beach, California. He was a former major league baseball outfielder. He was a switch hitter, who played with the following teams:

New York Mets   1969-1970
San Diego Chargers   1971, 1974

He played college baseball at Long Beach State University. Gasper played a total of 178 games in the big leagues.

Most of them came his rookie year in 1969. He played 118 games that season. He began the years, as a starting right-fielder, until in mid season when Ron Swoboda, replaced him. He then became an utility outfielder, playing all three outfield positions. That season, he .228, drove in 14 RBI's, and hit his only career home run off Mike McCormick of San Francisco on May 30th, 1969. He excelled defensively, leading all Mets outfielders in assists with 12 and douple plays with 6.

Gasper was a member of the '69 New York Mets team that defeated Baltimore in 5 games in the World Series. In Game 4 of the Series, Gasper scored the winning run after a controversial bunt by pinch hitter J.C. Martin in the 10th inning that provided te margin of victory, 2-1. Pete Richert's throw ricocheted away off Martini's arm that allowed Gasper to come around to score. Replays showed that Martin had been running on the inside side of the baseline, which might have been called catcher's interference. It was not called, allowing the winning run to score. Manager, Earl Weaver of Baltimore was not in the dugout to argue, having been thrown out earlier for arguing - balls and strikes.

Gaspar's son, Cade is a former minor league pitcher. Today, Gaspar owns an insurance company in Mission Viejo, California.

Rod Gaspar
Rodney Earl Gaspar
Positions: Outfielder and Pinch-Hitter
Bats: Both, Throws: Left
Height: 5'11", Weight: 165 pounds
Born: April 3rd, 1946 in Long Beach, CA
High School: Lakewood (Lakewood, California)
School: California State University, Long Beach, CA
Drafted: April 8th, 1969
Teams: Mets / Padres - 1969-1974
Final Game: July 19, 1974

Year	Team	Lg	G	AB	R	H	HR	RBI	BA	SB
1969	New York	NL	118	215	76	49	1	14	.228	7
1970	New York	NL	11	14	4	0	0	0	.000	1
1971	San Diego	NL	16	17	1	2	0	2	.118	0
1974	San Diego	NL	33	14	4	3	0	1	.214	0
4 Seasons			178	260	85	54	1	17	.208	8

Did not play in post-season in 1969.

Bud Harrelson

Daniel McKinley "Bud" Harrelson was born June 6th, 1944 - "D-Day". He grew up in Hayward, CA and attended Sunset High School. He is a former big league player for the following teams:

New York Mets	**1965-1977**
Philadelphia Philles	**1978-1979**
Texas Rangers	**1980**

He then was a manager of the New York Mets in 1990 and 1991. After retiring in 1980, he served as coach for the World Champion Mets in 1986. He was inducted into the New York Mets Hall of Fame in 1982.

Bud Harrelson anchored the New York Mets' infield for 13 years, including their 1969 championship season and 1973 pennant winning seasons. Harrelson was a typical short stop of that era - good fielder and poor hitter. He had a lifetime batting average of .236 and hit a total 7 home runs during his major league career. He had a .963 fielding average and won a gold glove at short stop in 1971. His only All-Star appearance was in 1970.

On May 28th, 1969 after a 5 game losing streak that saw the New York Mets fall into a 4th place in the National League, Jerry Koosman of the Mets and Clay Kirby, Padres engaged in a pitcher's duel at Shea Stadium. After 9 scoreless innings by Kirby and 10 by Koosman, the game was turned over to the bullpen for both teams. Then end finally came after 11 innings, when Harrelson hit a single to drive in Cleon Jones. This led to an 11 game winning streak that brought New York within 7 games of Chicago, the first place team.

On September 10th, the Mets swept a double header against Montreal. Coupled with a loss by Chicago, the Mets jumped into first for the first time in their history. For that season, Bud .248 with no home runs, 24 RBI's, and 42 run scored. He had a .969 fielding percentage in 119 games at short stop. He shared the position with Al Weis.

Harrelson had only two hits for Mets in the '69 NLCS. He hit a big go-ahead, triple in the 4th inning of the first game, and a RBI double in the 3 game sweep of the Atlanta Braves. In the World Series against Baltimore, Harrelson went 3 - 17 with 2 RBI's for a .176 batting average.

Harrelson's light hitting became the subject of controversy during the 1973 NL Championship Series. Mets' starter, Jon Matlack held the Cincinnati Reds to two hits in a 5-0 complete game victory in game 2 at Riverfront Stadium.

Following the game, Harrelson commented, "He made the Big Red Machine look like me hitting, today." Inadvertently, providing the Reds with bulletin board material. Harrelson was confronted by Reds' second baseman, Joe Morgan during pre-game warmups for game three. During this confrontation, he received the warning that the 1973 batting champion, Pete Rose was not happy with quote.

In the fifth, Joe Morgan hit a double play grounder to first baseman, John Milner with Rose on first. Whether Rose slid hard into second base to break up the double play, or if Harrelson was overly sensitive due to the warning from Morgan is a matter of debate. Anyway, a fight between the two erupted, resulting in a bench clearing brawl. The game was nearly cancelled at Shea Stadium, when The Reds took the field the next inning. Fans in left field threw objects from the stands at Rose, causing Cininnati manager, Sparky Anderson to take his team off the field. Then, Mets manager, Yogi Berra, players-Tom Seaver, Cleon Jones, and Rusty Staub were actually, summoned by NL President, Chub Feeney to go out in left field to calm the fans. The Mets went on to beat Cincinnati in five games, in a great upset for the NL pennant. The Mets went onto the World Series, only to lose in seven games to the Oakland Athletics.

The season by season records of the New York Mets when Bud Harrelson played on the team are as follows:

Year	W.	L.	Pct.	GB.
1965	50	112	.309	47
1966	66	95	.410	28 ½
1967	61	101	.377	40 ½
1968	73	89	.451	24
1969	100	62	.617	--
1970	83	79	.512	6
1971	83	79	.512	12
1972	83	73	.532	13 ½
1973	82	79	.509	--
1974	71	91	.438	17
1975	82	80	.506	10 ½
1976	86	76	.531	15
1977	64	98	.395	37

After reacquiring former number 1 pick, Tim Foli, the Mets dealt Harrelson to the Phillies prior to the start of the '78 season. Rose and Harrelson actually, became teammates when Rose signed with Philadelphia before the 1979 season. After two seasons in Philadelphia, Harrelson was traded to the Texas Rangers, and then retired after the 1980 season. In 1986, Harrelson was inducted into the New York Mets Hall of Fame.

After his retirement, Harrelson managed the Little Falls Mets in 1984 an the Columbia Mets in 1985. When Mets, 3rd base coach, Bobby Valentine accepted a managerial position with

Texas Rangers, half way through the 1985 season, Harrelson was added, as coach.

Harrelson was a Mets' coach during the 1986 championship season, and eventaully replaced Dave Johnson, following his dismissal, as Mets' manager-42 games into 1990 season. He led the Mets to their seventh consecutive winning season - 91-71. Although the Mets were contenders for most of the first half of the '91 season, the team collapsed in the 2nd half and Harrelson was then fired with one week left in the season. He ws replaced by his third base coach, Mike Cubbage. His second season ended at 75-80. The Mets finished '91 at 78-84 in 4th place.

During the 1991 season, Harrelson hosted his own radio show in New York, but ended it prematurely during the season because of the teams' poor record.

He currently, resides in Hauppauge, NY, and is co-owner, Senior Vice President for baseball operations and first base coach of the Long Island Ducks, an unaffiliated, minor league baseball team. He appeared on a TV sitcom called *Everyone Loves Raymond* with some of the '69 Mets team.

Bud Harrelson
Derrel McKinley Harrelson
Positions: Shortstop and 2nd baseman
Bats: Both, Throws: Right
Height: 5'11", Weight: 160 lbs.
Born: June 6th, 1944 in Niles, CA (Age 67)
High School: Sunset (Hayward, CA)
School: San Francisco State University
Signed by the NY Mets, as an amateur free agent in 1963
Debut: September 2nd, 1965
Teams: Mets, Phillies, Rangers - 1965-1980
Final Game: October 5th, 1980

Year	Team	Lg	G	AB	R	H	HR	RBI	BA	SB
1965	New York	NL	19	37	3	4	0	0	.108	0
1966	New York	NL	33	99	20	22	0	4	.222	7
1967	New York	NL	151	540	59	137	1	28	.254	12
1968	New York	NL	111	402	38	88	0	14	.219	4
1969	New York	NL	123	395	42	98	0	24	.248	1
1970	New York	NL	157	564	72	137	1	42	.243	23
1971	New York	NL	142	547	55	138	0	32	.252	28
1972	New York	NL	115	418	54	90	1	24	.215	12
1973	New York	NL	106	356	35	92	0	20	.258	5
1974	New York	NL	106	331	48	75	1	13	.227	9
1975	New York	NL	34	73	5	16	0	3	.219	0
1976	New York	NL	118	359	34	84	1	26	.234	9
1977	New York	NL	107	269	25	48	1	12	.178	5
1978	Phila.	NL	71	103	16	22	0	9	.214	5
1979	Phila.	NL	53	71	20	20	0	7	.282	3
1980	Texas	AL	87	180	49	49	1	9	.272	4
Seasons			1533	5516	539	1120	7	267	.236	127

Post-Season

Year	Team	Lg	G	AB	R	H	HR	RBI	BA	SB
1969	New York	NLCS	3	11	2	2	0	3	.182	0
1969	New York	WS	5	17	1	3	0	0	.176	0
1973	New York	NLCS	5	18	1	3	0	2	.167	0
1973	New York	WS	7	24	2	6	0	1	.250	0
2 Seasons			20	70	6	14	0	6	.200	0

Managerial Record

Year	Team	W.	L.	Pct.	Finish
1990	New York	71	49	.592	2nd
1991	New York	74	80	.481	5th
2 Seasons		**155**	**129**	**.529**	**3rd**

Cleon Jones

Cleon Joseph Jones was born on August 4th, 1942, in Plateau, Alabama. He is a former major league baseball, left-fielder, who is best remembered, as a man who caught the final out of the ***Miracle Mets*** improbable World Series Championship over the Baltimore Orioles in 1969.

Jones played football and baseball at Mobile County Training School in Mobile, Alabama, and Alabama A & M University. With the Bulldogs, James scored 26 TD's in 9 games. Jones signed, as an amateur free agent in 1963. After batting over .300 for both the Carolina League, Raleigh Mets, and New York-Penn League-Auburn Mets, he received a September call up to New York.

He was called up to the big club without having played double A or triple A baseball. He got two hits in 15 at bats for a .133 batting average during September with New York.

After spending all of 1964 with AAA - Buffalo Bisons, Jones made the Mets out of spring training and was the 1965 season opener the Los Angeles Dodgers. Jones went back down to Buffalo on May 2nd with a .156 batting average. He again, received a call-up to New York that September 22nd against Pittsburgh. He finished with a batting average of .149.

Jones was the starting center fielder in 1966 and hit for a .275 batting average with 8 home runs and 57 RBI's. He also, had 16 stolen bases to finish 4th in the NL Rookie of the Year balloting. Following the season, the Mets acquired Jones' childhood friend - Tommie Agee from the Chicago White Sox. Jones moved to left field with former, Gold Glove winner, Agee playing center field.

Jones began the '68 season platooning with Art Shamsky in left-field. He was batting .205 on May 18th, when he went 3 for 4 with a home run, 2 RBI's, and a run scored to lift the Mets to a 5-2 win over the Atlanta Braves. From there Jones began to hit. His finest game of his career occurred on July 16th, 1969 at Shibe Park in Philadelphia, when Jones went four for six with 3 RBI's and a run scored . He played all three outfield positions. He ended the season with a .297 batting average, which was 6th in the NL.

Jones was batting .341 with 10 home runs and 56 RBI's in the first half of 1969, earning the starting left-field position for the All- Star Game. He went 2 for 4 with 2 runs scored in the NL's, 9-3 victory. He hit a home run in the first game after the break, and emerged, as the hitting star of the surprising Mets, with a team leading batting average of .341.

The Mets won 39 of their last 50, and finished the season 100 wins against 62 losses, eight games in front of Chicago. Jones ended the season with a .340 batting average, which was third behind Pete Rose and Roberto Clemente. He was second on the Mets in home runs, RBI's, and runs scored, behind Tommy Agee in those categories.

Jones hit .429 in the Mets - three game sweep of Atlanta in the NLCS. In game two of the series, Jones went 3 for 5 with a home run, 2 runs scored, and 3 RBI's in the Mets' 11-6 victory.

The Mets were big underdogs in the 1969 World Series, but took a 3 games to 1 Series lead. The Orioles were ahead, 3-0 in game 5, when Jones led off the sixth inning. Dave McNally struck Jones in the foot with a pitch. However, home plate home plate umpire, DiMuro ruled that the ball missed Jones. Gil Hodges came out of the dugout to argue, and showed DiMuro the shoe polish smudged ball. DiMuro reversed his call and awarded Jones first base. The following batter, Donn Clendenin, hit a two run home run to make it, 3-2 Baltimore.

Following an Al Weis solo home run in the seventh to tie the game, Jones led off the eighth with a double and scored Ron Swoboda's double two batters, later. With the Mets leading 5-3 in the ninth inning. Orioles second baseman, Davey Johnson lifted a lazy fly ball to left field that Cleon Jones caught to win the World Series for New York.

Early in the 1970 season, Jones suffered through the worst slump of his career that saw his batting average go down to .167 on May 26th. His average improved to .251 by the time he began a then club record 23 game hitting streak on August 25th. For the season, he hit .277 with 10 home runs and 63 RBI's. In 1971, Jones hit for a .319 batting average with 14 home runs and 69 RBI's. Both seasons, the Mets finished with 83 - 79 records behind Pittsburgh.

In 1972, Jones platooned with John Milner in left field. He played 20 games at first base, but not very well. He had one of his worst seasons. He hit for a .245 batting average with 5 home runs and 52 RBI's. The following year, Milner was shifted to 1st base with Jones, again in left field.

In the 1973 season opener, Jones had his first career 2 home run game against Philadelphia. He had his second on September 19th against the Pittsburgh Pirates in the first of a crucial 3 game series with Pittsburgh at Shea for first place. The following day, Jones started one of the most memorable plays in Mets history, what is known as ***The Ball on the Wall Play.*** In the top of the 13th inning, with Richie Zisk on at first, Dave Augustine belted what appeared to be a home run over the left field wall. Jones turned to play the ball off the wall. The ball hit the top of the wall and went into Jones glove. He turned to throw to relay man, Wayne Garrett, who threw to home plate to catcher, Ron Hodges to get Zisk out at home plate. Following this play, the Mets won the game in the bottom of the 13th to within ½ game of the first place, Pirates.

The Mets won the NL East on the last day of the season with an 82-79 record (.508 Pct.) and then upset "the Big Red Machine" in the NLCS in 5 games. Jones went 3 for 5 with 2 RBI's and scored the Series clinching run. In '73, Jones hit for a .260 batting average, with 11 home runs and 48 RBI's.

The Mets lost in seven games to the Oakland Athletics in the '73 Series. In the Series, Jones hit .286 with a home run in game 2 and scored one of the 4 runs the Mets scored in the 12th inning of their game 2 victory.

In 1974, Jones hit 13 home runs with 60 RBI's, along with a .282 batting average. In 1975, Jones suffered a knee injury and was used mostly, as a pinch-hitter - hitting .240 with only 2 runs batted in. He was released after an altercation with manager, Yogi Berra on July 18th. He was picked up by the Chicago White Sox in 1976. He was released after 13 games, hitting .200. He retired afterwards.

Jones was inducted into the Mets Hall-of-Fame in 1991. His .340 batting average in 1969 remained a Met club record until John Olerud hit .354 in 1998. Jones remains among the Mets' leaders in games played, at-bats, and hits.

Jones had a reputation, as an outfielder with one of the strongest arms in the National League. For his career, he had 64 assists, including 10 in '66 and '70.

Cleon Jones
Cleon Joseph Jones
Position: Left Field
Bats: Right, Throws: Left
Ht: 6'0", Wt: 185 lbs.
Born: August 4th, 1942 in Plateau, Alabama (Age 69)
School: Alabama A & M University
Signed by NY Mets, as an amateur free agent in 1963.
Teams: Mets / White Sox 1963-1976
Final Game: May 1st, 1976

Year	Team	Lg	G	AB	R	H	HR	RBI	BA	SB
1963	New York	NL	6	15	1	2	0	1	.133	0
1965	New York	NL	30	74	2	11	1	9	.149	1
1966	New York	NL	139	495	74	136	8	57	.275	16
1967	New York	NL	129	411	46	101	5	30	.246	12
1968	New York	NL	147	509	63	151	14	55	.297	23
1969	New York	NL	137	483	92	164	12	75	.340	16
1970	New York	NL	134	506	71	140	10	63	.277	12
1971	New York	NL	136	505	63	161	14	69	.319	6
1972	New York	NL	106	375	39	92	5	52	.245	1
1973	New York	NL	92	339	48	88	11	48	.260	1
1974	New York	NL	124	461	62	130	13	60	.282	3
1975	New York	NL	21	50	50	12	0	2	.240	0
1976	Chicago	AL	12	40	40	8	0	3	.200	0
13 Seasons			1213	4263	565	1196	93	524	.281	91

Post-Season - Cleon Jones

Year	Team	Lg	G	AB	R	H	HR	RBI	BA	SB
1969	New York	NLCS	3	14	4	6	1	4	.429	2
1969	New York	WS	5	19	2	3	0	0	.158	0
1973	New York	NLCS	5	20	3	6	0	3	.300	0
1973	New York	WS	7	28	5	8	1	1	.286	0
2 Seasons			20	81	14	23	2	8	.284	2

Cal Koonce

Calvin Lee Koonce was born on November 18th, 1940 in Fayetteville, North Carolina. He was a professional baseball player, who played on the following teams, as mostly a left-handed relief pitcher:

    Chicago Cubs 1962-1967
    New York Mets 1967-1970
    Boston Red Sox   1970-1971

He pitched relief for the 1969 champion - New York Mets.
He died in Winston-Salem, NC on October 28th, 1993 at the age of 52.

Cal Koonce
Calvin Lee Koonce
Position: Pitcher
Ht: 6'1", Wt.: 185 pounds
Born: November 18th, 1940 in Fayetteville, NC
High School: Hope Hills (Hope Hills, NC)
School: Campbell University
Signed by Chicago Cubs as an amateur free agent in 1961
Debut: April 14th, 1962
Teams: Cubs, Mets, Red Sox - 1962-1971

Final Game: August 18th, 1971
Died: October 28th, 1993 - Winston-Salem, NC

Year	Team	Lg	W	L	Pct.	ERA	G	IP	H	R	BB	SO
1962	Chicago	NL	10	10	.500	3.97	35	191	200	93	86	84
1963	Chicago	NL	2	6	.250	4.58	21	73	75	43	32	44
1964	Chicago	NL	3	0	1.000	2.03	6	31	30	8	7	17
1965	Chicago	NL	7	9	.438	3.69	38	173	181	83	52	88
1966	Chicago	NL	5	5	.500	3.81	45	109	113	57	35	65
1967	Chi./NY	NL	5	5	.500	3.75	45	96	97	43	28	52
1968	New York	NL	6	4	.600	2.42	55	97	80	27	32	50
1969	New York	NL	6	3	.667	4.99	40	83	85	53	42	48
1970	NY/Bos.	NL/AL	3	6	.333	3.48	36	98	89	41	43	47
1971	Boston	AL	0	1	.000	5.57	13	21	22	16	11	9
10 Seasons			47	49	.490	3.78	334	971	972	464	368	504

Cal Koonce did not appear in the 1969 post-season with New York.

Jerry Koosman

Jerome Martin Koosman was born on December 23rd, 1942. He was a former left-handed starting pitcher in big league baseball. Koosman pitched for the following major league teams:

New York Mets 1967-1978
Minnesota Twins   1979-1981
Chicago White Sox 1981-1983
Philadelphia Pillies 1984-1985

He was the Mets number 2 starter behind Tom Seaver, when they won the World Series in 1969.

Koosman was discovered by the son of a Shea Stadium usher, who caught Koosman when he pitched in the Army at Fort Bliss, Texas. He had written his dad about Koosman. The Mets offered Koosman a contract after discharge. Koosman was about to be cut from the Mets in 1966, when Joe McDonald, the Assistant Farm Director requested Koosman be retained atleast until his final payday because he owed the Mets money . The money was wired by the Mets because his car broke down en-route to spring training.

After leading all International League pitchers in strikeouts in 1967. Koosman broe into the Mets starting rottion in 1968 and went 19-12 with seven shutouts, 178 strikeouts, and a 2.08 ERA. The wins, shutouts, and ERA set franchise records that were in their seventh year in existence.

Koosman also, made the first of two all-star teams in his career. The NL won the game, 1-0 on a Willie Mays RBI in the ***Year of the Pitcher.*** The game was at the Astrodome in Houston, a pitcher's park. Koosman pitched a scoreless ninth inning for the save, striking out Boston's, Carl Yaztremski for the finl out. Koosman finished runner up in the NL Rookie of the Year balloting to Cincinnati's, John Bench, a catcher.

In 1969, Koosman posted a 17-9 record with a 2.28 ERA and 180 strikeouts, while making his second All Star game appearance. That year Koosman was a key member of the 1969 World Champion New York Mets. Koosman lost a game, 9-8 to Houston on August 13th, 2011, then won 8 of his final 9 decisions.

In Game 2 of the NLCS with Atlanta, Koosman was rocked for 6 runs in 4 2/3 innings, including a three run home run by Hank Aaron. The Mets won, 11-6, however, then won Game 3 to sweep the series.

Koosman was the star pitcher in the '69 World Series with Baltimore. After Tom Seaver was defeated in game 1, Koosman defeated Baltimore, 2-1. Koosman held the O's hitless until the seventh, when Paul Blair singled to lead off. He scored later, on a single by Brooks Robinson, his only hit of the series in 19 at bats. The Mets scored in the top of the ninth and held on to win with Ron Taylor reolacing Koosman with two out. He got Brooks Robinson to ground out to end te game.

With the Series shifting to Shea Stadium in New York, the Mets won games 3 and 4, then Koosman took the mound for Game 5. He fell behind 3-0 on home runs by pitcher, Dave Mc Nally and Frank Robinson. Mets' Donn Clendenon hit a 2 run home run in the sixth to make it 3-2. Then Al Weis hit home run to tie it in the seventh. The Mets scored 2 runs in the eighth to take the lead, 5-3. After walking Frank Robinson to start the ninth, Koosman retired three Orioles to end the game and complete the Mets' improbable World Series win.

After catching Davey Johnson's fly out for the final out of the World Series, left fielder, Cleon Jones gave the ball to Koosman. That ball, as well, as his game ball from Game 2, was stored safe in Koosman's residence. In the early 1990's, Koosman sold the ball from Game 5. The Game 5 ball's current whereabouts is unknown.

In 1970, Koosman posted a 12-7 record with a 3.14 ERA. The Mets finished 83-79 behind the Pirates. Over the next two seasons, he posted losing records : 6-11, a season when he had arm trouble. He went 11-12 in 1972 with a 4.14 ERA. The Mets went 83-73 in a strike shortened season.

In 1973, Koosman went 5-0 in his first 6 starts, but finished 14-15. The Mets won the NL East with an 82-79 record, 1 ½ games in front of St. Louis, who led most of the way. Again, pitching was the difference for New York - Seaver, Koosman, and the previous year's NL Rookie of the Year - Jon Matlack.

In a game 3 of the NLCS with Cincinnati, Koosman pitched a complete game, 9-2 win that fatured a fight at second base between Pete Rose and Mets' shortstop, Bud Harrelson. This put New York up, 2-1 in games. They would win the NL Pennant two days, later in 5 games.

Koosman was the winning pitcher in game 5 of the World Series against the defending champion, Oakland Athletics. He held Oakland scoreless through 6 1/3 innings. This gave the Mets a 3 - 2 games lead in the Series. However, Oakland would rally to win the next two games in Oakland to repeat, as World Champions.

Koosman went 15-11 in 1974 and 14-13 in 1975. The Mets were 71-91 in '74 and 82-80 in '75.

In 1976, Koosman had his best season, establishing career bests with 21 wins (10 losses) and 200 strikeouts. He also, was runnerup to Randy Jones for NL Cy Young Award. The Mets finished 86-76 behind Philadelphia. In 1977, the Mets traded Tom Seaver to Cincinnati in block buster trade. The Mets floundered after that, especially Koosman. He went 8-20, finishing tied with Atlanta's, Phil Niekro for most losses in the National League. The '77 Mets finished 64-98 (.395 Pct.) - 37 games behind Philadelphia.

After a 3-15 season in New York in 1978, Koosman, seeing no improvement in the team, requested a trade. He was dealt to the Minnesota Twins for left-handed reliever, Jesse Orosco in December 1978. The Mets finished 66-98 (.407 Pct.) in '78. His departure left Ed Kranepool, as the only Met left from the 1969 Mets team. It should be noted that Tom Seaver returned to the Mets prior to the 1983 season.

Koosman rebounded in Minnesota in 1979 by going 20-13. Then he went 16-13 in 1980. The Twins went 82-80 and 77-84, respectfully in those two seasons.

On August 30th, 1981, less than a month after the players' strike ended, the Twins traded Koosman to the Chicago White Sox. He went 4-13 on the season, again finishing tied in the AL for most losses.

Koosman went 11-7 in both 1982 and 1983. In 1983, the White Sox American League West Division under manager, Tony LaRussa. This was their first post-season appearance since the 1959 World Series against Los Angeles. In the ALCS, Baltimore defeated Chicago in 4 games. Baltimore would go on to win the World Series against Philadelphia, known as the ***Weez Kids.***

After the season the White Sox traded Koosman to Phildelphia, where he went 14-15 in 1984. The Phillies finished that season - 81-81 (.500 Pct.).

Koosman's final career stats are 222 wins and 209 losses with a 3.36 ERA in 612 games. He struck out 2,556 batters in 3,839 innings pitched.

Jerry Koosman

Jerome Martin Koosman
Position: Pitcher
Bats: Right, Throws: Left
Ht: 6'2", Wt: 205 lbs.
Born: December 23rd, 1942 in Appleton, Minnesota (Age 68)
High School: West Central School Agriculture (Morris Minnesota)
Signed by New York Mets as a free agent in 1964
Debut: April 14th, 1967
Teams: Mets, Twins, White Sox, Phillies - 1967-1985

Year	Team	Lg	W	L	Pct.	ERA	G.	IP	H	R	BB	SO
1967	NY	NL	0	2	.000	6.04	9	22	22	17	19	11
1968	NY	NL	19	12	.613	2.08	35	263	221	72	69	178
1969	NY	NL	17	9	.654	2.28	32	241	187	66	68	180
1970	NY	NL	12	7	.632	3.14	30	212	189	87	71	118
1971	NY	NL	6	11	.353	3.04	26	166	160	66	51	96
1972	NY	NL	11	12	.478	4.14	34	163	155	81	52	147
1973	NY	NL	14	15	.483	2.84	35	263	234	93	76	156
1974	NY	NL	15	11	.577	3.36	35	265	258	113	85	188
1975	NY	NL	14	13	.519	3.42	36	240	234	106	98	173
1976	NY	NL	21	10	.677	2.69	34	247	205	81	66	200
1977	NY	NL	8	20	.286	3.49	32	227	195	102	81	192
1978	NY	NL	3	15	.167	3.75	38	235	221	110	84	160
1979	Minn.	AL	20	13	.606	3.38	37	264	268	108	83	157
1980	Minn.	AL	16	13	.552	4.03	38	243	252	119	69	149
1981	Minn./Chi	AL	4	13	.235	4.01	27	121	125	59	41	76
1982	Chicago	AL	11	7	.611	3.84	42	173	194	81	38	88
1983	Chicago	AL	11	7	.611	4.77	37	170	176	96	53	90
1984	Phila.	NL	14	15	.483	3.25	36	224	232	95	60	137
1985	Phila.	NL	6	4	.600	4.62	19	99	107	56	34	60
19 Seasons			222	209	.515	3.36	612	3839	3635	1608	1198	2516

Post-Season

Year	Team	Lg	W	L	Pct.	ERA	G.	IP	H	R	BB	SO
1969	NY	NLCS	0	0	.000	11.57	1	5	7	6	4	5
1969	NY	WS	2	0	1.000	2.04	2	18	7	4	4	9
1973	NY	NLCS	1	0	1.000	2.00	1	9	8	2	0	9
1973	NY	WS	1	0	1.000	3.12	2	9	9	3	7	8
1983	Chicago	ALCS	0	0	.000	54.00	1	1/3	1	3	2	0
3 post-seasons			4	0	1.000	3.79	7	40	32	18	17	31

Ed Kranepool

Edward Emil Kranepool was born on November 8th, 1944. He is a former major league first baseman, who spent his entire career - 1962 - 1979 with the New York Mets.

Born in Bronx, New York, Kranepool attended James Monroe High School, where he played basketball and baseball. Mets' scout, Bubba Jonnard signed Kranepool in 1962 at the age of 17, as an amateur free agent.

After batting a combined .301 at three different levels of minor league ball in 1962, Kranepool received a call-up in September his first professional season. At the age of 17, Kranepool was 6 years younger than the next nearest Met in age, who was 23.

He made his first appearance, as a Mets player wearing number 21 on September 22nd, 1962, as a late inning defensive replacement for first baseman, Gil Hodges in a 9-2 loss in New York's, Polo Grounds. He grounded out to Cubs - second baseman, Ken Hubbs in his at-bat. He made his first start the next day, September 23rd, where again he started at first base, and went 1 for 4 with a double.

Kranepool began 1963, splitting time between "Marvelous" Marv Throneberry at first base and Duke Snider in right field.

By May 5th. Throneberry's .143 batting average and 1 RBI in 23 games, was wearing thin with Mets' fans and the management. He was then, demoted to the Mets' AAA affiliate team, the Buffalo Bisons. Tim Harkness was given the first base job with Duke Snyder moving to left field, and Kranepool, the everyday first baseman. However, Kranepool did not hit enough (.190 batting average) and was sent down to Buffalo in July. He again, surfaced in a September call-up, and went 4 for 5 with a RBI and runs scored in his first game up from the minors. He continued to improve in hitting the rest of September and brought his batting average up to .209 for the season.

With Harkness, Dick Smith, and Frank Thomas all sharing time at first base, Kranepool played mostly right field to start the 1964 season. On May 24th, Joe Christopher, batting .303, was awarded the right field position by manager, Casey Stengel. Then Kranepool was demoted to Buffalo after batting .139 to that point.

Kranepool played just 15 games at Buffalo. He hit 3 home runs and had a .352 batting average to earn a trip back to New York. In first game back, he started both ends of a doubleheader with San Francisco on May 31st. The second game of the twin bill went 23 innings. Kranepool ended up playing all the innings of both games, going 4 for 14 in their 2 games. The record setting double header in time lasted, nearly 10 hours and ended at 11:20 PM. These two games started Ed Kranepool on a 13 game hitting streak.

For the season in 1964, Kranepool hit for a .257 batting average with 10 home runs and 45 RBI's. Prior to the 1965 season, the Mets acquired future Hall of Famer, Warren Spahn from the Milwaukee Braves. Kranepool gave up his number 21 to Spahn, who ha worn the number his whole career in Milwaukee. Kranepool was given number 7 to wear.

Kranepool was batting .287 with 7 home runs and 37 RBI's at the All Star break in 1965. He was named the sole representative for the Mets' team, though he did not appear in the game. By the end of the season, Kranepool's batting average fell to .253, but that was still enough to lead the team that lost 112 games and finish in last place in the NL. He also, led the team with 133 base hits and 24 doubles. He hit 10 home runs and had 53 RBI's.

In 1966, Kranepool paced the Mets with 16 home runs and helped the Mets avoid last place for the first time by going 67-95.

Moving forward in Met history - 1969, the Miracle Year, on May 21st, 1969, the Mets won their third game in a row to go to the .500 mark at 18 and 18. The Mets then went on an 11 game winning streak that included a two home run game by Kranepool against Los Angeles. By the end of the 11 game streak, the Mets were just 7 games behind the Cubs.

Another big couple of hits for Kranepool came on July 8th, when he hit a home run off Cubs' ace pitcher, Fergie Jenkins to give New York a 1-0 lead. Going into the ninth inning, Chicago led 3-1. The Mets scored three in the ninth to win the game, with Cleon Jones scoring the winning run on a line drive single to center field by Kranepool.

The Mets completed their "Miacle" 1969 season, in which the team of Koosman, Seaver, Kranepool, and others won the franchise's first World Series title against Baltimore in 5 games. Kranepool hit a home run in game 3 of the World Series, a 5-0 victory.

On June 23rd, 1970, Kranepool was batting just .118 and was demoted to the Mets' - AAA affiliate, Tidewater Tides. He considered retirement, but instead reported and batted .310 in 47 games at Tidewater. He was back in New York in August, but saw limited playing time - only 52 at bats in 43 games.

Kranepool would bouce back in 1971 and have his best season. He hit for a .280 batting average with 14 home runs, and 58 RBI's. He led all NL first baseman with a .998 fielding percentage.

In 1973, Kranepool lost his first base position to rookie, John Milner. Kranepool still played in 100 games with 320 at bats, backing up Milner at first base and Cleon Jones in left field. He hit 1 home run and 35 RBI's to go with a .269 batting average. The Mets in 1973 would go on to their second World Series with the Oakland A's, but lost in seven games. They upset the storied, Cincinnati Reds in five games to get there. Kranepool's only appearance in the NLCS was in game 5, when he drove in the first two runs in the clinching victory to put the Mets in the Series.

Kranepool batted .300 in 1974 and 1975, sharing first base with Milner and Dave Kingman. When Mets owner, Joan Payson passed away on October 4th, 1975, she left the team to her husband, Charles. Charles delegated his authority to his three daughters, who left control of the franchise to club chairman, M. Donald Grant. According to an interview with Kranepool, he was the only Met player invited to Mrs. Payton's funeral.

The Mets enjoyed their second best record in history in 1976 by going 86 and 76 to finish third in the NL East. Kranepool was the regular first baseman that season hitting for a .292 batting average with 10 home runs and 49 RBI's. He compiled his best offensive years from 1974 through 1977, hitting .299 in 431 games with 28 home runs and 156 RBI's those 4 seasons.

Matinee idol, center-fielder, Lee Mazzili became the face of the Mets' organization. Kranepool was the link to past glories in 1969 and 1973. He emerged as a fan favorite, now being used mostly, as a pinch - hitter. He batted .486 (17 hits in 35 at-bats) in that role in 1974. That is still a major league record for btting average of a pinch hitter.

When he retired after the 1979 season at the age of 34, he left, as the all-time club leader in 8 offensive categories, of which 3 he currently still owns (at bats - 5436, hits - 1418, and sacrifice flies - 58). He also, has played in more games than any other Met player (1853 games). He would become a legend among Met fans for playing 18 seasons, all of them with the Mets. No other Met player ever played that long with the team - 18 seasons - (1962-1979).

Though still relatively young at this time, he was only useful, as long as he was a successful pinch hitter. When the team was sold in 1979 after the season to a group, headed by Nelson Doubleday, Jr. and Fred Wilpin, Kranepool was part of one of the groups offering a losing bid.

Ed Kranepool also, appeared on Saturday Night Live-a TV show, in a cameo appearance, being interviewed by Bill Murray during a skit filmed during the '79 spring training, regarding Chico Secular's (Garrett Morris) tell all book, "Bad Stuff 'bout the Mets", which was a parady of Sparky Lyle's tell all book about the New York Yankees - "The Bronz Zoo".

Ed Kranepool made a living after retirement, as a stockbroker and restauranteur. He currently, is living in New York city. He was inducted into the Mets - Hall of Fame in 1990.

Ed Kranepool
Edward Emil Kranepool
Positions: First Baseman and outfielder
Bats: Left, Throws: Left
Ht: 6'3", Wt: 205 lbs.
Born: November 8th, 1944 in New York, New York
(Age 67)
High School: James Monroe (Bronz, NY)
Signed by NY Mets, as an amateur free agent in 1962
Debut: Sept. 22nd, 1962
Team: Mets - 1962-1969
Final Game: September 30th, 1979

Year	Team	Lg	G	AB	R	H	HR	RBI	BA	SB
1962	New York	NL	3	6	0	1	0	0	.167	0
1963	New York	NL	86	273	22	57	2	14	.209	4
1964	New York	NL	119	420	47	108	10	45	.257	0
1965	New York	NL	153	525	44	133	10	53	.253	1
1966	New York	NL	146	464	51	118	16	57	.254	1
1967	New York	NL	141	469	37	126	10	54	.269	0
1968	New York	NL	127	373	29	86	3	20	.231	0
1969	New York	NL	112	353	36	84	11	49	.238	3
1970	New York	NL	43	47	2	8	0	3	.170	0
1971	New York	NL	122	421	61	118	14	58	.280	0
1972	New York	NL	122	327	28	88	8	34	.269	1
1973	New York	NL	100	284	28	68	1	35	.239	1
1974	New York	NL	94	217	20	65	4	24	.300	1
1975	New York	NL	106	325	42	105	4	43	.323	1
1976	New York	NL	123	415	47	121	10	49	.292	1
1977	New York	NL	108	281	28	79	10	40	.281	1
1978	New York	NL	66	81	7	17	3	19	.210	0
1979	New York	NL	82	155	7	36	2	17	.232	0
18 Seasons			1853	5436	536	1418	118	614	.261	15

Post-Season

Year	Team	Lg	G	AB	R	H	HR	RBI	BA	SB
1969	New York	NLCS	3	12	2	3	0	1	.250	0
1969	New York	WS	1	4	1	1	1	1	.250	0
1973	New York	NLCS	1	2	0	1	0	2	.500	0
1973	New York	WS	4	3	0	0	0	0	.000	0
2 Seasons			9	21	3	5	1	4	.238	0

J.C. Martin

Joseph Clifton Martin was born on December 13th, 1936 in Axton, Virginia.

He is a former major league catcher, who hit left handed and played with the following teams:

Chicago White Sox	**1959-1967**
New York Mets	**1968-1969**
Chicago Cubs	**1970-1972**

Martin was scouted by the Chicago White Sox, as an amateur free agent in 1956. After 5 seasons in the White Sox' farm system, which included September call ups in 1959 and 1960, Martin became a regular in 1961. He split time between first base and third base. He hit for a .230 batting average with 5 home runs and 32 RBI's.

Martin was converted to catcher after Al Lopez, manager convinced him to go to the minors and learn how to catch. Regular catcher - Sherm Lollar was ending his career at 37 years old. Also, the White Sox traded Earl Battey an John Romano and had no other catchers in their farm system. As the team's regular catcher, Martin batted only .205 in 1963 and .197 in 1964. However, he had great value to Chicago in handling a pitching rotation that had Gary Peters, Juan Pizarro, Joel Horlen, Roy Herbert, and closer - Hoyt Wilhelm. Joel Horner threw a no-hitter in 1967 with J.C. Martin catching.

In 1965, Martin hit a career best .261. However, he set a major league record with 33 passed balls due to catching knuckleball pitchers - Hoyt Wilhelm and Eddie Fisher. This record stood until Geno Petralli committed 35 passed balls in 1987.

In 1967, Martin batted .234 on a team that was involved in 4 way photo finish at the wire pennant race with the Minnesota Twins, Detroit Tigers, and Boston Red Sox for the American League pennant. The Red Sox won the pennant on the last day. They had triple crown winner and MVP - Carl Yaztremski. The White Sox had been eliminated on September 27th after losing a double header to Kansas City. After the World Series, the White Sox traded Martin to the Mets to complete a deal that had been made earlier in July.

The White Sox records with Martin, mostly catching are as follows:

Year	W.	L.	Pct.	Finish
1959	94	60	.610	____
1960	87	67	.565	3rd
1961	86	76	.531	4th
1962	85	77	.525	5th
1963	94	68	.580	2nd
1964	98	64	.605	2nd
1965	95	67	.586	2nd
1966	83	79	.512	4th
1967	89	73	.549	4th

The White Sox were bridesmaids a lot of the years Martin caught on the team.

Back to completing the trade, on July 22nd, 1967, the Mets traded Ken Boyer to Chicago for Bill Southworth. Both teams received a player to be named, later. Sandy Alomar, Sr. ws dealt to the White Sox on August 15th to complete one side of the trade, and the trade of Martin to the Mets on Novemeber 27th completed the other. In a separate deal, the White Sox traded Tommie Agee and Al Weis to the Mets with 4 players for Tommie Davis, outfielder and pitcher, Jack Fisher going to the White Sox.

In 1969, J.C. Martin was a back-up catcher for Jerry Grote on a team that surprised in the NL East. In Game one of the NLCS with Atlanta, Martin pinch hit for Tom Seaver and then singled to center to drive in Weis and Kranepool during a 5 run 8th inning. The Mets won, 9-5 and swept Atlanta in 3 straight games. The Mets than beat the Orioles in the World Series in 5 games.

In Game 4 of that Series with the Mets up 2-1 in games, Martin was involved in a controversial play. With the score tied 1-1 in the bottom of the 10th and pinch runner, Rod Gaspar on second base, Martin, pinch hitting for Seaver, bunted toward pitcher, Pete Richert. While J.C was running toward first base, he was hit on the arm by Pete Richert's throw. The error allowed Gaspar to score from second base with the winning run. Replays later showed that Martin had been running inside the baseline, close to the grass. This could have been called runner's interference. However, the umpires said they did not call Martin out because he did not intentionally interfere with play.

Martin was traded to the Chicago Cubs on March 29th, 1970 for catcher, Randy Bobb. After being released by Chicago during spring training, 1973, Martin served on their coaching staff in 1974. He was also a White Sox broadcaster alongside, Harry Caray on WSNS-Chicago in 1975.

In his career, Martin batted .222 with 32 home runs and 230 RBI's.

J. C. Martin
Joseph Clinton Martin
Position: Catcher, First Baseman, and Third Baseman
Ht: 6'2", Wt: 188 lbs.
Born: December 13th, 1936 in Axton VA (74)
Signed by the Chicago White Sox, as an amateur free agent in 1956.
Debut: September 10th, 1959
Teams: White Sox, Mets, Cubs - 1959-1972
Final Game: August 12th, 1972

Year	Team	Lg	G	AB	R	H	HR	RBI	BA	SB
1959	Chicago	AL	3	4	0	1	0	1	.250	0
1960	Chicago	AL	7	20	0	2	0	2	.100	0
1961	Chicago	AL	110	274	26	63	5	32	.230	1
1962	Chicago	AL	18	26	0	2	0	2	.077	0
1963	Chicago	AL	105	259	25	53	5	28	.205	0
1964	Chicago	AL	122	294	23	58	4	22	.197	0
1965	Chicago	AL	119	230	21	60	2	21	.261	2
1966	Chicago	AL	67	157	13	40	2	20	.255	0
1967	Chicago	AL	101	252	22	59	4	22	.234	4
1968	New York	NL	78	244	20	55	3	31	.225	0
1969	New York	NL	66	177	12	37	4	21	.209	0
1970	Chicago	NL	40	77	11	12	1	4	.156	0
1971	Chicago	NL	47	125	13	33	2	17	.264	1
1972	Chicago	NL	25	50	3	12	0	7	.240	1
14 Seasons			908	2189	189	487	32	230	.222	9

Post-Season

Year	Team	Lg	G	AB	R	H	HR	RBI	BA	SB
1969	New York	NLCS	2	2	0	1	0	2	.500	0
1969	New York	WS	1	0	0	0	0	0	.000	0
1 post-season			3	2	0	1	0	2	.500	0

Jim McAndrew

James Clement McAndrew was born on January 11th, 1944 in Lost Nation, Iowa. He was a major league baseball pitcher from 1968 to 1974. He pitched for the following big league teams:

New York Mets 1968-1974
San Diego Padres   1974

McAndrew started 12 games for the Mets in 1968. He went 4 - 7 with an ERA of 2.28. He pitched in 161 games in his career, starting 160 of them. His won / loss record was 37 - 53, with an ERA of 3.65.

His best season was 1972 when McAndrew went 11-8 with an ERA of 2.80. His nickname during his big league career was, "The Pride of Lost Nation, Iowa."

Jim McAndrew
James Clement McAndrew
Positions: Pitcher
Bats: Right, Throws: Right
Ht: 6'2", Wt: 185 lbs.
Born: January 11th, 1944 in Lost Nation, Iowa (Age 67)
School: University of Iowa
Drafted by the New York Mets in the 11th round of the 1965 amateur draft
Debut: July 21st, 1968
Teams: Mets and Padres 1968-1974
Final Game: May 29th, 1974
Relatives: Father of James McAndrew

Year	Team	Lg	W	L	Pct.	ERA	G	IP	H	R	BB	SO
1968	New York	NL	4	7	.364	2.28	12	79	66	20	17	46
1969	New York	NL	6	7	.462	3.47	27	135	112	57	44	90

1970	New York	NL	10	14	.417	3.56	32	184	166	77	38	111
1971	New York	NL	2	5	.286	4.38	24	90	78	50	32	42
1972	New York	NL	11	8	.579	2.80	28	161	133	54	38	81
1973	New York	NL	3	8	.273	5.38	23	80	109	60	31	38
1974	San Diego	NL	1	4	.200	5.62	15	42	48	30	13	16
7 Seasons			37	53	.411	3.65	161	771	712	348	213	424

Tug McGraw

Frank Edwin "Tug" McGraw, Jr. was born on August 30th, 1944. He was a major league relief pitcher and father of country singer-Tim McGraw and actor / TV personality - Mark McGraw, and Cari McGraw. He pitched for the following major league teams:

New York Mets   **1965-1974**
Philadelphia Phillies   **1975-1984**

He is likely best remembered for recording the final out by striking out - Kansas City Royals, Willie Wilson in the 1980 World Series, bringing Philadelphia Phillie fans their first World Series title. He was the last active major league player to play for Mets' manager, Casey Stengel.

Tug was born in Martinez, California to Frank Edwin "Big Mac" McGraw, Sr. and Mable McKenna. Frank was the great grandson of Irish immigrants. They graduated from St. Vincent high school in Vallejo, CA in 1962. He went to Solano Community College, and signed with the New York Mets, as an amateur free agent on June 12th, 1964 after graduation.

McGraw was used both, as a starting pitcher and reliever in the minors. After the first season in the Mets farm system, he went 6-4 with a 1.64 ERA in Rookie and Class A ball. McGraw then made the big club, the Mets out of spring training in 1965 without pitching in AA or AAA baseball.

McGraw made the Mets, as a reliever, and was 0-1 with a 3.12 ERA with one save. He then made first big league start on July 28th against Chicago in his second game of a double header at Wrigley Field. He lasted on 2/3 of an inning, giving up 3 runs on his way to a 9-0 loss. The first game the Mets also, lost 7-2. On August 22nd, in his second start, also in a second game of a twin bill against St. Louis at Shea Stadium, McGraw pitched a complete game win, his first win in the big leagues. He won his next start, 5-2 over Los Angeles', Sandy Koufax, future Hall of Famer. It was the only time the Mets defeated Koufax. McGraw continued, as a starting pitcher the rest of the season, and went 2-6, as a starter and 0-1, as a reliever with a 3.32 ERA.

The Mets used McGraw, as a starter, again in 1966, and went 2-9 with a 5.52 ERA. Though he made 4 starts with the Mets in 1967, McGraw spent most of the season, and all of 1968 in the minors with the Jacksonville Suns. By the time he returned to the Mets in 1969, manager - Gil Hodges had a very capable starting rotation that included, Seaver, Koosman, and Gentry. Hodges had no need to use McGraw in the starting rotation until Koosman injured his arm in May. McGraw then, went

1-1 with a 5.23 ERA, filling in for Koosman.

Koosman returned to the rotation at the end of May. McGraw got a big victory in relief against San Diego, 1-0 when McGraw came in for Koosman who pitched 10 scoreless innings. In the 11th inning, the only run scored when Bud Harrelson singled in Cleon Jones with the winning run. This victory led to an eleven game winning streak that brought them back into contention - second place behind Chicago - 11 games back.

During the Mets improbable, 1969 title run, McGraw's first post-season experience came in game two of the NLCS with

Atlanta. After the Braves' batters lit up Koosman for 6 runs in 4 2/3 innings, Ron Taylor, and McGraw held the Braves scoreless the rest of the way to preserve the Mets' 11-6 victory. He did not appear in the World Series with Baltimore. McGraw went 9-3 with a 2.24 ERA in 42 games, 100 innings and 12 saves.

McGraw emerged as one of the best closers in the National League in the early 1970's, enjoying a career year in 1972. He was 3-3 with a 2.01 ERA and 15 saves at the All-Star break to earn his first all-star game selection. McGraw pitched 2 innings, striking out four and giving up only 1 hit to get the win in the NL's, 4-3, come from behind victory. For the season, McGraw went 8-6 with a 1.70 ERA, giving up just 71 hits in 106 innings. He also, set a Mets' record for saves that lasted until 1984, 27 saves. John Franco broke the record.

Whereas 1973 was not a good year stats wise for McGraw, he was a leader for the National League champs. The Mets had fallen into last place of the NL East on August 30th. McGraw was the winning pitcher for the Mets on August 31, when the Mets emerged from last place with an extra innings victory over the St. Loui Cardinals. The win improved McGraw's record to 2-6 with a 5.05 ERA.

For the remainder of the season, McGraw went 3-0 with a 0.57 ERA and ten saves. The Mets meanwhile, went 20-8 from that point forward to pull off the stunning NL East title. McGraw adopted the saying in September, "You gotta believe!" He said the famous phrase when only he believed the Mets could get to the World Series. But soon enough, having McGraw keep saying it, and McGraw pitching the ninth in games, the Mets moved into first place on September 21st with a 10-2 victory over Pittsburgh, and clinched the division on the final day of the season. This marked the only time between 1970 and 1980 that the NL East was not won between Philadelphia or Pittsburgh.

McGraw continued his dominant pitching into the post-season, when he pitched 5 scoreless innings over two games in 1973 NLCS with Cincinnati. He also, pitched 5 of 7 World Series games against Oakland, though he did blow a save in game 2, he pitched 3 shutout innings in the extra frames to get the victory. Tug went 5-6 in 1973 with a 3.87 ERA in 60 games with 27 saves.

On December 4th, 1974, the Mets traded McGraw and outfielders, Don Hahn and Dave Schneck to the Philadelphia Phillies for pitcher, Mac Scarce, outfielder - Del Unser, and catcher-John Stearns, when the Phillies drafted number 7 overall in the amateur draft in 1973. McGraw developed shoulder problems during 1974 at the time of the trade. It appeared the Phillies had received damaged goods. After the trade, doctors determined that McGraw had a small cyst and after successful surgery to remove it. He was now, completely recovered. McGraw led the Mets, as the saves leader and games pitched leader, also.

With the Phillies, he continued his role, as a good closer. He earned his second All-Star game. After the Phillies finished second to Pittsburgh in '75. McGraw's Phillies won division titles in '76, '77, and '78. They were swept by Cincinnati in 1976, then fell to Los Angeles in '77 and '78.

The Phillies were battling back and forth for first place with Montreal in 1980, when the Expos came in for a three game set on September 25th. The Phillies won 2 of 3 with Tug winning the second game, to put them up ½ games in front. By the time the Phillies returned to Montreal for the final series of the season, the two teams were tied for first place.

The Phillies won the game, 2-1, McGraw got the save by striking out 5 of 6 batters he faced. The following day with score tied, 4-4, McGraw pitched three innings, only giving up a scratch single by Jerry White. It was also, one of just two balls to leave the infield once McGraw entered the game.

After Mike Schmidt's, 11 inning home run put Philadelphia up, 6-4, McGraw pitched a 1-2-3 11th, striking out Lance Parrish to end the game. This clinched the NL East Title for the fourth time.

For the 1980 season, McGraw went 5-4 with a 1.46 ERA, 75 strikeouts, and 20 saves. Phillies ace starting pitcher, "Lefty", Steve Carlton won the NL Cy Young award and third baseman - Mike Schmidt was unaminous, National League MVP. McGraw received consideration in balloting for both awards, as well.

Mike Schmidt had a monster year - 48 home runs, 121 RBI's, and .286 batting average. Bake McBride was the best batting average hitter - .309 with 9 home runs and 87 RBI's. Steve Carlton went 24 and 9 with a 2.34 ERA. Dick Ruthven went 17-10 and 3.55 ERA. The Phillies finished 91-71 (.561 Pct.).

McGraw pitched in all 5 NLCS games with Houston. The Phillies won the first, 3-1, with McGraw earning a save. The Astros, however, came back in game 2 with an extra inning victory to knot the series at 1.

McGraw centered game 3 in the 8th inning with a runner on second, and one out. He managed to get out of the inning, and keep Houston scoreless until the 11th. Joe Morgan then, led off the inning with a triple. Rafael Landesty entered the game, as a pinch runner and then McGraw walked the next two, intentionally. Danny Walling hit a sacrifice fly to left fielder, Greg Luzinski to score Landesty from third to win the game for the Astros.

The final two games went into extra frames, also. McGraw got a save in game 4. However, he blew a save in the 9th in game 5, sending the game into extra innings. The Phillies scored in the 10th to win the game and advance to the World Series with Kansas City.

McGraw appeared in 4 of the 6 games of the 1980 World Series, striking out 10 batters in 8 innings. The Phillies won the first two games in Philadelphia, with McGraw saving game 1. The Royals came back to win games 3 and 4 in Kansas City, with McGraw picking up the loss in game 3.

In game 5, McGraw entered game 5 in the 7th inning with the Phillies behind, 3-2. He pitched 3 scoreless innings, while the Phillies scored to runs in the 9th off Dan Quisenberry, a submarine pitcher. The Series headed back to Philadelphia.

In game 6, McGraw came in the 8th inning with no outs, and two runners on with the Phillies leading, 4-0. He allowed one run to score, but managed to get through the inning unscathed. After giving up a walk and 2 singles to load the bases in the ninth, he struck out Willie Wilson to win the Philadelphia Phillies first World Series.

The next day, at the victory rally at JFK, McGraw summed up his speech with some controversial comments about New York sports teams championships. The fans of the Philadelphia Phillies waited 97 years for this championship. The Philadelphia Athetics had a championship in the 1929. The A's moved to Kansas City in 1954. The Phillies won their second World Series in 2008 against Tampa Bay.

McGraw went 2-4 with a 2.66 in 1981 that was player strike shortened. The Phillies won the first half season crown, then lost the NLDS to Montreal. The Phillies finished 59-48 (.551 Pct.) both halves.

In 1982, McGraw shifted into more of a set-up role with Ron Reed and Ed Farmer closing games.

Prior to the start of the 1983 season, the Phillies acquired Al Holland from the San Francisco Giants to assume the closer role. Following the 1984 season, McGraw retired. Tug, as a favor from former Philadelphia Eagle quarterback, Roman Gabriel, returned to pitch minor league baseball. Gabriel quarterbacked Philadelphia in the 1970's and LA Rams in the '60's. Tug started games for attendance during 1989 and 1990 with the Class A Gastonia Rangers of the South Atlantic League.

Tug had a brief relationship in 1966 with Betty D'Agostino, which resulted in a son, country singer, Tim McGraw . Tim did not acknowledge his son until Tim was 17 years old, but the two later became very close.

In the 1980's and 1990's, Tug was a reporter for Action News on WPVI, TV feed on Channel 6 - Philadelphia. He usually reported on sports and strange stories.

In the mid-1970's, McGraw collaborated with artist Michael Witte on a nationally syndicated comic strip "Scroogie". McGraw, Witte, David Fisher, and Ned Offer produced 2 books - Scroogie (1976) and Hello, there, ball (1977).

On March 12th, 2003, McGraw was working, as an instructor for the Phillies during spring training, when he was hospitalized with a brain tumor. When surgery was performed to remove it, it revealed the tumor malignant and inoperable. Given three weeks to live by doctors, he managed to live nine months. During this time, he went to closing ceremonies of Veterans' Stadium, when he reenacted the final out of the Phillies' World Series in 1980. Ted died of cancer on January 5th, 2004.

Tug McGraw
Frank Edwin McGraw
Position: Pitcher
Bats: Right, Throws: Left
Ht: 6'0", Wt: 170 lbs.
Born: August 30th, 1944 in Martinez, CA
High School: St. Vincent's (Petaluma, CA)
Signed by the Mets as an amateur free agent in 1964
Debut: April 18th, 1965
Teams : Mets / Phillies - 1965-1984
September 25th, 1984
Died: January 5th, 2004 - Brentwood, Tennessee (Age 59)

Year	Team	Lg	W	L	Pct.	ERA	G	IP	H	R	BB	SO
1965	New York	NL	2	7	.222	3.32	37	98	88	47	48	57
1966	New York	NL	2	9	.182	5.34	15	62	72	38	25	34
1967	New York	NL	0	3	.000	7.79	4	17	13	16	13	18
1969	New York	NL	9	3	.750	2.24	42	100	89	31	47	92
1970	New York	NL	4	6	.400	3.28	57	91	77	40	49	81
1971	New York	NL	11	4	.733	1.70	51	111	73	22	41	109
1972	New York	NL	8	6	.571	1.70	54	106	53	26	40	92
1973	New York	NL	5	6	.455	3.87	60	119	106	53	55	81
1974	New York	NL	6	11	.353	4.16	41	89	96	43	32	54
1975	Phila.	NL	9	6	.600	2.98	56	103	84	38	36	55
1976	Phila.	NL	7	6	.538	2.50	58	97	81	34	42	76
1977	Phila.	NL	7	3	.700	2.62	45	79	62	25	24	58
1978	Phila.	NL	8	7	.533	3.21	55	90	82	39	23	63
1979	Phila.	NL	4	3	.571	5.16	65	84	83	56	29	57
1980	Phila.	NL	5	4	.556	1.46	57	92	62	16	23	75
1981	Phila.	NL	2	4	.333	2.66	34	44	35	13	14	26
1982	Phila.	NL	3	3	.500	4.31	34	40	50	19	12	25
1983	Phila.	NL	2	1	.667	3.56	34	56	58	24	19	30
1984	Phila.	NL	2	0	1.000	3.79	25	38	36	17	10	26
19 Seasons			96	92	.511	3.14	824	1513	597	582	1109	1318

Post-Season

Year	Team	Lg	W	L	Pct.	ERA	G	IP	H	R	BB	SO
1969	New York	NLCS	0	0	.000	0.00	1	3	1	0	1	1
1973	New York	NLCS	0	0	.000	0.00	2	5	4	0	3	3
1973	New York	WS	1	0	1.000	2.63	5	14	8	5	9	14
1976	Phila.	NLCS	0	0	.000	11.57	2	2	4	3	1	5
1977	Phila.	NLCS	0	0	.000	0.00	2	3	1	0	2	3
1978	Phila.	NLCS	0	1	.000	1.59	3	6	3	2	5	5
1980	Phila.	NLCS	0	1	.000	4.50	5	8	8	4	4	5
1980	Phila.	WS	1	1	.500	1.17	4	8	7	1	8	10
1981	Phila.	NLDS	1	0	1.000	0.00	2	4	2	0	0	2
7 Seasons			3	3	.500	2.24	26	52	38	15	33	48

The following are career accomplishments for Tug McGraw:

2 time All-Star - 1972 and 1975
2 time World Series Champion - 1969 and 1980
24 th on the all-time major league list of games pitched (824).
22nd on the all-time major league list of games finished (541).
4th on New York Mets career list games saved (86).
4th on Mets career list in games finished (228).
5th on the Mets career list in most games pitched (761).
7th on the Mets career list hits per 9 innings (7.78).
1st in all-time Phillies list in games finished (313).
3rd in all-time Phillies list in games pitched (500).
Fourth in all time Phillies list in saves (94).
8th in all-time Phillies in least hits per 9 innings (7.02)

Amos Otis

Amos Joseph Otis was born April 26th, 1947 in Mobile, Alabama. He is a former center fielder in major league baseball, who played for the following teams:

New York Mets	1967, 1969
Kansas City Royals	1970-1983
Pittsburgh Pirates	1984

Otis was initially drafted by the Boston Red Sox in 1965, as shortstop. However, he put in some time in the outfield, third baseman, and first baseman, while playing in the minors. In November 1966, the Mets drafted him and then put him in class AAA for 1967. He saw some time with the Mets, late in the 1967, but spent 1968 in AAA, also. He made the big club, New York in 1969. The Mets recognized his potential, so much that when Atlanta asked for Amos Otis, when they tried to acquire Joe Torre, the Mets refused. Instead, Torre was traded to St. Louis for 1st baseman, Orlando Cepeda.

However, Otis immediately clashed with Mets' manager, Gil Hodges, who tried to convert him to third baseman. After only 4 games, Otis was sent back to the minors for a month. At the end of a season, Royals' general manager, Cedric Tallis sent seemingly hot, third base prospect, Joe Foy to the Mets, in exchange for Otis. In the 1969 championship year, Otis in 48 games, hit only .151 with 4 RBI's.

The deal turned out to be an epach-making deal for the Royals, as well as one of the worst deals in Mets history. Foy was having personal problems and was out of baseball by 1971. Meanwhile, the Royals immediately moved Otis to center field and became an All-Star and a fixture at his position for most of the 1970's. The made the all-star team each of his first 4 seasons and won 3 Gold Gloves. His very good speed worked out well with the Royals' team philosophy of speed and defense. On September 7th, 1971, he became the first player since 1927 to steal 5 bases in one game. He led the AL with 52 stolen bases that year.

By the late 1970's and early 1980's, his fielding skills had declined somewhat, and he lost his center field job to Willie Wilson. He was still an important contribution, though hitting .478 with 3 home runs and 7 RBI's in the 1980 World Series loss to Philadelphia.

Otis best season was 1973, when he hit 26 home runs and drove in 93 RBI's with a 300 batting average. He spent one season in with Pittsburgh in 1984, before he retired.

In a 17 season career, Otis posted a .277 batting average with 193 home runs and 1007 RBI's in 1998 games. He stole 341 bases in his career.

Amos Otis
Amos Joseph Otis (A.O.)
Position: Centerfielder
Bats: 5'11", Wt: 165 lbs.
Born: April 26th, 1947 in Mobile, Alabama (Age 64)
High School: Williamson (Mobile, AL)
Drafted by the Boston Red Sox in the 5th round of the amateur draft
Debut: September 6th, 1967
Teams: Mets/ Royals/ Pirates - 1967-1984
Final Game: August 5th, 1984

Year	Team	Lg	G	AB	R	H	HR	RBI	BA	SB
1967	New York	NL	19	59	6	13	0	1	.220	0
1969	New York	NL	48	93	6	14	0	4	.151	1
1970	KC	AL	159	620	91	176	11	58	.284	33
1971	KC	AL	147	555	80	167	15	79	.301	52

MICKEY STRUNAK

Year	Team	Lg	G	AB	R	H	HR	RBI	BA	SB
1972	KC	AL	143	540	75	158	11	54	.293	28
1973	KC	AL	148	583	89	175	26	93	.300	13
1974	KC	AL	146	552	87	157	12	73	.284	18
1975	KC	AL	132	470	87	116	9	46	.247	39
1976	KC	AL	153	592	93	165	18	86	.279	26
1977	KC	AL	142	478	85	120	17	78	.251	23
1978	KC	AL	141	486	74	145	22	96	.298	32
1979	KC	AL	151	577	100	170	18	90	.295	30
1980	KC	AL	107	394	56	99	10	53	.251	16
1981	KC	AL	99	372	49	100	9	57	.269	16
1982	KC	AL	125	475	73	136	11	88	.286	9
1983	KC	AL	98	356	35	93	4	41	.261	5
1984	Pittsburgh	NL	40	97	6	16	0	10	.165	0
17 Seasons			**1998**	**7299**	**1092**	**2020**	**193**	**1007**	**.277**	**341**

Post-Season (Amos Otis)

Year	Team	Lg	G	AB	R	H	HR	RBI	BA	SB
1976	KC	ALCS	1	1	0	0	0	0	.000	0
1977	KC	ALCS	5	16	1	2	0	2	.125	2
1978	KC	ALCS	4	14	2	6	0	1	.429	4
1980	KC	ALCS	3	12	2	4	0	0	.333	2
1980	KC	WS	6	23	4	11	3	7	.478	0
1981	KC	ALDS	3	12	0	0	0	1	.000	0
5 Seasons			**22**	**78**	**9**	**23**	**3**	**11**	**.295**	**8**

Bobby Pfeil

Robert Raymond Pfeil was born on November 13th, 1943 in Passaic, New Jersey. He is a former major league baseball - third baseman, who played for the following teams:

New York	**1969**
Philadelphia	**1971**

He attended Resedor High School.

Originally, he was signed, as an undrafted free agent by the Chicago Cubs in 1961. He was traded with Hal Gilson to the St. Louis Cardinals for Bob Humphreys on April 7th, 1965. Before the start of the 1968 season, he was sent from the Cardinals to the Mets for cash.

He made his big league debut at age 25 on June 26th, 1969 against pitcher, Grant Jackson and the rest of the Philadelphia Phillies. Pfeil went 1 for 4 in his debut, although Jackson shut down the Mets, 2-0 on four hits. He ended up hitting .232 for 1969 in 211 at bats. He also scored 20 runs and had 10 RBI's.

Although the Mets, eventually reached the World Series in 1969, Pfeil neither, appeared in the playoffs, or Fall Classic. On May 26th, 1970, Pfeil was sent, as the player to be named later to the Phillies to complete a trade that occurred originally, on April 10th of that year. In return for Pfeil, the Mets received Ron Allen.

Pfeil was sent to the minors in 1970, however in 1971 he appeared in 44 games for Philadelphia. He collected 19 hits in 70 at-bats for a .271 batting average. He played his final game on September 6th against St. Louis, as a defensive replacement. He made his big league debut against Philadelphia, while playing for the Mets. Coincidently, he ended up facing the Mets, while playing for the Phillies in his final at bat on September 5th.

Overall in his big league career, he played in 106 games, he had 68 hits in 281 at bats for a .242 batting average. He ended up with 12 doubles and 2 home runs with 19 RBI's. He had a .976 fielding percentage.

Although he did not play in the major leagues after 1971, he still played minor league baseball. On February 8th, 1972, he was traded to the Milwaukee Brewers for a player to be named later, who ended up being minor leaguer, Chico Vaughn. On March 20th of 1972, he was purchased by the Boston Red Sox from the Milwaukee organization.

Bobby Pfeil
Robert Raymond Pfeil
Positions: third baseman, pinch hitter, and second baseman
Bats: Right, Throws: Right
Ht: 6'1", Wt: 180 lbs.
Born: November 13th, 1943 in Passaic, NJ (68 years old)
High School: Reseda (Reseda, CA)
Signed by the Chicago Cubs, as an amateur free agent in 1961.
Debut: June 26th, 1969
Teams: Mets and Phillies - 1969 - 1971

Year	Team	Lg	G	AB	R	H	HR	RBI	BA	SB
1969	New York	NL	62	211	20	49	0	10	.232	0
1971	Phila.	NL	44	70	5	19	2	9	.271	1
2 Seasons			106	281	25	68	2	19	.242	1

Nolan Ryan

Lynn Nolan Ryan, Jr. was born on January 31st, 1947, nicknamed "The Ryan Express", is a former major league baseball pitcher. He is currently, principal owner, president of the Texas Rangers.

During his major league baseball -record 27 year career, he pitched for 4 different teams, as follows:

New York Mets	1966-1971
California Angels	1972-1979
Houston Astros	1980-1988
Texas Rangers	1989-1993

He was inducted into the Hall of Fame in 1999. Ryan, a flame throwing right-handed pitcher, threw pitches that were regularly recorded above 100 miles per hour, similar to Randy Johnson. The high velocity was still there, even at 40 years old, he could still reach 95 miles per hour.

While his lifetime winning percentage was low at .526, he still won 324 games and lost 292 games with an ERA of 3.19. Ryan was an 8 time all-star . His 5,714 career strikeouts - first in big league history. Randy Johnson is 839 strikeouts behind him in second place with Steve Carlton in third place. Ryan is the only major league player to have his number retired for three teams - the Angels, Astros, and Rangers.

Ryan is the all-time leader in no-hitters with seven, three more than any other pitcher. He is tied with Bob Feller with 12 one hitters pitched. He also, has 18 two hitters. Despite pitching 7 no-hitters, he never threw a perfect game, nor did he win a Cy Young Award.

Ryan was born in Refugo, Texas, the youngest of 6 children to Lynn Nolan Ryan, Sr. and Martha Lee Howard Ryan. His family lived in nearby Woodsboro, Texas until they moved to Alvin, Texas, when he was 6 weeks old. As a boy, he enjoyed throwing objects at any target. His father thought baseball was better usage of his arm. He encouraged his son to be a pitcher.

Ryan joined the Alvin little league, when he was 9 and pitched his first no-hitter of his life at 11.

Ryan played baseball for Coach Jim Watson at Alvin High School for all his high school days. Ryan held the senior league strikeout record for 44 years, retiring 21 batters in a game. The record was tied by Alvin High School pitchers, Aaron Stewart and Josh Land in the same week in 2009.

In 1965, after graduating from Alvin high school, Ryan was drafted by the New York Mets in the 12th round of the 1965 major league baseball draft. He was assigned to the minor league - Appalachian League, called the Marion Mets, in Marion, Virginia. When Ryan was called up to the New York club the following year, he was the second youngest player in the league. His first strike out victim was Pat Jarvis. First home run given up was against - Joe Torre of Atlanta.

Ryan missed much of the 1967 season due to an illness, an arm injury, and service with the Army Reserve. He pitched only 7 innings with the Mets' affiliate in Jacksonville, FL. Ryan was not in the majors for good until 1968. Despite his excellent fastball, the Mets used Ryan in relief and as a spot starter. He went 6-3 with a 3.53 ERA in 89 innings in '69. He was a member of the 1969 Champion Mets.

Ryan pitched well, in the 1969 post-season for the Mets against the Braves in the NLCS, Ryan completed a sweep of Atlanta by pitching 7 shutout innings of relief in Game 3, getting his first playoff win. Then in the World Series with Baltimore, Ryan saved game 3 pitching 2 1/3 shutout innings against the Baltimore Orioles. The Game 3 victory gave the Mets a 2-1 lead in the Series, which New York won in 5 games. It was Ryan's only appearance in the World Series in his 27 year career.

On April 18th, 1970, Ryan tried a Mets record by striking out 15 batters in one game. Four days later, Ryan's teammate, Tom Seaver, topped it with 19 strikeouts against San Diego. Ryan has credited his time with New York and Tom Seaver in developing him from the basic flame thrower to a pitcher that uses certain pitches to set up hitters.

Ryan had become increasingly frustrated and was considering quitting baseball. His record was just 10-14. He told management that he was not happy in New York and wanted a trade to another team.

On December 10th, 1971, Ryan was sent to the California Angels, along with Don Rose, catcher Francisco Estrada, and outfielder, Larry Stanton for shortstop, Jim Fregosi (who later managed Nolan in Anaheim with the Angels). Fregosi was an all star in 6 of 7 years between 1964 and 1970. He was only 30 years old and Fregosi was rated by baseball historian, Bill James as the 15th best short stop in major league history. Fregosi played less than 150 games in New York and never had a productive season, again. The deal remains one of the worst in New York Mets' history.

In his first season with the Angels, Ryan was given a chance to pitch regularly, as a starting pitcher for the first time in his career. He had a league leading - 329 strike outs, nearly one third more than the AL runnerup. This was the fourth highest total through 1972. Within the next 5 years, Ryan would top 329 strike outs, three times. He also, set a still standing major league record by allowing 5.26 hits per 9 innings, breaking Cleveland's, Luis Tiant 5.30 in 1968. Meanwhile, Fregosi failed in his seasons in New York, making no big contribution in the 1973 National League pennant. He was sold to the Texas Rangers in the midseason. Ryan went 19-16 in 1972 with a sparkling ERA of 2.28.

Although, the Rangers were a sub - .500 team, Ryan had winning records, 21-16 in '73 and 22-16 in '74. The 22 victories tied Clyde Wright's club record in 1970. Ryan also, led the American League in losses, when he went 17-18 in 1976.

On July 9th, 1972, Ryan struck out 3 batters on just 9 pitches in the second inning of a 3-0 win over the Boston Red Sox. He became the seventh AL pitcher to accomplish this and first to do that in both leagues. On April 19th, 1968, he also accomplished the feat with the Mets in the second inning of a 2-1 victory over St. Louis, becoming the eighth National League pitcher to record 3 strikeouts on 9 pitches.

On a personal note, I did this once, closing a game in the Babe Ruth league of 5-1 victory, when I was 14 years old. The last two batters were called out on strikes. I never did it though in high school or college baseball.

In 1973, Ryan set his first big league record, when he struck out 383 batters in one season, beating Sandy Koufax's, 1965 mark by one strike out.

Ryan threw two no-hitters in 1973. In the second one on July 15th, against the Tigers, he struck out 17 Tiger hitters, the most ever in a no-hitter.

Ryan added a third no-hitter in 1974 and fourth in 1975, tying another Koufax's records. In 1974, he twice struck out 19 batters, tying Tom Seaver and Steve Carlton for the single game record for a 9 inning game. Roger Clemens, Boston would become the first pitcher to strike out 20 in a game in 1986.

The California Angels finally made the playoffs in Ryan's final season, his eighth in 1979. He started game one of the ALCS with Baltimore and pitched seven strong innings against Orioles, Jim Palmer. However, neither starter was involved in the decision, as Baltimore won in the 10th inning. Ryan would have pitched game 5, but the Angels were eliminated in 4 games. Ryan was a free agent after the season and signed with the Houston Astros. The California Angels records when Nolan Ryan was there is as follows:

Year	W.	L.	Pct.	Finish
1972	75	80	.484	5th
1973	79	83	.488	4th
1974	68	94	.420	6th
1975	72	89	.447	6th
1976	76	86	.469	4th
1977	74	88	.457	5th
1978	87	75	.537	5th
1979	88	74	.543	1st
ALCS				

Ryan led the American League in strikeouts every year during 8 seasons with California . However, he also, led the AL in walks in 6 of those 7 years. Aside from Bob Feller in 1938, Ryan is the only pitcher since 1900 to walk 200 batters in a season in 1974 and 1977.

Though Ryan's strikeouts and no-hitters got him media attention, he did win over the Angels General Manager, Buzzie Bavassi, who said Ryan was nothing more than a flashy .500 picture. Ryan was 26-27 in his first two years. When Bavassi let Ryan leave after a 16-14 record in 1979, Bavassi said, "He only needed to find two 8-7 pitchers to replace Nolan Ryan. He later admitted that signing Nolan Ryan was the biggest mistake he made, as Angels' GM. Ryan's best years were '73 and '74, when he went 21-16 and 22-16 with ERA's of 2.87 and 2.89. What Bavassi does not understand is the Angels were not a very good team, leading to records under .500, most seasons. Also, Ryan sold tickets, when he pitched. Everyone in Los Angeles wanted to see Nolan Ryan pitch over 100 miles per hour on the radar gun. The Dodgers also, were doing very well during this period of time, it should be noted.

Koufax, once remarked, "Yeah, he broke my strikeout record by one (383 in 1973), he also, topped my record for base on balls in a single season by 91.

Ryan signed a lucrative free-agent contract with the Houston Astros after the 1979 season. The normally, light hitting Ryan got his Houston years started with a bang in a nationally television game against Los Angeles on April 12th, 1980, when he hit a three run home run off Don Sutton. It was the first of the two home runs he hit in his career. Ryan had not hit since, September 1971 with the New York Mets because the American League has the Designated Hitter in their league games.

On July 4th of that season at Riverfront Stadium, Ryan recorded his 3,000 career strikeout. The victim was Cesar Geronimo, Cincinnati outfielder. Geronimo was also, Bob Gibson's 3,000 strikeout victim. In 1974, Ryan got his third taste of the post-season play in 1980, but the Astros lost in 5 games to Philadelphia.

In the 1980 NLCS versus the Phillies, Ryan threw well in game 2, leaving with the game tied 2-2 in the 7th. He helped in the 2 Houston runs scoring - a walk and sacrifice bunt. He got no decision in the game that went extra innings. In the 5th and final game of the NLCS, Ryan and Houston led, 5-2 entering the 8th inning. But Ryan allowed 3 consecutive singles before walking in the third run. The Houston bullpen allowed two more runs to make it, 7-5 Phillies. Only a game tying Astros rally prevented Ryan from absorbing the loss. Ryan only, went 11-10 in 1980 with a 3.35 ERA.

On September 26th, 1981, Ryan threw his fifth no-hitter, breaking Koufax's mark, while becoming the third pitcher to throw a no-hitter in each league. That season, his 1.69 ERA won the NL ERA title. The 1981 season was interrupted by the players' strike.

Facing the Los Angeles Dodgers in the 1981 NLDS, Ryan threw a complete game 2-hitter in the opener against Dodgers' rookie sensation, Fernando Valenzuela. It was Ryan's second and last post-season victory.

By the end of 1982, both Nolan Ryan and "Lefty" Steve Carlton were approaching Washington's, Walter Johnson all-time career strikeout record. Both pitchers sometimes passing one anothers' career total on successive starts. On April 27th, 1983, Ryan won the race with his 3509 strikeout against Brad Mills of Montreal. Phillies, Steve Carlton would pass the same mark, two weeks after Ryan.

In 1986, the Astros won the NL West title and faced the New York Mets in the NLCS. Ryan had a shaky second start in game 2, and took the loss. He returned to the mound for game 5 and pitched 9 innings of 2 hit, 1 run ball with 12 strikeouts. However, one of those hits was a solo home run by Darryl Strawberry that tied the score at 1 apiece. New York's, Dwight Gooden matched Ryan, pitch for pitch. Ryan got a no decision, as his Astros lost in 12 innings.

The Mets went on to win the NLCS in seven games over Houston and the World Series in seven games over the Boston Red Sox. The Red Sox legacy of losing World Series continued until 2004, when they beat St. Louis in 4 straight games.

In 1987, Ryan led the major leagues in both ERA (2.76) and strikeouts (270) at the age of 40. He finished 8-16, as a result of a lack of hitting by Houston bats.

The Astros records with Nolan Ryan by season are listed below:

1980	W	L	Pct.	GB	Finish
1980	93	70	.571	___	1st
1981-	28	29	.491	8	3rd
1981-	33	20	.565	___	1st

1982	77	85	.475	12	5th
1983	85	77	.525	6	3rd
1984	80	82	.494	12	2nd
1985	83	79	.512	12	3rd
1986	96	66	.593	___	1st
1987	76	86	.469	14	3rd
1988	82	80	.506	12½	5th

Ryan left Houston in a contract dispute following the 1988 season. He signed, as a free agent with the Texas Rangers. In 1989, Ryan went 16-10 and led the AL with 301 strikeouts. Against the Oakland A's on August 22nd, Ryan struck out Ricky Henderson to become the only pitcher with 5,000 career strikeouts.

Two years, later in 1990, Ryan threw his 6th no-hitter at age 44 on June 11th, against Oakland. On July 31st against Milwaukee, Nolan got his 300th win. On May 1st, 1991, Ryan set a major league record by throwing his 7th no-hitter of his career by striking out Toronto's, Roberto Alomar for the final out. On August 6th, 1992, Ryan had the first and only ejection of his career, when he got kicked kicked out after getting in a shouting match with Oakland's, outfielder, Willie Wilson with two outs in the 9th inning.

Before the 1993 season, Ryan announced his retirement, effective end of the season. Ryan's very durable arm gave out in Seattle on September 22nd, 1993, when he tore a ligament in his arm, ending his career two starts sooner than planned. Briefly trying to pitch with the injury, Ryan threw one more pitch. With the damaged arm, his final pitch was clocked at 98 MPH. That last start was the worst of his career because he allowed a single, four walks, and a grand slam in the top of the first without getting an out. It was his 10th grand slam given up, which leads all big league pitchers. Ryan left the game trailing, 5-0.

Ryan finished his career, playing in 27 seasons. He was the final player to retire from the 1960's, besting Carton Fisk by three months.

Ryan threw a record seven no-hitters in his career as follows:

Date	Result	Venue	Att.	Catcher	Time
5-15-73	Cal. 3, KC 0	Royals Stadium	12,205	Jeff Torberg	2:20
7-15-73	Cal. 6, Det. 0	Tigers Stadium	41,411	Art Kusnyer	2:21
9-28-74	Cal. 4, Min. 0	Anaheim St.	10,872	Tom Egan	2:22
6-1-75	Cal. 1, Min. 0	Anaheim St.	18,492	Ellie Rodriguez	2:01
9-26-81	LA 0, Hous. 5	Astrodome	32,115	Alan Ashby	2:46
6-11-90	Texas 5, Oak. 0	Oakland AC	33,436	John Russell	2:49
5-1-90	Texas 3, Tor. 0	Arlington St.	33,439	Mike Stanley	2:25

Nolan's post-retirement business, included ownership of 2 minor league teams: Corpus Cristi Hooks, which play in the AA Texas League and the Round Rock Express, a Class AAA team in the Pacific Coast League. Both were affiliates of the Houston Astros for whom Ryan, also served as a special assistant to the GM until he became president of the Texas Rangers in 2008.

Ryan threw out the ceremonial "first pitch" before game 3 of the 2005 World Series between Houston and the Chicago White Sox. It was the Astros first World Series appearance. The game went 14 innings, equaling the longest Word Series game in innings. The 5:41 time in length minutes / hours was the longest in Series history.

Nolan Ryan has co-authored 6 books as follows:

> **Miracle Men with Jerry Jenkins, 1992 - autobiographer**
> **Throwing Heat with Harvey Frommer, 1988-autobiographer**

The Road to Cooperstown with Mickey Herskowitz and T.R. Sullivan, 1999 - autobiography
Kings of the Hill with Mickey Herskowitz, 1992
Pitching and Hitting with Joe Torre and Joel Cohen, 1977
Nolan Ryan's Pitching Bible (with Tom House, 1991)

In addition, to his baseball activities, Ryan was majority owner and Chairman of Express Bank of Alvin, but sold his interest in 2005.

In February 2008, Nolan Ryan was hired, as President of the Rangers. After the 2009 season, Ryan and Chuck Greenberg partnered to place the winning bid to purchase the Texas Rangers from owner, Tom Hicks. The deal was completed just before the 2010 season started. At midnight on August 5th, 2010, the Ryan / Greenberg group was announced, as the winner auction to purchase the Rangers. Greenberg sold his share in the Rangers in 2011 to Nolan Ryan, making him principal owner.

Ryan is often compared to the Los Angeles Dodgers' - Sandy Koufax. They are linked because Ryan broke two of Koufax's records - most no-hitters and the single season and strike out record. There are other similarities . Both Ryan and Koufax started in the majors at a very young age and struggled early in their careers. Also, both were reserved and quiet.

Ryan had the longest career of any pitcher, whereas Koufax sterling career was ended short at 31 years old because arthritis and arm trouble. Nonetheless, both stand out, as the best known "Power Pitchers" of their times. Koufax won 27 games in 1966 for the World Series Champs - Dodgers, his final season.

In 1992, the US Mint produced a $1 commemorative coin, often referred to as the ***Nolan Ryan Dollar.***

In 1995, the Texas State Legislature declared State Highway 288, which passes Alvin, his hometown, as Nolan Ryan Expressway.

Ryan married his Alvin High School sweetheart, the former Ruth Holdorff on June 25th, 1967. They had three children - Reid, Reese, and Wendy. Reid and Reese were both pitchers for the TCU Horned Frogs.

Nolan Ryan currently, resides in Cimarron Hills community, near Forth Worth, Texas.

Nolan Ryan
Lynn Nolan Ryan
(Ryan Express)
Position: Pitcher
Bats: Right Throws: Right
Born: January 31st, 1947 in Refugio, TX (Age 65)
High School: Alvin Texas High School
Drafted by New York Mets in the 12th round
Of 1965 amateur draft
Debut with the New York Mets on September 11th, 1966
Teams: Angels, Astros, Rangers, and Mets 1966-1993
Final Game: September 22nd, 1993 with Texas

Year	Team	Lg	W	L	Pct.	ERA	G	IP	H	R	BB	SO
1966	NY	NL	0	1	.000	15.00	2	3	5	5	3	6
1968	NY	NL	6	9	.400	3.09	21	134	93	50	75	133
1969	NY	NL	6	3	.667	3.53	25	89	60	38	53	92
1970	NY	NL	7	11	.389	3.42	27	132	86	59	97	125
1971	NY	NL	10	14	.417	3.97	30	152	125	78	116	137
1972	Cal.	AL	19	16	.543	2.28	39	284	166	80	157	329
1973	Cal.	AL	21	16	.568	2.87	41	326	238	113	162	383
1974	Cal.	AL	22	16	.579	2.89	42	333	221	127	202	367
1975	Cal.	AL	14	12	.538	3.45	28	198	152	90	132	186
1976	Cal.	AL	17	18	.486	3.36	39	284	193	117	183	327

Year	Team	Lg	W	L	Pct.	ERA	G	IP	H	R	BB	SO
1977	Cal.	AL	19	16	.543	2.77	37	299	198	110	204	341
1978	Cal.	AL	10	13	.435	3.72	31	235	183	106	148	260
1979	Cal.	AL	16	14	.533	3.60	34	223	169	104	114	226
1980	Hous.	NL	11	10	.524	3.35	35	234	205	100	98	200
1981	Hous.	NL	11	5	.688	1.69	21	149	99	34	68	140
1982	Hous.	NL	16	12	.571	3.16	35	250	196	100	109	245
1983	Hous.	NL	14	9	.609	2.98	29	196	134	74	101	183
1984	Hous.	NL	12	11	.522	3.04	30	184	143	78	69	197
1985	Hous.	NL	10	12	.455	3.88	35	232	205	108	95	209
1986	Hous.	NL	12	8	.600	3.34	30	178	119	72	82	194
1987	Hous.	NL	8	16	.333	2.76	34	212	154	75	87	270
1988	Hous.	NL	12	11	.522	3.52	33	220	186	98	87	228
1989	Texas	AL	16	10	.615	3.20	32	239	162	96	98	301
1990	Texas	AL	13	9	.591	3.44	30	204	137	86	74	232
1991	Texas	AL	12	6	.667	2.91	29	173	102	58	72	203
1992	Texas	AL	5	9	.357	3.72	27	157	138	75	69	157
1993	Texas	AL	5	5	.500	4.88	13	66	54	47	40	46
27 Seasons			324	292	.526	3.19	807	5386	3923	2178	2795	5714

Post-Season (Nolan Ryan)

Year	Team	Lg	W	L	Pct.	ERA	G	IP	H	R	BB	SO
1969	NY	NLCS	1	0	1.000	2.57	1	7	3	2	2	7
1969	NY	WS	0	0	.000	0.00	1	2	1	0	2	3
1979	Cal.	ALCS	0	0	.000	1.29	1	7	4	3	3	8
1980	Hous.	NLCS	0	0	.000	5.40	2	13	16	8	3	14
1981	Hous.	NLDS	1	1	.500	1.80	2	15	6	4	3	14
1986	Hous.	NLDS	0	1	.000	3.86	2	14	9	6	1	17
5 Post-Seasons			2	2	.500	3.19	9	59	39	23	14	63

Career accomplishments of Nolan Ryan:

World Series champion - New York Mets in 1969.
1977 Amrican League - *The Sporting News* - **Pitcher of the Year.**
LA Angels of Anaheim - retired # 30.
Houston Astros - retired #34.
Texas Rangers - retired #34.
Texas Rangers' Hal o Fame.
Major League All - Century Team.
5,714 career strikeouts- leads ML baseball.
Seven No-Hitters.
Member of Hall-of-Fame - Cooperstown, NY - 1999.
98.79% of vote by baseball writers.

Tom Seaver

George Thomas "Tom" Seaver was born on November 17th, 1944. He is a former big league pitcher, who pitched for the following teams:

New York Mets	1967-1977,1983
Cincinnati Reds	1977-1982
Chicago White Sox	1984-1986
Boston Red Sox	1986

Tom Seaver was born in Fresno, California to Betty Lee Cline and Charles Henry Seaver. Pitching for Fresno High School, Seaver compensated for his lack of size and strength by developing control on the mound. Despite being an all-city basketball player, he hoped to play baseball in college.

He joined the US Marine Corps Reserve on June 28th, 1967. He served with AIRFMFPAC 29 Palms, California through July

1963. After 6 months of active duty in the reserves, Tom enrolled at Fresno City College.

With the following baseball season starting, he was recruited to pitch for USC by legendary Trojan coach, Rod Dedeaux. Not sure as to whether Seaver should get a scholarship, Tom was sent to pitch for for the Alaska Goldpanners, at Fairbanks, Alaska, in 1964. After a stellar season, in which he won a game in the National tournament with a grand slam, home run, he was awarded a scholarship to USC. His sophomore year, Seaver posted a 10-2 record. He was then drafted in the 10th round of the 1965 amateur draft by the Los Angeles Dodgers. Seaver wanted $70,000 to sign, but the Dodgers refused.

In 1966, he signed a contract with the Atlanta Braves, who had drafted him in the first round of the secondary draft (20th overall). However, the contract was voided baseball commissioner, William Eckert because his college team had played two exhibitions with big league clubs. Seaver then, wanted to finish the college season, but because he signed a pro contract was ruled ineligible by the NCAA. After Seaver's father complained to Eckert about the unfairness of the situation, the commissioner ruled other teams could match Atlanta's offer. The Mets were awarded the signing rights in a lottery drawing among 3 teams (Philadelphia and Cleveland) that were willing to match Atlanta's offer.

Seaver spent one season with the Jacksonville Suns of the International League, then joined New York in 1967. He won 16 games for the last place Mets, with 18 complete games, 176 strikeouts, and a 2.76 ERA. He also, was named National League Rookie of the Year. He was named to the 1967 All-Star Game and got into the game in the 15th inning in a 2-1 victory by the NL. Tony Perez, Cincinnati home run won it in Anaheim.

In 1968, he again, won 16 games and recorded over 200 strikeouts for the first of 9 consecutive seasons. The Mets finished in ninth place in 1968.

In 1969, Seaver and the New York Mets won their first World Series Championship. Seaver won a league high 25 games and first Cy Young Award. He finished second to Willie McCovey for the league's MVP Award. On July 9th, before a crowd of 59,000 at New York's Shea Stadium, Seaver threw 8 1/3 perfect innings against the division leading Cubs. The Cubs' backup rookie outfielder, Jimmy Qualls lined a clean single to left field, breaking up the perfect game.

The Mets went on to win the NL East with 100 wins and 62 losses. In the first game of the NLCS, Seaver bested Atlanta's, Phil Niekro for a sloppy 9-5 victory. Seaver was also, the starter for the first game of the World Series - game with Baltimore, but lost a 4-1 decision to Mike Cuellar. Seaver then, pitched a 10 inning complete game for a 2-1 victory in game 4 that put the Mets up, 3-1 in games.

At years' end, Seaver was presented the Hickory Belt, as top professional athlete of the year. He was also, named Sports Illustrated magazine *Sportsman of the Year* award.

On April 22nd, 1970, Seaver set a major league record by striking out the final 10 batters of a 2-1 victory over expansion team, San Diego at Shea Stadium. Al Ferraro, former Dodger, who had homered in the second inning was the final strikeout of the game. Seaver tied Steve Carlton's record of 19 strikeouts in a game. Since then, Kerry Wood, Chicago, Randy Johnson, Seattle, and Roger Clemons - twice, Boston and Toronto all had 20 strikeout games. By mid August, Seaver's record was 17-6 and seemed like a sure 20 game winner, again. But, he would win only one of ten final starts. Four of the starts were on three days rest. He finished 18-12. Seaver led the league in both ERA (2.82) and strikeouts (283).

His 1971 season was arguably Seaver's finest year, when he led the league in ERA (1.76) and strikeouts (289 in 286 innings), while going 20-10. He finished second in the Cy Young award voting to Fergie Jenkins of Chicago due to Jenkin's winning 24 games and 325 innings pitched. Also, Fergie had exceptional control numbers. Seaver has stated his 1971 season was his best.

Seaver had four 20 game seasons (20 in '71, 21 in '72, 22 in '75, and 21 in '77). In 1977, he was traded to Cincinnati (7 wins in New York and 14 with Cincinnati). He won two more Cy Young Awards in 1973 and 1975 with the Mets.

During his tenure with the Mets, Seaver made 108 starts in which he pitched 9 or more innings and allowed 1 run, or less. His record in those starts is 93-3 with 12 no decisions. In 7 of 12 no decisions, he pitched 10 or more innings . In the 12 no decisions, he hurled a total of 117 innings, allowing 56 hits and just 5 earned runs, compiling an ERA of 0.38.

Between 1970 and 1976, Seaver led the National League in ERA - 3 times. He led the NL in strikeouts-5 of 7 seasons, finishing second in 1972 and third in 1974. Seaver was frequently compared with fellow-Hall of Fame pitcher, Christy Mathewson. Seaver's longevity is a result to his powerful legs that saved his arm. The delivery is called "drop and drive" overhand delivery.

By 1977, the free agency period had begun and contract negotiations between Mets ownership and Seaver were at a standstill. Seaver wanted a new contract that brought him in line with other top pitchers in baseball. Chairman of the Board M. Donald Grant, who had been given *carte blanche* by Mets' management to do what he wished. He refused to budge. Longtime New York **Daily News** columnist, Dick Young wrote columns of Seaver's excessive money demands. Seaver tried to resolve the impasse going to owner, Lorinda de Roulet, who along with GM, Joe McDonald, had negotiated in principal a three contract extension by mid June. But, before the contract was signed, Dick Young wrote that Seaver was goaded by his wife into asking for more money because she was jealous of the money Nolan Ryan was making with the California Angels. Upon hearing about Young's column in the paper, Seaver informed de Roulet that he wanted out of the contract and asked McDonald for an immediate trade.

In the trade that was called "the Midnight Massacre", the other involving Dave Kingman. Seaver was traded to the Cincinnati Reds on June 15th, 1977, for pitchers-Pat Zachary and Fred Norman, outfielder-Steve Henderson, and infielder-Doug Flynn. Seaver went 14-3 with Cincinnati to finish with 21 victories. One victory was an emotional, 5-1 victory over the Mets in Shea Stadium. Seaver struck out 11 in his return and also, hit a double. Seaver, very popular in New York, received a lengthy standing ovation in Yankee Stadium at the 1977 All-Star game. His departure from the Mets sustained negative fan reaction because the Mets became the worst team in the NL, finishing in last place three straight seasons. Combined with the Yankees resurgence in New York, attendance dipped in 1978, and GM-Joe McDonald was fired fired following the sale of the team. The new owner was publishing magnate, Nelson Doubleday, Jr.

After having pitched 5 one hitters for New York, including 2 no-hitters broken up in the 9th inning. Seaver finally, pitched one, a 4-0 no-hitter against the St. Louis Cardinals on June 16th, 1978 at Riverfront Stadium. It was Seaver's only no-hitter of his career.

Seaver was 75-46 during his time at Cincinnati. He led the Cincinnati staff, especially in 1979, when the Reds won the NL West crown. Mario Soto was also, a very good pitcher with Seaver on that staff.

In the 1981 strike shortened season, the Reds posted the best overall record in baseball. They did not qualify for post-season because of the season being split into 1st half and 2nd half. Seaver was a close second in the Cy Young award voting to Dodger's Fernando Valenzuela after going 14-2 in 1981. Tom suffered through injuries in 1982 and finished 5-13.

The Reds' records during Seaver's stay in Cincinnati are as follows:

Year	W	L	Pct.	GB.	Finish
1977	88	74	.543	10	2nd
1978	92	69	.571	2½	2nd
1979	90	71	.559	___	1st
1980	89	73	.549	3½	3rd
1981	66	42	.611	½	----
1982	61	101	.377	28	6th

On December 16th 1982, Seaver was traded back to the Mets for Charley Puleo, Lloyd McClendon, and Jesse Felice. On April 5th, 1983 he tied Walter Johnson's record of 14 opening day starts, shutting out the Phillies for 6 innings in a 2-0 win. He made two more opening day starts for the Chicago White Sox in 1985 and 1986 for a record 16 total opening day starts. Despite a 9-14 record in 1983, he had high expectations going into 1984, expecting to finish his career with the Mets.

Seaver and the Mets were stunned on January 20th, 1984, when he was claimed in a free agent draft by the Chicago White Sox. The Mets GM- Frank Cashen had incorrectly assumed that no one would claim a high salaried 39 year old starting pitcher. With Seaver going to Chicago, Dwight Gooden was given a starting pitcher position on the team.

Seaver pitched 2 ½ seasons in Chicago, getting his last shutout on July 19th, 1985 against the visiting Cleveland Indians. In an anomaly, Seaver won two games on May 9th, 1984. He pitched the 25th inning of a suspended game from the night before, picking up the win. Then started the regularly schedule game and won that one. He was now at 298 victories. Fellow teammate, Carlton Fisk wanted Seaver to notch number 300 against his old club Boston.

On August 4th, 1985, Seaver recorded his 300th victory at Yankee Stadium, pitching a complete game. Coincidently, it was Phil Rizzuto day. Tom Seaver would later become Rizzuto's broadcast partner for Yankee games.

Later in 1985, his next to last season, Seaver almost became a Met, again. General Manager, Fran Cashen was poised to make a late season trade for Seaver. Manager, Davey Johnson vetoed the trade and Seaver ended up in Boston after being traded for catcher, Steve Lyons in mid July. The White Sox's records during Seaver's stay in Chicago are as follows:

Year	W.	L.	Pct.	Finish
1984	74	88	.457	5th
1985	85	77	.525	3rd
1986	72	90	.444	5th

Seaver's 311th and last victory came on August 18th, 1986 against the Minnesota Twins.

On a personal note, I saw Tom Seaver pitch the start before on August 13th in Cleveland Stadium in front of 40,000 plus. He got a no decision in a 5-4, Indians' win by Tom Candiotti, knuckleball pitcher. The following afternoon, I saw another 300 game winner, Phil Niekro of Cleveland defeat Boston to move Cleveland within 8 games of Boston.

At the time of his retirement, Seaver was third on the all-time list for strikeouts (3,640) behind only Steve Carlton and Nolan Ryan. Seaver's won / loss percentage of .605 is one of the highest for Hall of Fame pitchers. A knee injury prevented Seaver from appearing with Boston against his old team the New York Mets in the 1986 Series. He received one of the loudest ovations prior to game 1.

The Red Sox did not offer Seaver a contract to his liking prior to 1987. He made $1 million in 1986. The Red Sox offered 500,000 dollars for 1987. Seaver refused and was then, granted free agency on November 12th, 1986.

In 1987, with the Mets starting rotation decimated by injury. New York sought help from Seaver. Though no contract was actually signed, Seaver joined the club on June 6th, and was hit hard in an exhibition game with the Tidewater Tides, an AAA team of the Mets. After more of the same in his next two starts, Seaver announced his retirement.

The Mets retired his number 41 in 1988 in a Tom Seaver ceremony. He is the only Met player with a retired number. Managers, Casey Stengel (37) and Gil Hodges (14), also have retired numbers.

Seaver was elected to the Baseball Hall of Fame on January 7th, 1992. He got 98.84% of the vote (425 of 430 cast ballots). He was inducted into the Marines Sports Hall of Fame in 2003, and the Cincinnati Reds Hall of Fame in 2006.

In 1999, Seaver ranked 32nd on the *Sporting News* list of 100 greatest players. Seaver, a pretty good hitting pitcher and bunter, hit 12 home runs during his career.

Since retirement, Seaver has sometimes been a color commentator, working for the Mets, the Yankees, and with Vin Scully in 1989 for NBC. He has also, worked as a part-time scout and as a spring training pitching coach for the Mets.

Seaver married the former Nancy Lyons McIntyre on June 9th, 1966. They are the parents of two daughters. They live in Calistoga, California, where he has 3.5 acre (14,000 square meter) vineyard called Seaver Family Vineyards. This is part of the 116 acre (0.47 square kilometers) estate in 2002. His first vintage was produced in 2005.

Tom Seaver
George Thomas Seaver (Tom Terrific)
Position: Pitcher
Bats: Right, Throws: Right
Ht: 6'1", Wt: 195 lbs.
Born: November 17th, 1944 in Fresno, California (age 67)
High School: Fresno (Fresno, California)
School: University of Southern California (USC)
Signed by the New York Mets, as an amateur free agent in 1966.
Teams: Mets, Reds, White Sox, and Red Sox (1967-1986)
Final Game: Sept. 19th, 1986

Year	Team	Lg	W	L	Pct.	ERA	G	IP	H	R	BB	SO
1967	New York	NL	16	13	.552	2.76	35	251	224	85	78	170
1968	New York	NL	16	12	.571	2.20	36	278	224	73	48	205
1969	New York	NL	25	7	.781	2.21	36	273	202	75	82	208
1970	New York	NL	18	12	.600	2.82	37	291	230	103	83	283
1971	New York	NL	20	10	.667	1.76	36	286	210	61	61	289
1972	New York	NL	21	12	.636	2.92	35	262	215	92	77	249
1973	New York	NL	19	10	.655	2.08	36	290	219	74	64	251
1974	New York	NL	11	11	.500	3.20	32	236	199	89	75	201
1975	New York	NL	22	9	.710	2.38	36	280	217	81	88	243
1976	New York	NL	14	11	.560	2.59	35	271	211	83	77	235
1977	NY/Cinci.	NL	21	6	.778	2.58	33	261	197	78	66	196
1978	Cincinnati	NL	16	14	.533	2.88	36	260	218	97	89	226
1979	Cincinnati	NL	16	6	.727	3.14	32	215	187	85	61	131
1980	Cincinnati	NL	10	8	.556	3.64	26	168	140	74	59	101
1981	Cincinnati	NL	14	2	.875	2.54	23	166	120	51	66	87
1982	Cincinnati	NL	5	13	.278	5.50	21	111	136	75	44	62
1983	New York	NL	9	14	.391	3.55	34	231	201	104	86	135

Year	Team	Lg	W	L	Pct.	ERA	G	IP	H	R	BB	SO
1984	Chicago	AL	15	11	.577	3.95	34	237	216	108	61	131
1985	Chicago	AL	16	11	.593	3.17	35	239	223	103	69	134
1986	Chi./Bos.	AL	5	7	.417	3.80	16	104	114	46	29	72
20 Seasons			311	205	.603	2.86	656	4783	3971	1674	1390	3640

Post-Season

Year	Team	Lg	W	L	Pct.	ERA	G	IP	H	R	BB	SO
1969	New York	NLCS	1	0	1.000	6.43	1	7	8	5	3	2
1969	New York	WS	1	1	.500	3.00	2	15	12	5	3	9
1973	New York	NLCS	1	1	.500	1.62	2	17	13	4	5	17
1973	New York	WS	0	1	.000	2.40	2	15	13	4	3	18
1979	Cincinnati	NLCS	0	0	.000	2.25	1	8	5	2	2	5
2 Post-Seasons			3	3	.500	2.77	8	62	51	20	16	51

Career accomplishments of Tom Seaver:

Pitched no-hitter at Riverfront Stadium against St. Louis, 4-0 on June 16th, 1978.

12 time all-star ('67, '68, '69, '70, '71, '72. '73, '75 '76, '77, '78, and '81)

3 time NL Cy Young Award Winner (1969, 1973, and 1975).

Member of 1969 World Series Champion - New York Mets.

Retired # 41 - New York Mets.

Hall of Fame - 1992 induction - first ballot - 98.8% vote.

Art Shamsky

Arthur Shamsky was born on October 14th, 1941 in St. Louis, Missouri. He is a former big league player, who played for the following teams:

Cincinnati Reds	**1965-1967**
New York Mets	**1968-1971**
Chicago Cubs	**1972**
Oakland Athletics	**1972**

Shamsky is Jewish and was born in St. Louis, Missouri. He attended University High School in St. Louis and played on the school's baseball team, as did fellow major league pitcher, Ken Holtzman, for years later. After playing baseball with the University of Missouri in 1958 and 1959, he was signed by Cincinnati, as a free agent in 1959.

Art began his professional baseball career, as an 18 year old with the Geneva Redlegs. He hit a home run in his first at-bat. A roomate of Pete Rose that year, he hit for a .271 batting average, slugging percentage of .480, and hit 18 home runs which was second in the league. Also, in the league were Dick Allen and Tony Perez which he was well ahead of in home runs. Shamsky led the league's outfielders in assists and made the all-star game.

He moved up to the Topedo Reds in 1961 and hit .288 with 15 home runs.

In 1962, he was with the Macon Peaches. Shamsky played with Pete Rose, Lee May, Darron Johnson, and Mel Queen on the Peaches. The Reds won the National League pennant in 1961, so some players had to stay in the minors.

By 1963, Shamsky made it up to the AAA level with the San Diego Padres. He hit .267 with 18 home runs. In 1964 at San Diego the next season, he hit for a .272 batting average with 25 home runs to finish 8th in home runs. The Pacific Coast League (PCL) was known as a home run league. He was second in home runs on the Padres behind Tony Perez's - 34 home runs.

In 1965, Shamsky finally, made the Cincinnati Reds, as a sub and hit .260. The Reds finshed 89-73 (.549 Pct.) - 8 games behind Los Angeles.

Shamsky tied a major league record by hunting in 4 consecutive at bats for the Reds on August 12th and 14th in 1966 against Pittsburgh at Crosley Field. Perhaps most memorable, the first three home runs were hit in a game, in which he was inserted in the 8th inning, as part of a double switch. He homered in the bottom half of that inning and stayed in the game to hit home runs in two extra-inning at bats, extending the game each home run. He hit the 4th home run, pinch-hitting in the next game for four straight. He is also, the only player in history to hit 3 home runs in a game, who was not in the starting lineup, when the game started. The bat he used is on display in Baseballs Hall of Fame in Cooperstown, New York.

He finished the year with 21 home runs (second on Cincinnati) and 47 RBI's, and a .521 slugging percentage in only 234 at-bats. The Reds finished in seventh place - 76 and 84, .475 Pct. - 18 games.

Shamsky was traded to the New York Mets for pitcher, Bob Johnson before the season in 1968. Originally, he was unhappy with being traded to New York because the city was big and intimidating. He eventually, warmed up to the city and became a fan favorite for the Jewish fans in New York city.

In 1969, Shamsky hit .300, as part of a right field platoon with Ron Swoboda for the World Champion Mets. Art started against right handed pitchers and Swoboda started against left-handers. He batted .385, as a pinch-hitter, and .388 in games decided by one run.

Shamsky's torrid hitting continued into the post-season. He hit .538 in the NLCS with Atlanta, in which he started all three games of a 3 game sweep. In the World Series with Baltimore, he only played in game 3 on his 28th birthday .

In 1970, he hit .293. Despite batting only 402 times, he was issued 13 intentional walks. He hit 11 home runs and 49 RBI's.

He remained with Mets until 1972, when he played 22 games with the Chicago Cubs and the Oakland A's. Nagging back problems caused this to behis last season. He retired from baseball after 13 big league seasons with 68 home runs and a World Series championship ring.

Art Shamsky is a member of the New York Jewish Sports Hall of Fame. He was inducted into the National Jewish Sports Hall of Fame in 1994.

Shamsky was the manager of the Modi'in Miracle in 2007, the first season of Israel baseball league. Shamsky faced Ken Holtzman, as opposing manager for the first all-star game of the Israel baseball league. The Miracle finished the season, 22-19 (.557 Pct.) in third place. After upsetting the #2 Tel Aviv Lightning, they lost to Bet Shemesh Blue Sox, 3-0 in the championship game.

After his baseball career, Shamsky bcame a real-estate consultant with First Realty Reserve. He also, was a sports radio and TV broadcaster for WFAN, WNYW TV, ESPN television WNEW television - Channel 5 in New York City. He also did play by play commentator with the New York Mets radio and television. In addition, he hosted a sports talk show on WFAN Sports Radio. He has writte guest columns for the New York Times - sports section.

He owns a restaurant in New York City called "Legends".

He has co - authored a book called *The Magnificent Seasons, How the Jets, Mets and Knicks made sports history and uplifted a city and a country* with Gary Zeman.

Art Shamsky is currently divorced, having been married two times.

He now, runs Bravo Properties in South Orange New Jersey.

Art Shamsky
Arthur Louis Shamsky
Positions: Outfield, Pinch-Hitter, and 1st Baseman
Bats: Left, Throws: Left
Ht: 6'1", Wt.: 168 lbs.
Born: October 14th, 1941 in St. Louis, Missouri (Age 70)
High School: University City (University City, Missouri)
School: University of Missouri
Signed by the Cincinnati Reds, as an amateur free agent in 1959
Debut: April 17th, 1965
Teams: Mets, Reds, Cubs, Athletics-1965-1972
Final Game: July 18th 1972

Year	Team	Lg	G	AB	R	H	HR	RBI	BA	SB
1965	Cincinnati	NL	64	106	13	25	2	10	.260	1
1966	Cincinnati	NL	96	271	41	54	21	47	.331	0
1967	Cincinnati	NL	76	164	6	29	3	13	.197	0
1968	Cincinnati	NL	116	381	30	82	12	48	.238	1
1969	New York	NL	100	349	42	91	14	47	.300	1
1970	New York	NL	122	458	48	118	11	49	.293	1
1971	New York	NL	68	157	13	25	5	18	.185	1
1972	Chi./Oak.	NL/AL	23	27	1	2	0	1	.087	0
8 Seasons			665	1686	194	426	68	233	.253	5

Post-Season

Year	Team	Lg	G	AB	R	H	HR	RBI	BA	SB
1969	New York	NLCS	3	13	3	7	0	1	.558	0
1969	New York	WS	3	6	0	0	0	0	.000	0
1 Post-Season			6	19	3	7	0	1	.368	0

Ron Swoboda

Ronald Allen Swoboda was born on June 30th, 1944. He is a former major league ball player best remembered, as a right fielder on the 1969 World Series Champion New York Mets.

He played on the following baseball teams:

New York Mets   1965-1970
Montreal Expos   1971
New York Yankees 1971-1973

After graduating from Sparrows Point High School. He played a season at the University of Maryland. He starred in the AAABA tournament in Johnstown, PA. Swoboda was offered a $35,000 contract to sign with the New York Mets and scout Pete Gebrian on September 5th 1963.

He spent only one season in the Mets' farm system - AA Williamsport, PA before making the Mets out of spring training out of spring training-1965. He made his first major league at-bat as a pinch-hitter in the '65 season opener with Houston and line out to left. He pinch-hit again, in the second game of the season and hit a home run in the 11th inning. The Mets still lost to Houston, as they rallied to win. He hit a home run, again on April 18th, giving him 2 home runs in his first four big league at bats.

He had 15 home runs to at the all star break, the most by a Mets' rookie at the half way point, ahead of Benny Agbayani

(11 in '99) and Ike Davis (11 in '2010). He comented on a TV interview that he loved to hit fastballs. Pitchers threw a steady diet of breaking pitches after that. He hit 4 home runs the rest of 1965 to finish with 19.

Still his 19 home runs stood, as Met rookie record until Darryl Strawberry hit 26 home runs in 1983. He recorded 9 assists in the outfield in 1965 due to his strong throwing arm.

Swoboda wore # 14, as a rookie in 1965. When the Mets acquired Ken Boyer from St. Louis to play third base for 1966, they gave Boyer #14, the same number he wore in St. Louis. Ron Swoboda then, switched to # 4. Swoboda hit 8 home runs and 58 RBI's to g with a .222 batting average in 1966.

During his early years with New York he was called **Rocky** because of the problems in catching the ball in left field that Swoboda had. However, he did possess a powerful throwing arm. After having spent most of his time left field his first two years, Swoboda was moved to first base to make room for newly acquired Tommy Davis in left field. Davis came from Los Angeles before the 1967 season. Swoboda had trouble fielding at first base, so he was moved to right field. Offensively, he had his best season, hitting for a .281 batting average with 13 home runs and 53 RBIs.

In 1968, he led the Mets with 6 triples. He hit 11 home runs with 59 RBI's and a .242 batting average. He also had 14 assists in right field.

By May 21st, 1969, the Mets won their third consecutive game to put them at .500 (18-18). On September 13th, 1969, Swoboda hit a grand slam against Pittsburgh to propel the Mets to a 5-2 victory Two days later against Cardinals', Steve Carlton, the Mets won 4-3 on 2- two run home runs by Swoboda. Carlton struck out 19 Mets in a losing effort at Busch Stadium in St. Louis. The Cardinals, defending NL champs, never recovered. The Mets won

39 of their last 50, a blistering pace .780 winning percentage to win the NL East Crown, easily.

Swoboda did not play in NLCS with Atlanta that was three game sweep for New York. The Orioles and Mets would play in the '69 World Series.

In Game 4 of the World Series, Swoboda made a spectcular catch of a fly ball hit by Brooks Robinson in the ninth inning to stop a Baltimore rally. The Mets won the game in the 10th inning, 2-1 . They then, won game 5 and the World Series. Swoboda hit .400 in the Series with one RBI that was the game winner in game 5.

A photograph of Swoboda's, stretched almost horizontally just inches off the ground, became a iconic image for Mets fans. The new ball park, Citi Field, features a metal silohoutte of Swoboda making his great catch in game 4 of the Series.

In 1971, Swoboda and minor leaguer, Rich Hacker were traded to the Montreal Expos in exchange for center fielder, Don Hahn. Later in 1971, Swoboda was traded to the New York Yankees. He then, was released by the Yankees in 1973. He signed with Atlanta in 1974 for spring training, but was released on March 25th. He then, retired from baseball.

After his retirement, Swoboda worked as the television sportscaster in New York city on WCBS-TV and for many years with WVUE in New Orleans. He also, worked on Cox Sports TV. He currently, works as a color commentator for telecasts of games played by the New Orleans Zephyrs, a AAA team for the Florida Marlins.

He received the Thurman Munson award in February 2009.

Ron Swoboda
Ronald Alan Swoboda
Bats: Right, Throws: Right
Ht: 6'2", Wt: 195 lbs.
Born: June 30th, 1944 in Baltimore Maryland (Age 67)
High School: Sparrows Point (Baltimore, MD)
School: University of Maryland
Signed by New York Mets, as an amateur free agent in 1963.
Debut: April 12th, 1965
Teams: Mets, Yankees, Expos 1965-1973
Final Game: September 30th, 1973

Year	Team	Lg	G	AB	R	H	HR	RBI	BA	SB
1965	New York	NL	135	399	52	91	19	52	.228	2
1966	New York	NL	112	342	32	76	8	50	.222	4
1967	New York	NL	134	449	48	126	13	53	.281	3
1968	New York	NL	132	450	46	109	11	59	.242	8
1969	New York	NL	109	327	38	77	9	52	.235	1
1970	New York	NL	115	245	29	57	9	40	.233	2
1971	Mont/NY	NL	93	213	24	55	2	38	.258	0
1972	New York	AL	63	113	28	28	1	12	.248	0
1973	New York	AL	35	43	5	5	1	2	.116	0
9 Seasons			928	2581	285	624	73	344	.242	20

Post-Season (Ron Swoboda)

Year	Team	Lg	G	AB	R	H	HR	RBI	BA	SB
1969	New York	WS	4	15	1	6	0	1	.400	0

Ron Taylor

Ron Taylor was born December 13th, 1939, in Toronto, Canada. He is a former professional baseball player over the parts of 11 seasons with the following teams:

Cleveland Indians	1962
St. Louis Cardinals	1963-1965
Houston Astros	1965
New York Mets	1967-1971
San Diego Padres	1972

Taylor was a member of two World Series champion teams, 1964 St. Louis Cardinals and 1969 New York Mets. For his career, he completed a 45-43 record with 3.93 ERA. He had 464 strikeouts in 493 appearances, mostly as a reliever.

He closed games for the 1969 Champion Mets - 2.72 ERA in 59 games and saved 13 games.

Ronald Wesley Taylor
Position: Pitcher
Bats: Right, Throws: Right
Signed by the Cleveland Indians,
as an amateur free agent in 1956.
Debut: April 11th, 1962
Teams: Mets, Cardinals, Astros, Indians,
and Padres - 1962-1972

MICKEY STRUNAK

Year	Team	Lg	W	L	Pct	ERA	G	IP	H	R	BB	SO
1962	Cleve.	AL	2	2	.500	5.94	8	33	36	23	13	15
1963	St. Louis	NL	9	7	.563	2.84	54	133	119	44	30	91
1964	St. Louis	NL	8	4	.667	4.62	65	101	109	56	33	69
1965	St. L./Hous.	NL	3	6	.333	5.60	57	101	111	66	31	63
1966	Houston	NL	2	3	.400	5.71	36	65	89	47	10	29
1967	New York	NL	4	6	.400	2.34	50	73	60	21	23	46
1968	New York	NL	1	5	.167	2.70	58	77	64	24	18	49
1969	New York	NL	9	4	.692	2.72	59	76	61	23	24	42
1970	New York	NL	5	4	.556	3.93	57	66	65	31	16	28
1971	New York	NL	2	2	.500	3.65	45	69	71	28	11	32
1972	New York	NL	0	0	.000	12.60	4	5	9	7	0	0
11 Seasons			45	43	.511	3.93	491	800	794	370	209	464

Post-Season (Ron Taylor)

Year	Team	Lg	W	L	Pct.	ERA	G	IP	H	R	BB	SO
1964	St. Louis	WS	0	0	.000	0.00	2	5	0	0	0	2
1969	New York	NLCS	1	0	1.000	0.00	2	3	3	0	0	4
1969	New York	WS	0	0	.000	0.00	2	2	0	0	1	3
2 Post-Seasons			1	0	1.000	0.00	6	10	3	0	1	9

Al Weis

Al Weis was born on April 2nd, 1938 in Franklin Square, New York. He is a former major league baseball player, who played infield. He played fo the following teams:

    Chicago White Sox   1962-1967
    New York Mets   1968-1971

He grew up in Bathpage, New York and graduated high shool from Famingdale High School, New York in 1955. He was a high school temmate of Jack Lamabe, who pitched with Boston, the Mets, Pittsburgh, and St. Louis.

Weis was a switch-batter until 1968 with the Mets. Then, he hit just right handed.

He was signed, as a free agent by the Chicago White Sox in 1959. After 4 years in the minors, he played 99 games, as a rookie utility infielder in 1963. In 1964, he and Don Buford shared second base duties after the trade of popular, Nellie Fox. Weis batted .247 and established a career high with 81 hits and 22 stolen bases. He was part of the Go-Go Sox that finished in second place, one game behind the New York Yankees for the American League pennant. The Yankees would not win another American League pennant until 1978, when George Steinbrenner was an owner of the franchise. The Yankees were helped by new free-agency that just started in baseball. They made a big splash by signing "Catfish" Hunter and Reggie Jackson, stars from Oakland.

Back to Weis. Weis continued, as an utility infielder (2B-SS) the next three seasons . His most at-bats came in 1966, when he had 187 at-bats. He suffered a broken leg in a collision at second base with the Orioles' Frank Robinson in mid season, 1967.

After the 1967 season, he and Tommie Agee were traded to the New York Mets for 4 players (including Tommie Davis and Jack Fisher).

Weis was a member of the '69 **Miracle Mets** that upset Baltimore in the '69 World Series. He played a major role in the Series in the two Jerry Koosman victories. Baltimore pitcher Dave McNally was the victim both times.

In game 2, his ninth inning single scored Ed Charles from second with the winning run in a 2-1 victory. Then in game 5 at Shea Stadium, after hitting just 6 home runs in his career, he hit a home run off McNally to knot the score at 3-3. The Mets then, scored 2 runs in the bottom of the eighth to complete the Series victory.

The 1969 World Series was the last moment in the spotlight for Al Weis. He batted .417 for the Series on 5 hits in 11 at-bats. He was released from the Mets July 1st, 1971. He ended his career with a .218 batting average on 346 hits. He hit 7 home runs and 115 RBI's in 800 career games.

Al Weis
Albert John Weis
Positions: 2nd baseman and shortstop
Bats: Both, Throws: Right
Ht: 6'0", Wt: 160 lbs.
Born: April 2nd 1938 in Franklin Square New York (Age 73)
Signed by Chicago White Sox as a free agent in 1959
Debut: September 15th 1962
Teams: White Sox / Mets - 1962-1971
Final Game: June 23rd, 1971

Year	Team	Lg	G	AB	R	H	HR	RBI	BA	SB
1962	Chicago	AL	7	12	2	1	0	0	.083	1
1963	Chicago	AL	99	210	41	57	0	18	.271	15
1964	Chicago	AL	133	328	36	81	2	23	.247	22
1965	Chicago	AL	103	135	24	40	1	12	.296	4
1966	Chicago	AL	129	187	20	29	0	9	.155	3
1967	Chicago	AL	50	53	9	13	0	4	.245	3
1968	New York	NL	90	224	15	47	1	14	.172	3
1969	New York	NL	103	247	20	53	2	23	.215	3
1970	New York	NL	75	121	20	25	1	11	.207	1
1971	New York	NL	11	11	3	0	0	1	.000	0
10	Seasons		800	1578	195	346	7	115	.219	55

Post-Season

Year	Team	Lg	G	AB	R	H	HR	RBI	BA	SB
1969	New York	NLCS	3	1	0	0	0	0	.000	0
1969	New York	WS	5	11	1	5	1	3	.455	0
1 Post-Season			**8**	**12**	**1**	**6**	**1**	**3**	**.417**	**0**

CHAPTER 8

VARIOUS STATISTICS AND GAME BY GAME RESULTS

Major League Standings
May 14th, 1969

NL East	W	L	Pct.	GB	NL West	W	L	Pct.	GB
Chicago	23	11	.676	___	Atlanta	21	10	.677	___
Pittsburgh	17	15	.531	5	San Fran.	19	13	.594	2 1/2
New York	15	17	.469	7	Los Ang.	18	13	.581	3
St. Louis	14	18	.438	8	Cincinnati	15	16	.484	6
Phila.	12	17	.414	8 ½	San Diego	15	21	.417	8 ½
Montreal	**11**	**19**	**.367**	**10**	Houston	13	23	.361	10 ½

SUMMER OF '69

AL East	W	L	Pct.	GB	AL West	W	L	Pct.	GB
Baltimore	23	12	.657	---	Minnesota	19	10	.655	---
Boston	20	11	.645	1	Oakland	20	11	.645	---
Wash.	17	18	.486	6	Chicago	13	12	.520	4
Detroit	14	16	.467	6½	KC	15	16	.484	5
New York	13	21	.382	9½	Seattle	13	18	.419	7
Cleveland	6	21	.222	13	California	11	18	.329	8

Major League Standings
June 15th, 1969

NL East	W	L	Pct.	GB	NL West	W	L	Pct.	GB
Chicago	41	19	.683	---	Atlanta	34	24	.586	---
New York	30	26	.536	9	San Fran.	33	25	.569	1
Pittsburgh	30	30	.500	11	Los Ang.	33	25	.569	1
St. Louis	28	31	.475	12½	Cincinnati	29	26	.527	3½
Phila.	23	32	.418	15½	Houston	29	33	.468	7
Montreal	15	41	.268	24	San Diego	25	38	.397	11½

AL East	W	L	Pct.	GB	AL West	W	L	Pct.	GB
Baltimore	43	17	.721	---	Minnesota	31	26	.544	---
Boston	36	22	.621	6½	Oakland	30	25	.544	---
Detroit	31	23	.574	9 1/2	Seattle	26	31	.456	5
Wash.	31	32	.492	14	Chicago	23	32	.418	7
New York	30	32	.484	14 1/2	KC	24	34	.414	7½
Cleveland	20	35	.364	21	California	19	36	.345	11

Major League Standings
July 15th 1969

NL East	W	L	Pct.	GB	NL West	W	L	Pct.	GB
Chicago	58	35	.624	---	Los Ang.	51	38	.573	---
New York	50	37	.575	5	Atlanta	52	40	.565	½
St. Louis	47	46	.505	11	San Fran.	50	41	.549	2

	W	L	Pct.	GB.		W	L	Pct.	GB.
Pittsburgh	44	47	.484	13	Cincinnati	46	40	.535	3½
Phila.	38	50	.432	17½	Houston	47	46	.505	6
Montreal	28	62	.311	28½	San Diego	32	61	.344	21

AL East	W	L	Pct.	GB.	AL West	W	L	Pct.	GB.
Baltimore	63	27	.700	___	Minnesota	54	35	.607	___
Boston	50	42	.543	14	Oakland	48	38	.538	4½
Detroit	47	40	.540	14½	KC	39	52	.429	16
Wash.	50	45	.526	15½	Seattle	38	51	.428	16
New York	43	50	.462	21½	Chicago	38	51	.428	16
Cleveland	36	54	.400	27	California	34	55	.382	20

Major League Standings
September 3rd, 1969

NL East	W	L	Pct.	GB.	NL West	W	L	Pct.	GB.
Chicago	84	53	.613	___	San Fran.	76	59	.563	___
New York	77	56	.579	5	Los Ang.	74	59	.556	1
Pittsburgh	71	61	.538	10½	Cincinnati	73	59	.553	1½
St. Louis	72	63	.533	11	Atlanta	74	63	.540	3
Phila.	54	79	.406	28	Houston	70	64	.522	5½
Montreal	41	95	.301	42	San Diego	40	95	.296	36

AL East	W	L	Pct.	GB.	AL West	W	L	Pct.	GB.
Baltimore	92	44	.676	___	Minnesota	82	52	.612	___
Detroit	79	56	.585	12½	Oakland	75	58	.564	6½
Boston	72	62	.537	19	California	56	76	.424	25
Wash.	71	66	.578	21½	Chicago	53	79	.402	28
New York	67	67	.500	24	KC	54	80	.403	28
Cleveland	54	82	.393	38	Seattle	50	83	.376	31½

SUMMER OF '69

Game by Game Results of the 1969 New York Mets

Date	Team	Result	Record	Winner	Loser
April 8	Montreal	L 10-11	0-1	Shaw	Koonce
April 9	Montreal	W 9-5	1-1	McGraw	Stoneman
April 10	Montreal	W 4-2	2-1	Gentry	Jaster
April 11	St. Louis	L 5-6	2-2	Carlton	Koosman
April 12	St. Louis	L 0-1	2-3	Giusti	Cardwell
April 13	St. Louis	L 1-3 &	2-4	Gibson	Seaver
April 14	at Phila.	L 1-5	2-5	Fryman	McAndrew
April 15	at Phila.	W 6-3	3-5	Gentry	Wagner
April 16	at Pitts.	L 3-11	3-6	Moose	Koosman
April 17	at Pitts.	L 0-4	3-7	Bunning	Cardwell
April 19	at St. Louis	W 2-1	4-7	Seaver	Gibson
April 20	at St. Louis	W 11-3	5-7	Ryan	Briles
April 21	Phila.	L 2-11	5-8	Fryman	Taylor
April 23	Pittsburgh	W 2-0	6-8	Koosman	Bunning
April 25	Chicago	L 1-3	6-9	Jenkins	Seaver
April 26	Chicago	L 3-9	6-10	Hands	Cardwell
April 27	Chicago	L 6-8	6-11	Ryan	Koonce
April 27	Chicago	W 3-0	7-11	McGraw	Nye
April 29	at Mont.	W 2-0	8-11	Ryan	Grant
April 30	at Mont.	W 2-1	9-11	Seaver	Wegener

Record in April 10-10

May 2	at Chicago	L 4-6	9-13	Holtzman	Gentry
May 3	at Chicago	L 2-3	9-14	Rogers	Koosman
May 4	at Chicago	W 3-2	10-14	Seaver	Hands
May 4	at Chicago	W 3-2	11-14	McGraw	Selma
May 6	Cincinnati	W 8-1	12-14	Cardwell	Nolan
May 7	Cincinnati	L 6-3	12-15	Merritt	Gentry
May 10	Houston	W 3-1	13-15	Seaver	Lemasters
May 11	Houston	L 1-4	13-16	Dierker	Cardwell
May 11	Houston	W 11-7	14-16	Koonce	Wilson
May 13	Atlanta	L 3-4	14-17	Reed	Gentry
May 14	Atlanta	W 9-3	15-17	Seaver	Niekro
May 15	Atlanta	L 5-6	15-18	'Jarvis	Cardwell
May 16	at Cinci.	W 10-9	16-18	Koonce	Culver
May 17	at Cinci.	W 11-3	17-18	Gentry	Maloney
May 21	at Atlanta	W 5-0	18-18	Seaver	Niekro
May 22	at Atlanta	L 3-15	18-19	Jarvis	McGraw
May 23	at Houston	L 0-7	18-20`	Griffin	Gentry
May 24	at Houston	L 1-5	18-21	Dierker	Koosman

MICKEY STRUNAK

May 25	at Houston	L 3-6	18-22	Lemasters	Seaver
May 27	San Diego	L 2-3	18-23	Santorini	McAndrew
May 28	San Diego	W 1-0+	19-23	Mc Graw	McCool
May 30	San Fran.	W 4-3	20-23	Seaver	Linzy
May 31	San Fran.	W 4-2	21-23	Gentry	Perry

Record in May 12-12

June 1	San Fran.	W 5-4	22-23	Taylor	Gibbon
June 2	Los Ang.	W 2-1	23-23	Koosman	Osteen
June 3	Los Ang.	W 5-2	24-23	Seaver	Foster
June 4	Los Ang.	W 1-0x	25-23	Taylor	Mikkelsen
June 6	at SD	W 5-3	26-23	Gentry	Ross
June 7	at SD	W 4-1	27-23	Koosman	Podres
June 8	at SD	W 3-2	28-23	Seaver	Santorini
June 10	at SF	W 9-4	29-23	Cardwell	McCormick
June 11	at SF	L 2-7	29-24	Perry	Gentry
June 13	at LA	L 0-1	29-25	Foster	Koosman
June 14	at LA	W 3-1	30-25	Seaver	Sutton
June 15	at LA	L 2-3	30-26	Drysdale	DiLauro
June 17	at Phila.	W 1-0	31-26	Gentry	Champion
June 17	at Phila.	L 3-7	31-27	Cardwell	Jackson
June 18	at Phila.	W 2-0	32-27	Koosman	Wise
June 19	at Phila.	W 6-5	33-27	Taylor	Raffo
June 20	St. Louis	W 4-3	34-27	Ryan	Gibson
June 21	St. Louis	L 3-5	34-28	Briles	DiLauro
June 22	St. Louis	W 5-1	35-28	Gentry	Cardwell
June 22	St. Louis	W 1-0	36-28	Koosman	Torrez
June 24	Phila.	W 2-1	37-28	Seaver	Fryman
June 24	Phila.	W 5-0	38-28	McAndrew	Johnson
June 25	Phila.	L 5-6	38-29	Wilson	Taylor
June 26	Phila.	L 0-2	38-30	Jackson	Cardwell
June 27	Pittsburgh	L 1-3	38-31	Blass	Koosman
June 28	Pittsburgh	L 4-7	38-32	Bunning	Gentry
June 29	Pittsburgh	W 7-3	39-32	Seaver	Veale
June 30	at St. Louis	W 10-2	40-32	McAndrew	Briles

June record 19-9

SUMMER OF '69

Date	Team	Result	Record	Winner	Loser
July 1	at St. Louis	L 1-4	40-33	Carlton	Ryan
July 1	at St. Louis	L 5-8	40-34	Torrez	DiLauro
July 2	at St. Louis	W 6-4&	41-34	McGraw	Willis
July 3	at St. Louis	W 8-1	42-34	Gentry	Grant
July 4	at Pitts.	W 11-6	43-34	Seaver	Veale
July 4	at Pitts.	W 9-2	44-34	Cardwell	Ellis
July 6	at Pitts.	W 8-7	45-34	Taylor	Hartenstein
July 8	Chicago	W 4-3	46-34	Koosman	Jenkins
July 9	Chicago	W 4-0	47-34	Seaver	Holtzman
July 10	Chicago	L 2-6	47-35	Hands	Gentry
July 11	Montreal	L 4-11	47-36	Wegener	McAndrew
July 13	Montreal	W 4-3	48-36	Koosman	Robertson
July 13	Montreal	W 9-7	49-36	Koonce	McGraw
July 14	at Chicago	L 0-1	49-37	Hands	Seaver
July 15	at Chicago	W 5-4	50-37	Gentry	Selma
July 16	at Chicago	W 5-2	51-37	Koonce	Jenkins
July 18	at Mont.	W 5-2	52-37	Koosman	Robertson
July 19	at Mont.	L 4-5	52-38	Stoneman	Seaver
July 20	at Mont.	L 2-3	52-39	Waslewski	Gentry
July 20	at Mont.	W 4-3	53-39	DiLauro	Face
July 24	Cinci.	L 3-4	53-40	Ramos	McGraw
July 25	Cinci.	W 4-3	54-40	Taylor	Carroll
July 26	Cinci.	W 3-2	55-40	Seaver	Cloninger
July 27	Cinci.	L 3-6	55-41	Arroyo	Cardwell
July 30	Houston	L 3-16	55-42	Wilson	Koosman
July 30	Houston	L 5-11	55-43	Dierker	Gentry
July 31	Houston	L 0-2	55-44	Griffin	Seaver
July record 15-12					
August 1	Atlanta	W 5-4	56-44	Koonce	Niekro
August 2	Atlanta	W 1-0	57-44	McAndrew	Reed
August 3	Atlanta	W 6-5+	58-44	Taylor	Raymond
August 4	at Cinci.	L 0-1	58-45	Maloney	Koosman
August 5	at Cinci.	L 5-8	58-46	Nolan	Seaver
August 5	at Cinci.	W 10-1	59-47	Ryan	Arrigo
August 6	at Cinci.	L 2-3	59-48	Merritt	McAndrew
August 8	at Atlanta	W 4-1	60-48	Koosman	Pappas
August 9	at Atlanta	W 5-3	61-48	Seaver	Stone
August 10	at Atlanta	W 3-0	62-48	Cardwell	Britton
August 11	at Houston	L 0-3	62-49	Griffin	McAndrew
August 12	at Houston	L 7-8	62-50	Wilson	Koosman
August 13	at Houston	L 2-8	62-51	Dierker	Gentry

MICKEY STRUNAK

August 16	San Diego	W 2-0	63-51	Seaver	Sisk
August 16	San Diego	W 2-1	64-51	McAndrew	Ross
August 17	San Diego	W 3-2	65-51	Koosman	Niekro
August 17	San Diego	W 3-2	66-51	Cardwell	Kirby
August 19	San Fran.	W 1-0&	67-51	McGraw	Marichal
August 20	San Fran.	W 6-0	68-51	McAndrew	Perry
August 21	San Fran.	L 6-7+	68-52	McMahon	Taylor
August 22	Los Ang.	W 5-3	69-52	Koosman	Singer
August 23	Los Ang.	W 3-2	70-52	Taylor	Brewer
August 24	Los Ang.	W 7-4	71-52	Koonce	Sutton
August 26	at SD	W 8-4	72-52	Seaver	Sisk
August 26	at SD	W 3-0	73-52	McAndrew	Niekro
August 27	at SD	W 4-1	74-52	Koosman	Kirby
August 29	at SF	L 0-5	74-53	Marichal	Gentry
August 30	at SF	W 3-2*	75-53	McGraw	Perry
August 31	at SF	W 8-0	76-53	Seaver	McCormick
August 31	at SF	L 2-3+	76-54	Linzy	McGraw

August record 21-9

Sept. 1	at LA	L 6-10	76-55	Bunning	Koosman
Sept. 2	at LA	W 5-4	77-55	Gentry	Sutton
Sept. 3	at LA	L 4-5	77-56	Mikkelsen	DiLauro
Sept. 5	Phila.	W 5-1	78-56	Seaver	Jackson
Sept. 5	Phila.	L 2-4	78-57	Wise	McAndrew
Sept. 6	Phila.	W 3-0	79-57	Cardwell	Johnson
Sept. 7	Phila.	W 9-3	80-57	Ryan	Champion
Sept. 8	Chicago	W 3-2	81-57	Koosman	Hands
Sept. 9	Chicago	W 7-1	82-57	Seaver	Jenkins
Sept. 10	Montreal	W 3-2#	83-57	Taylor	Stoneman
Sept. 10	Montreal	W 7-1	84-57	Ryan	Reed
Sept. 11	Montreal	W 4-0	85-57	Gentry	Robertson
Sept. 12	at Pitts.	W 1-0	86-57	Koosman	Moose
Sept. 12	at Pitts.	W 1-0	87-57	Cardwell	Ellis
Sept. 13	at Pitts.	W 5-2	88-57	Seaver	Walker
Sept. 14	at Pitts.	L 3-5	88-58	Blass	Ryan
Sept. 15	at St. Louis	W 4-3	89-58	McGraw	Carlton
Sept. 17	at Mont.	W 5-0	90-58	Koosman	Waslewski
Sept. 18	at Mont.	W 2-0	91-58	Seaver	Stoneman
Sept. 19	Pittsburgh	L 2-8	91-59	Veale	Ryan
Sept. 19	Pittsburgh	L 0-8	91-60	Walker	McAndrew
Sept. 20	Pittsburgh	L 0-4	91-61	Moose	Gentry
Sept. 21	Pittsburgh	W 5-3	92-61	Koosman	Ellis
Sept. 21	Pittsburgh	W 6-1	93-61	Cardwell	Blass

Sept. 22	St. Louis	W 3-1&	94-61	Seaver	Briles
Sept. 23	St. Louis	W 3-2+	95-61	McGraw	Gibson
Sept. 24	St. Louis	W 6-0	96-61	Gentry	Carlton
Sept. 26	at Phila.	W 5-0	97-61	Koosman	Fryman
Sept. 27	at Phila.	W 1-0	98-61	Seaver	Jackson
Sept. 28	at Phila.	W 2-0	99-61	Gentry	Johnson
Oct. 1	at Chicago	W 6-5#	100-61	Taylor	Selma
Oct. 2	at Chicago	L 3-5	100-62	Dierker	Cardwell

September Record 25-7 *10 inn. +11 inn. &12 inn. X 13 inn. # 14 inn. @15 inn. games

Batting Leaders National League

Player Team	G	AB	R	H	HR	RBI	BA	SB
Pete Rose, Cinci.#	156	627	120	218	16	82	.348	7
Roberto Clemente, Pitt	138	507	87	175	19	91	.345	4
Rico Carty, Atlanta	104	304	47	104	16	58	.342	0
Cleon Jones, NY	137	483	92	164	12	75	.340	16
Matty Alou Pitts. +	162	695	105	231	1	48	.331	22
Willie McCovey, SF+	149	491	101	157	45	126	.320	0
Alex Johnson, Cinci.	139	523	86	165	17	88	.315	8
Willie Davis, LA +	129	498	66	155	11	59	.311	24
Willie Stargell, Pitts.+	145	522	89	160	29	92	.307	1
Bobby Tolan, Cinci.+	152	637	104	194	21	93	.305	26
Rusty Staub Mont.+	158	549	89	166	29	79	.302	3
Rich Hebner Pitts.+	129	459	72	138	8	47	.301	4
Henry Aaron Atl.	147	547	100	164	44	97	.300	9
Lou Brock St. L.+	157	655	97	195	12	47	.298	53
Tony Perez, Cinci.	160	629	103	185	37	122	.294	4
Johnny Bench Cinci.	148	532	83	156	26	90	.293	6
Billy Williams, Chi. +	163	642	103	188	21	95	.293	3

Batting Leaders American League

Player Team	G	AB	R	H	HR	RBI	BA	SB
Rod Carew, Minn.	123	458	79	152	8	56	.332	19
Reggie Smith Bost.#	143	543	87	168	25	93	.309	7
Tony Oliva, Minn.+	153	637	97	197	24	101	.309	10
Frank Robinson, Balt.	148	539	111	166	32	100	.308	9
Boog Powell, Balt.+	152	533	83	162	37	121	.304	1
Walt Williams, Chi.	135	471	59	143	3	32	.304	6
Rico Petrocelli, Bost.	154	535	92	159	40	97	.297	3
Frank Howard, Wash.	161	592	111	175	48	111	.296	4
Jim Northrup, Det.+	148	543	79	160	25	66	.295	4
Mike Andrews, Bost.	121	464	79	136	15	79	.293	1
Don Buford, Balt.+	144	554	99	161	11	64	.291	19
Roy White, NY +	130	448	55	130	7	74	.290	18
Cesar Tovar, Minn.	158	535	99	154	11	52	.288	45
Mark Belanger Balt.	150	530	76	152	2	50	.287	14
Del Unser, Wash. +	153	581	69	166	7	57	.286	8

Pitching Leaders - National League 1969

Pitcher Team	W	L	Pct.	ERA	G	IP	H	R	BB	SO
Juan Marichal, SF	21	11	.656	2.10	37	300	244	90	54	245
Steve Carlton, St.L. +	17	11	.607	2.17	31	236	185	66	93	210
Bob Gibson, St.L.	20	13	.606	2.18	35	314	251	84	95	269
Tom Seaver NY	25	7	.787	2.21	36	273	202	75	82	208
Jerry Koosman, NY+	17	9	.654	2.28	32	241	187	66	68	180
Larry Dierker, Hous.	20	13	.606	2.33	39	305	240	97	72	232
Bill Singer LA	20	12	.625	2.34	41	316	316	96	74	247
Bill Hands, Chicago	20	14	.588	2.49	41	300	268	102	73	181
Gaylord Perry, SF	19	14	.576	2.48	40	325	290	115	91	233
Phil Niekro, Atl.	23	13	.639	2.57	40	284	235	93	57	193
Claude Osteen, LA+	20	15	.571	2.66	41	321	293	103	74	183
Jim Maloney, Cinci.	12	5	.706	2.77	30	179	135	64	86	102

Bob Moose Pitts.	14	3	.824	2.91	44	170	149	64	62	165
Denny Lemasters, H+	13	17	.433	3.16	38	245	232	97	72	173
Fergie Jenkins Chi.	21	15	.583	3.21	43	311	284	122	71	273

Pitching Leaders 1969-American League

Pitcher Team	W	L	Pct.	ERA	G	IP	H	R	BB	SO
Rich Bosman, Wash.	14	5	.737	2.19	37	193	152	59	39	99
Jim Palmer Balt.	16	4	.800	2.34	26	181	131	48	64	123
Mike Cuellar Balt.+	23	11	.676	2.38	39	291	213	94	79	182
Andy Messersmith, Cal.	16	11	.593	2.52	40	250	169	81	100	211
Fritz Peterson, NY+	17	16	.515	2.55	37	272	228	95	43	150
Casey Cox, Wash.	12	7	.632	2.77	52	172	161	62	64	73
Denny McLain, Det.	24	9	.727	2.80	42	325	288	105	67	181
Mel Stottlemyre, NY	20	14	.588	2.82	39	303	267	105	97	113
Jim Perry, Minn.	20	6	.769	2.82	46	262	244	87	66	153
John Odom, Oak.	15	6	.714	2.92	32	231	179	87	112	150
Sam McDowell, Cle+	18	14	.563	2.94	39	285	222	111	122	271
Mike Nagy Bost.	12	2	.857	3.11	33	197	183	84	106	84
Mickey Lolich, Det+	19	11	.633	3.14	37	281	214	111	122	279
Jim McGlothlin Cal.	8	16	.333	3.18	37	201	188	86	58	96
Dave McNally Balt.+	20	7	.741	3.21	41	269	232	103	84	166

Base Hit Leaders - 1969

National League	Hits	American League	Hits
Matty Alou, Pitts.+	231	Tony Oliva, Minn. +	197
Pete Rose, Cincinnati#	218	Horace Clark NY	183
Lou Brock, St. Louis+	195	Paul Blair, Balt.	178
Bobby Tolan, Cinci.+	194	Frank Howard Wash.	175
Billy Williams, Chi. +	188	Tony Horton, Cleve.	174
Tony Perez, Cincinnati	185	Sal Bando Oakland	171
Don Kessinger, Chi.	181	Reggie Smith, Boston	168
Roberto Clemente, Pit.	175	Luis Aparichio, Chicago	168
Joe Torre, St. Louis	174	Frank Robinson Balt.	166
Felix Millan, Atlanta	174	Leo Cardenas, Minn.	162
		Boog Powell, Balt.	162

Home Run Leaders - 1969

National League	HRs	American League	HRs
Willie McCovey SF	45	Harmon Killewbrew Min	49
Henry Aaron, Atlanta	44	Frank Howard, Wash.	48
Lee May, Cincinnati	40	Reggie Jackson, Oakland	47
Tony Perez, Cinci.	37	Rico Petrocelli Boston	40
Jimmy Wynn Houston	33	Carl Yastrzemski, Boston	40
Bobby Bonds, SF	32	Boog Powell Baltimore	37
		Frank Robinson, Balt.	32
		Sal Bando, Oakland	31
		Ken Harrelson, Bost./Cle.	30
		Mike Epstein, Wash.	30
		Tony Horton, Cleveland	27

Runs Batted In Leaders - 1969

National League	RBI's	American League	RBI's
Willie McCovey San Fran.	126	Harmon Killebrew,	140
Ron Santo, Chicago	123	Boog Powell Baltimore	121
Tony Perez Cincinnati	122	Reggie Jackson, Oakland	118
Lee May, Cincinnati	110	Sal Bando, Oakland	113
Ernie Banks, Chicago	106	Frank Howard, Wash.	111
Joe Torre, St. Louis	104	Carl Yastrzemski, Boston	111
Hank Aaron, Atlanta	97	Tony Oliva, Minn.	101
Billy Williams, Chicago	95	Frank Robinson, Balt.	100
		Rico Petrocelli, Boston	97
		Reggie Smith, Boston	93
		Tony Horton, Cleveland	93

APPENDIX

METS' CAREER STATISTICS

Career Batting Leaders - New York Mets
All Statistics through 2014 season

Player	Years	G.	AB.	R.	H.	HR.	RBI.	SB.	BA.
1. John Olerud	'97-'99	476	1662	288	524	63	291	5	.315
2. David Wright	'04-'14	1508	5707	907	1702	230	939	191	.297
3. Keith Hernandez	'83-'88	880	3164	455	939	80	468	17	.297
4. Mike Piazza	'98-'05	972	3478	532	1028	220	655	7	.296
5. Eduardo Alfonzo	'95-'02	1086	3897	614	1136	120	538	45	.292
6. Dave Magadan	'86-'92	701	2088	275	610	21	254	5	.292
7. Jose Reyes	'03-'11	1050	4453	735	1300	81	423	370	.292
8. Dan Murphy	'08-'14	773	2855	366	827	48	329	55	.289
9. Steve Henderson	'77-'80	497	1800	267	516	35	229	55	.287
10. Angel Pagan	'08-'11	393	1491	214	423	24	170	87	.284
11. Wally Backman	'80-'88	765	2369	359	670	7	165	106	.283
12. Ron Hunt	'63-'66	459	1683	207	474	20	127	21	.282
13. Cleon Jones	'63-'75	1213	4263	565	1196	93	524	91	.281
14. Carlos Beltran	'05-'10	839	3133	551	878	149	559	100	.280
15. Roger Cedeno	'99,'02-'03	452	1448	225	404	18	114	105	.279
16. Jeff Kent	'92-'95	498	1831	244	510	67	267	12	.279

Highest Season Batting Averages-Mets

Player	Year	BA
1. John Olerud	1998	.354
2. Mike Piazza	1998	.348
3. Moises Alou	2007	.341
4. Cleon Jones	1969	.340
5. Jose Reyes	2011	.337
6. Lance Johnson	1996	.333
7. Dave Magadan	1990	.328
8. Carlos Beltran	2007	.325
9. Bobby Bonnila	1995	.325
10. David Wright	2007	.325
11. Edgardo Alfonzo	2000	.324
12. Mike Piazza	2000	.324
13. Ed Kranepool	1975	.323
14. Wally Backman	1986	.320
15. Dan Murphy	2011	.320
16. Cleon Jones	1971	.319

Career Hits - Mets

Player	Years	Hits
1. David Wright	'04-'14	1713
2. Ed Kranepool	'62-'79	1418
3. Jose Reyes	'03-'11	1300
4. Cleon Jones	'63-'75	1196
5. Eduardo Alfonzo	'95-'02	1136
6. Mookie Wilson	'80-'89	1112
7. Bud Harrelson	'65-'77	1029
8. Mike Piazza	'99-'05	1028
9. Darryl Strawberry	'83-'90	1025
10. Howard Johnson	'85-'93	997
11. Jerry Grote	'66-'77	994
12. Keith Hernandez	'83-'88	939

Hit Leaders Season - Mets

Player	Year	Hits
1. Lance Johnson	1991	227
2. Jose Reyes	2008	204
3. John Olerud	1998	197
4. David Wright	1996	196
5. Jose Reyes	2006	194
6. Eduardo Alfonzo	1999	191
7. Felix Millan	1975	191
8. Jose Reyes	2005	190
9. Dan Murphy	2013	188
10. Felix Millan	1973	185
11. Keith Hernandez	1985	183
12. Tommy Agee	1970	182

Career Home Run leaders-Mets

Player	Year	HR's
1. Darryl Strawberry	'83-'90	252
2. David Wright	'04-'14	231
3. Mike Piazza	'99-'05	220
4. Howard Johnson	'85-'93	192
5. Dave Kingman	'75-'77	154
6. Carlos Beltran	'05-'10	149
7. Todd Hundley	'90-'98	124
8. Kevin McReynolds	'87-'91	122
9. Eduardo Alfonzo	'95-'02	120
10. Ed Kranepool	'62-'79	118
11. Carlos Delgado	'06-'09	104

Season Home Run leaders-Mets

Player	Year	HR's
1. Carlos Beltran	2006	41
2. Todd Hundley	1996	41
3. Mike Piazza	1999	40
4. Darryl Strawberry	'87-'88	39
5. Carlos Delgado	'06-'08	38
6. Howard Johnson	1991	38
7. Mike Piazza	2000	38
8. Dave Kingman	'76-'82	37
9. Darryl Strawberry	1990	37

Career RBI (Runs Batted In) leaders-Mets

Player	Year	RBI
1. David Wright	'04-'14	943
2. Darryl Strawberry	'83-'90	733
3. Mike Piazza	'98-'05	655
4. Howard Johnson	'85-'93	629
5. Ed Kranepool	'62-'79	614
6. Carlos Beltran	'05-'10	559
7. Eduardo Alfonzo	'95-'02	538
8. Cleon Jones	'63-'75	521
9. Keith Hernandez	'83-'88	468
10. Kevin McReynolds	'87-'91	456

Highest Season RBI Leaders -Mets

Player	Year	RBI
1. Mike Piazza	1999	124
2. David Wright	2008	124
3. Robin Ventura	1999	120
4. Bernard Gilkey	1996	117

5. Howard Johnson	1991	117
6. Carlos Beltran	2006	116
7. David Wright	2006	116
8. Carlos Delgado	2008	115
9. Mike Piazza	2000	113
10. Carlos Beltran	2007, 08	112
11. Todd Hundley	1996	112
12. Edgardo Alfanzo	1999	108
13. Darryl Strawberry	1990	108

Pitching Statistics New York Mets
Career ERA (Earned Runs allowed) - leaders - Mets

Player	Years	ERA	IP
1. Tom Seaver	'67-'77	2.57	3045
2. Jesse Orosco	'79, '81-'87	2.73	596
3. R. A. Dickey	'10-'12	2.95	617
4. Jon Matlack	'71-'77	3.03	1448
5. Jerry Koosman	'67-'78	3.09	2545
6. John Franco	'90-'04	3.10	703
7. Dwight Gooden	'84-'94	3.10	2170
8. Bob Ojeda	'86-'90	3.12	764
9. David Cone	'87-'92	3.13	1209
10. Sid Fernandez	'84-'93	3.14	1585

Season ERA Leaders - Mets

Player	Year	ERA
1. Jesse Orosco	1983	1.47
2. Dwight Gooden	1985	1.53
3. Tug McGraw	1971	1.70
4. Tug McGraw	1972	1.70
5. Tom Seaver	1971	1.76
6. Jerry Koosman	1968	2.08
7. Tom Seaver	1973	2.08

8. Tom Seaver	1968	2.20
9. Tom Seaver	1969	2.21
10. David Cone	1988	2.22

Career Wins Leaders - Mets

Player	Years	Wins	IP
1. Tom Seaver	'67-'77	198	3045
2. Dwight Gooden	'84-'94	151	2170
3. Jerry Koosman	'67-'78	140	2545
4. Ron Darling	'83-'91	99	1620
5. Sid Fernandez	'84-'93	98	1585
6. Al Leiter	'98-'04	95	1360
7. Jon Matlack	'71-'77	82	1448
8. David Cone	'87-'92	81	1209
9. Bobby Jones	'93-'00	74	1216
10. Steve Traschel	'01-'06	66	956

Season Wins Leaders - Mets

Player	Year	Wins
1. Tom Seaver	1969	25
2. Dwight Gooden	1985	24
3. Tom Seaver	1975	22
4. Jerry Koosman	1976	21
5. Tom Seaver	1972	21
6. David Cone	1988	20
7. R. A. Dickey	2012	20
8. Tom Seaver	1971	20
9. Frank Viola	1990	20
10. Dwight Gooden	1990	19
11. Jerry Koosman	1968	19
12. Tom Seaver	1973	19
13. Dwight Gooden	1988	18

14. Bob Ojeda	1986	18	
15. Tom Seaver	1970	18	
16. Ron Darling	1988	17	
17. Dwight Gooden	1984	17	
18. Dwight Gooden	1986	17	
19. Jerry Koosman	1967	17	
20. Al Leiter	1998	17	
21. Jon Matlack	1976	17	

Career Saves Leaders - Mets

Player	Years	Saves
1. John Franco	'90-'04	276
2. Armando Benitez	'99-'03	160
3. Jesse Orosco	'79, '81-'87	107
4. Billy Wagner	'06-'09	101
5. Tug McGraw	'65-'74	86
6. Roger McDowell	'85-'89	84
7. Francisco Rodriguez	'09-'11	83

Season Saves Leaders - Mets

Player	Year	Saves
1. Armando Benitez	2001	43
2. Armando Benitez	2000	41
3. Billy Wagner	2006	40
4. John Franco	1998	38
5. John Franco	1997	36
6. Francisco Rodriguez	2009	35
7. Billy Wagner	2007	34

www.ingramcontent.com/pod-product-compliance
Lightning Source LLC
LaVergne TN
LVHW011936070526
838202LV00054B/4676